Resistance

The Perpetual War 2

LEON STEELGRAVE

Published by Ice Pick Books

ISBN: 978-1-8384435-9-7

LEON STEELGRAVE

Books by Leon Steelgrave

Europa City 1: White Vampyre
Europa City 2: Though Your Sins Be Scarlet
Europa City 3: The Violet Hour
Europa City 4: A Life Owed

Europa City One-shot: Cocoa Psycho Killer
Europa City One-shot: Smack Upside The Head

The Perpetual War 1: Crusade
The Perpetual War 2: Resistance

Darkness Visible: The Complete Short Stories

CHAPTER 1

Jefferson Lynch cued the video feed on his HUD: the date stamp read '03:04:55 Apr 12 2090'. He swiped his right index finger in front of the glasses, splitting the display and initiating a session window with the studio engineer. The engineer gave Lynch the thumbs up and he swiped back to the main feed. A countdown appeared to the right of the display, below the Casablanca TV21 logo: 5… 4… 3… 2… 1… Live!

The shark-like profile of the SB Defiant XV attack helicopter filled the screen, a red cross pattée clearly visible on the fuselage. With the shot established, the camera pulled back to reveal a total of three helicopters flying in close formation over rubble-choked city streets, low to the ground, closing in on the walls of a large rectangular enclosure containing the domes and minarets of a mosque.

The lead helicopter skimmed across the northern courtyard, homing in on the sanctuary. It hovered for a second above the sanctuary's three arcades, prior to launching a pair of Hellfire missiles. The missiles streaked out on long tongues of flame, passing through the double arches of the second level to detonate against the supporting Corinthian columns inside. As the arcade collapsed in on itself, the feed cut to another of the attack helicopters as it launched a similar attack on the dome atop the prayer hall. A third jump-cut showed the destruction of the tallest of the mosque's three minarets, the octagonal spire appearing to telescope inside the rapidly expanding square-shaped lower body.

Lynch checked his microphone before starting to speak in his laconic Southern drawl. Arabic and French subtitles scrolled across the bottom of the screen.

'For the fourth day in a row, American forces continue their assault on Damascus. The attack, spearheaded by the First Templar Division's Combat Aviation Brigade, now under the command of Colonel James Willard, has deliberately targeted vital infrastructure, in addition to historic and religious sites – including the Umayyad Mosque, the Great Mosque of Damascus, where drone attack helicopters levelled the sanctuary's arcade and destroyed the Dome of the Eagle and the Minaret of Isa in an act of wanton cultural vandalism. In addition to regular sorties by unmanned aircraft systems, the city has been subject to a near continuous railgun bombardment, echoing the brutality of 2089's siege of Jerusalem. Civilian casualties are estimated to be in excess of half a million, but with no access for independent observers the figure may be far higher. Broadcasting earlier today from the Panopticon's Central Office, President Gerrard released the following statement.'

Lynch switched the feed to a wide shot of the Central Office. The camera zoomed in low across the floor to focus on the straight-backed figure sitting at the desk, flanked by a pair of flags. Each showed a red Christian cross on a blue background with twenty-nine white stars distributed across the four quarters, representing the individual Religious States of America. Gerrard was a man of middle years, his brown hair accented with grey, his body beginning to bloat from living too well.

'My fellow Americans, while this is still a time of national mourning following the cowardly assassination of my predecessor, intelligence reports have confirmed the presence of Omar El Zayyoud in the city of Damascus. El Zayyoud, leader of the Salafi-Jihadi terror organisation known as the Armed Islamic Group of Jordan, is the mastermind behind the assassination of President Hamilton. Despite repeated requests for El Zayyoud to be surrendered into our custody to stand trial for his heinous crimes, the forces of the Islamic Caliphate continue to protect him behind a human shield. Regrettably, we have no other recourse but to continue our assault on Damascus with extreme prejudice. Though the road be bloody and terrible we will not flinch in the relentless pursuit of our foes, for we are one nation under one God, and He knows our cause to be just. With His guidance, we will wipe the vile scourge of the Islamic Caliphate, a threat to our ideals, to the very existence of our glorious republic, from His Creation. This is my solemn promise to you, the people of America.'

Lynch switched the feed again and appeared for the first time in front of the camera: a tall, gangly man with a shaven head, wearing a wraparound HUD.

'The question on the lips of many of our viewers will be: who is Omar El Zayyoud? El Zayyoud is a Jordanian national and a former American ally. Following the American annexation of Kuwait in 2069, El Zayyoud was a member of one of the local militias trained and equipped by CIA operatives to assist in the fight against Kuwaiti insurgents. His whereabouts during the following six years are largely unknown, but evidence suggests he travelled to Iraq, where he became radicalised. Returning to his home country in 2081, he formed the Armed Islamic Group of Jordan. The terror group has since been responsible for several attacks on American forces.'

Lynch cued the final montage of the broadcast. The ruins of schools, hospitals and shops flitted across the screen; however, it was not the rubble that caught and held the viewer's eye, but the human detritus. Skulls, long since stripped of flesh by the rats who prospered in the wreckage, grinned mirthlessly from bomb craters. Shrunken blackened commas, the bodies of those burned alive by incendiaries, still smoked in the zones closest to the fighting. A solitary child, a girl no more than three years of age, killed by a blast shockwave, lay as if asleep in the centre of a street; the camera zoomed in to focus on her eyes, staring up into infinity, dispelling the illusion.

'This has been Jefferson Lynch, broadcasting live from Casablanca for TV Twenty-one, Morocco's eye on the world.'

Lynch killed the feed, pushed his HUD on top of his head and scrubbed his face with his hands.

'I need a cigarette. Or a drink. Or maybe just some kind of mental enema. Goddamn, this shit is depressing.'

Lynch unfolded his legs from beneath the desk and bounded across the broadcast room with an uneven, almost flailing walk. He used his thumb to call the elevator, turning side-on to enter the carriage before the doors had fully opened. His right leg jiggled with nervous energy as he shook a cigarette from its pack and placed it between his lips. He patted the various pockets of his gilet, eventually locating his lighter as the elevator reached the ground floor and bounced on its shocks before settling. Lynch sparked up and touched the flame to his cigarette as the elevator doors opened, ignoring the wagging finger of the security guard as he exited through a revolving door.

The glass and steel towers of downtown Casablanca rose on either side of Lynch, creating an artificial canyon. Land here, as it was the world over in the wake of the Great Flood, was at a premium. Few could afford to own it, but the developers were happy to sell airspace instead, and so the towers reached for the stars. And where there was building frontage there was advertising space; he was surrounded by a riot of holographic dioramas and vignettes bearing the logos of the African Tech Corps, premium suppliers of the world's cyberware and nanotech. Humankind had originated in Africa and it was here, in the aftermath of ecological disaster, that it sought to regain its previous heights.

Lynch wandered a half dozen steps to the right and then back to the left, smoking his cigarette and lighting a second from the smouldering butt of the first. The nicotine craving went away, leaving a kind of emptiness behind. But the emptiness didn't last, because the doubts were always waiting. What was he doing here? What difference was he making? Did anyone back home even see his broadcasts, let alone believe their content? He had cut and run in Jerusalem instead of going back home and speaking truth to power. But going home was the one thing he had no doubts about; home was a death sentence. Not the overt kind, rather the sort where you are found hanging naked in a hotel room with a wedge of lemon at your feet. An old playbook, perhaps, but accidents will happen. Particularly to political dissidents with a high public profile.

Lynch flicked the cigarette away and his com-unit beeped a second later. He unlocked it and saw a notification informing him he had been fined for public littering – the funds would be automatically debited from his account. He brushed his finger across the wallpaper image; a blonde-haired girl wearing an 'I AM 9' badge. Lynch remembered it well; it was the last time he was allowed to see his daughter, just prior to his divorce. Christine would be twelve now. Probably getting a hard time in school from the other kids about her father, the traitor and Caliphate sympathiser. Probably full of hate for the mean-spirited drunk who had been absent most of her life. He'd made the hard choices for the greater good. Hadn't he?

Lynch felt it first as a prickling in the back of his skull as the hairs rose on the nape of his neck. Then there was a roaring crackle of static as all the lights and holograms along the length of the street blinked out, plunging it into darkness. Lynch pulled down his HUD and switched it to infrared. A red and gold rose blossomed at the far end of the street as a missile streaked towards him. Lynch started to run, for all the good it would do. Limbs pumping furiously, he looked left and right, seeking some kind of cover, but the buildings would offer little protection from the missile's payload. His right hand brushed against his belt and he felt the camera drones nestled in their docking station. He pressed a finger against the implant behind his right ear and initiated the uplink between the drones and his HUD. The drones whirred softly as they detached from the docking station and flitted bat-like into the sky. Lynch activated the camera feed. If he was going down, he would go out broadcasting; beam his final moments to the world. He took shelter behind a parked truck, the missile filling more and more of the screen.

It hit him suddenly; one last, mad roll of the dice. He powered the drones to maximum throttle and directed them towards the missile, triggering its proximity detonator while it was still some twenty metres out. He closed his eyes and pressed himself to the ground as the fireball engulfed the truck, felt the first shards of shrapnel and glass pierce his flesh as the force of the blast propelled both him and the truck along the road. Then the darkness claimed him.

CHAPTER 2

Lynch paused in the middle of the Emergency Room's waiting area and, his right arm in a sling, struggled to open the pill bottle's plastic cap with his left hand. It finally flipped free, pinging across the room. He upended the bottle, tipped a half dozen strong painkillers into his mouth, and dry swallowed. A strip of tape covered the bridge of his nose, another ran parallel to his right eyebrow, while tape and gauze covered his exposed left arm. He felt as though he'd been run over by a truck; another foot or so to the left and that would have literally been the case. He had been lucky this time, but was under no illusion as to his chances of surviving a second attempt on his life.

He looked round for the missing cap and found it in the hand of a young man with red hair and freckles. The physical appearance of this good Samaritan didn't concern him so much as the dark blue uniform he wore. Lynch eyed the gold frogging and lieutenant's pips that identified him as a member of the *Sûreté Nationale*'s National Brigade, a branch of the Moroccan police that specialised in organised crime and counterterrorism.

The cop took out his wallet and flashed Lynch his badge and ID card.

'Lieutenant Rickhard Hirsch. I was wondering if you felt up to giving a statement concerning tonight's … incident?'

Lynch looked the man up and down again. Mid to late twenties at most; young to hold such a rank in the National Brigade, particularly when he was obviously a foreign national.

'That a Europa City accent I hear?'

'It is, originally. But I'm a Moroccan citizen now.'

Lynch shrugged. Squinted at the kid again; felt he should know him from somewhere, but couldn't place him in the current context. If it was important it would come back to him.

'So "incident" is the euphemism we're using for what amounts to a terrorist attack on foreign soil by the RSA?'

'Nobody died. Nobody got arrested. So, yes, we're dealing with an "incident". It's not as though you can prove the RSA was behind it. They certainly won't admit responsibility, as that would be a direct violation of Morocco's neutrality. You don't strike me as the kind of man who takes advice, but I'm going to give you some anyway. Whatever the issue between you and the RSA government is, it'd clearly be best for all concerned if you quit with the broadcasts.'

'After what those goddamn swine put me through? I don't think so. Blackmailing me into covering the Templar campaign to liberate Israel and retake Jerusalem wasn't enough for them; I had to film propaganda pieces portraying them as heroes while covering up the atrocities. Of which, let me tell you, there were plenty. Much to my shame, I went along with it to begin with. The promise of my freedom and viewing figures I hadn't enjoyed in over a decade silenced my conscience. When it finally got too much and I put the truth out there, implicating the Templars' commander, they tried to kill me. I was lucky to escape with my life. I dare say a smart man would have cut and run but, God help me, there's too much of the journalist in me to let the story rest. The world needs to learn the truth about what the Religious States are doing in the Middle East. Anyway, it's too late to stop now. I've already kicked up too much of a stink, embarrassed President Gerrard. His administration won't settle for anything less than a high-profile assassination – an example to discourage others.'

'You can't know that for certain.'

'No? Guess it was just bad luck a drone found me in the middle of Casablanca.'

'Okay, maybe you have a point there. But you need to understand the National Brigade won't assign men to protect a foreign national, particularly one intent on antagonising his own government. If you insist on continuing with your broadcasts, you're on your own. I'm sorry, but my bosses won't see it any other way.'

'And you're okay with that? Putting politics before the rule of law?'

A flush crept across Hirsch's face. He broke eye contact and then threw his hands up in the air.

'I know I'm gonna regret this. Contact Alia Tazi – she runs Red Phoenix Security. Among other services, they offer close protection.'

Lynch snorted. 'She do pro bono work?'

'Mention my name – Tazi owes me a favour. Besides, seems like you're kind of a celebrity. Protecting your ass from the RSA will be good publicity for her.'

Red Phoenix Security operated out of the twenty-fourth floor of an office block on the Boulevard de la Croix. The furnishings were cheap, generic, and bore the signs of hard use by the previous occupants. A layer of grime on the windows filtered and distorted the early morning sun, but at a certain angle you could, if you craned your neck, make out the waters of the Atlantic.

If the office disappointed Lynch, the woman who now stepped out from behind her desk and offered him her hand did not. She stood about five foot six; long black hair falling across the shoulders and down the back of a tactical vest, intelligent brown eyes measuring him coolly. Her hand was cool, the nails well-kept but short and practical, while the body encased in the matte black combat fatigues was lithe and muscular, honed by serious gym time. The butt of the pistol holstered just to the front of her right hip faced forward, marking her as a southpaw.

'Alia Tazi. Pleased to meet you.'

Lynch caught an odd inflection in her English, possibly a throwback to the country's historic status as a French protectorate. She waved a hand in the direction of a chair situated in front of the desk.

'Please take a seat, Mr Lynch.'

Lynch waited for Tazi to take her own seat before sitting himself. The courtesy appeared to amuse her. At least he assumed that's what the twitch of her lips meant. She swiped her datapad, eyes flitting rapidly in response to the various texts, and nodded.

'Lieutenant Hirsch tells me you're looking for a CPO. Got yourself in a spot of bother with the motherland.'

'You've watched my broadcasts?'

'Can't say as I have. I try not to concern myself with the politics of other countries. But don't worry.' She tapped the datapad. 'The details are all here.'

'And you understand I can't pay for your services?'

Tazi's shoulders stiffened, but she nodded. Private security tended to have an uneasy relationship with the law. Lynch surmised Hirsch had either got her out of a jam or, at the very least, cleared some obstacles for her.

'That's agreed. There are conditions. You don't follow them; we can't protect you. Simple as that. First and foremost, you do exactly what the CPO tells you. Seems like a no-brainer, but you'd be surprised. Next, avoid going out alone in public. If you absolutely can't avoid it, keep to densely populated areas where the collateral damage will be too great for more blunt methods of assassination. Having failed once, I doubt they'll try another drone strike. They'll send a professional to take care of you in person. As such, there's no point trying to conceal the CPO – they'll easily identify such subterfuge, so you might as well make a statement. One that will help deter any amateurs looking to win favour with the RSA by taking you out.'

'Sounds like you know your stuff.'

'You sound surprised?'

'Not at all, just making conversation. So, when do I meet my CPO?'

'You already have. I've decided to handle your case in person. I trust this meets with your approval?'

Lynch unfolded himself from the chair. The young woman, for all that he towered over her, looked more than up to the task.

'Of course. I'm in your hands, Ms Tazi.'

'Tazi will be sufficient.'

Lynch nodded. 'Okay if we head back to my apartment? I've a broadcast to prepare for – a special edition. Got to show those swine I'm taking no guff from them.'

'Not a problem. I've already prepared a car.'

'You have?' Lynch smiled wryly. Could be there was an upside to living with a death mark.

Lynch followed Tazi back to the elevator and rode it with her to the sub-basement's parking lot. She cut across to a bay on the far side, the lights of a Lincoln Continental XI blipping on in response to her biometrics when she got within two metres of the vehicle. He admired the black polished bodywork, performing a full 360 of the car before opening the front passenger door and climbing inside. The smell of new leather filled his nostrils as he felt the seat mould to his body. It was certainly a step up from the old Mercedes G-Wagon he was running.

Tazi slid in alongside him, the instrument panel lighting up simultaneously.

'Tahar El Alaoui, right?'

Lynch nodded and Tazi engaged the drive, allowing the Lincoln's AI to manoeuvre it through the parking lot and up the ramp to street level. She reviewed the route on the nav-comp, noted heavy congestion and keyed in an alternative route. The car veered suddenly to the right, cutting across the front of a courier truck and setting off its collision sensors before taking the exit ramp.

Lynch prised his fingers from the armrest.

'Jesus! What kind of auto-drive is this thing running?'

'I cracked the safety protocols myself and programmed the evasive system. Don't worry, you're surrounded by a crash safety zone.' She tapped her knuckles against the windscreen. 'Armoured glass, too. Will stop a point-fifty cal at close range. I've driven tanks less secure.'

'Uh-huh.' Lynch sought to settle his nerves by changing the subject. 'You always lived in Morocco?'

'All my days. My grandparents settled here following the Great Flood. It was the end of centuries of tradition.' Lynch's confusion must have showed, for she added, 'We were, still are in name at least, Roma. But the old ways were already under a great strain even before. People had long called us thieves and vagabonds, made our way of life difficult by limiting where we could camp, seeking to reduce our yearly migrations. Then came the Flood – no one wanted travellers moving across their borders and in and out of the shanty towns and refugee camps. With the police and army at their throats, my people had to make the choice between tradition and survival. Those who could not bear to be caged in cities were subsequently arrested and placed in internment camps, where disease did the work that their persecutors did not have the stomach for. Forty to fifty thousand are said to have died.'

'I'm sorry.'

'Why? You had no part in it. Besides, we are used to it. The Nazis murdered at least a quarter of a million of my people, perhaps closer to half a million. No one knows for sure. But at least we were free to travel afterwards. Now, with each generation fixed in place, more and more of our culture is erased. If I have children, what will they care for long-vanished traditions? I only know because my parents insisted on making me learn. My choices in life were a great disappointment to them.'

Lynch had no response to that. He turned and stared out of the window, taking in the streets of a foreign city while his thoughts bent towards the home he was exiled from. He wanted to walk the streets of Lexington again; to see his daughter. But both were impossible dreams and so he fought back in the only manner he knew, hoping against all reason that truth would somehow conquer his foes.

CHAPTER 3

Cooper took the bend at speed, the JLTV's nearside wheels lifting from the road. He peered ahead, his night-vision goggles transforming the dark into a luminous green. Beside him, Colonel Willard's attention remained fixed on his wrist-mounted com-unit as he viewed the real-time mission data. A series of ratcheting clicks and snaps from the rear of the JLTV informed Cooper that Jackson, Pedersen and Martinez were locked and loaded.

The dash readout told him they were now less than ten klicks from their objective, running in stealth mode. Cooper watched it count down apprehensively, the hollow sensation in his gut growing with every metre. He'd had his fill of fighting after Jerusalem, but President Hamilton's assassination had changed everything. With all leave cancelled as they pursued the retreating Caliphate forces, his request to cash out the end of his current tour was on hold until further notice. And so here he was in south-western Syria, thirty klicks north of Damascus, in the heart of Caliphate-held territory, tasked with extracting or killing the man said to be responsible for masterminding Hamilton's assassination.

Cooper checked the rear-view mirror; he couldn't see

anything but knew a second JLTV was following at a distance of twenty metres. His eyes flicked to Willard, his face eerily underlit by the glow from his com-unit. Their new CO was a very different beast from Tyler, lacking his naked ambition and fire. Doubtless the high command saw him as a steady pair of hands, an unimaginative but effective soldier who carried out his orders with brutal efficiency. He made Cooper's skin crawl.

Willard signalled for them to stop and Cooper slewed the JLTV round and braked to a halt. The second JLTV pulled up beside them, in the lee of a fortified compound wall that rose for three metres before angling outwards and terminating in coils of razor wire.

Both squads disembarked, a pair of two-man sentry teams taking up position either side of the parked vehicles and forming the backup team. Martinez launched the drones, initiating an uplink to the squad's HUDs. They rose silently, crossing over the top of the perimeter wall and feeding back images of the garden beyond.

Cooper tapped his com-unit, overlaying the drone footage with heat and motion detection data. Nothing moved in the garden, but he picked up a pair of heat signatures standing either side of the house's main doors on the west side of the garden.

Willard removed a small aerosol can from one of his belt pouches and, pulling a bandana up over his mouth and nose, sprayed a one metre diameter circle at the base of the wall.

Cooper stared, fascinated, as the nanotech ate its way silently through the reinforced plascrete, creating the perfect breach.

Willard motioned him, Jackson and Pedersen through, leaving Martinez to operate the drones.

Cooper rose from his belly to his haunches, senses alert as he scanned for danger. All clear. He followed Jackson at a crouching run to take up position by an acacia tree less than three metres from the house, Willard and Pedersen moving in parallel. Willard pointed to the sentry on the left and Jackson raised his rifle. The red dot of the laser sight found its target at the same moment as Willard's. Their rifles coughed in unison, the Templar strike team moving in before the bodies dropped.

Jackson slid open the left-hand door, allowing one of the drones to slip inside. Cooper scanned the sensor readout and identified three further guards within the main body of the house, one in the kitchen and two outside the master bedroom. There were an additional two heat signatures in the bedroom and two more in the adjoining room. Willard pointed towards the kitchen on the opposite side of the open-plan living area and drew his finger across his throat.

Cooper handed his rifle to Jackson and drew his knife. He crept forward, stepping over a discarded toy truck, and pressed himself flat against the wall to the left of the door. The drone feed showed the man standing at the kitchen table with his back to the door as he spooned some sort of filling into a flatbread. Cooper pushed conscious thought aside and let his training take over. He stepped through the door, crossed the floor, covered the guard's mouth with his hand and pulled it to the side as he drove the point of the knife deep into his neck with his right hand and cut forward, severing the carotid artery. He held him for the four seconds it took for him to lose consciousness before lowering his body to the floor. Death would follow a few seconds later.

Cooper wiped his knife on the man's tunic and returned it to the sheath inside his right boot. Jackson was waiting for him at the door. He handed Cooper his rifle and signalled for him to follow. They entered the corridor leading to the master bedroom in time to see Willard and Pedersen drop the guards. On his motion detector, Cooper watched one of the occupants of the master bedroom move to the adjoining room and then return with its occupants. All four figures now crowded together; there went the element of surprise.

Willard, drawing the same conclusion, kicked open the door and dived through. He rolled to the left, came up in a crouch with his assault rifle ready and uttered a terse, 'Fuck!'

El Zayyoud stood to the left of his wife; their two children, a boy and a girl, knelt in front of them. He held his right arm aloft, thumb pressed down on a dead man's switch, the cable of which snaked its way down to a suicide vest.

CHAPTER 4

Cooper struggled to read any expression in the woman's eyes, but the children's faces showed they were terrified. The boy, the eldest of the pair at maybe nine years of age, struggled to keep his bottom lip from trembling as he stared at the armed intruders. He gripped his sister's hand tightly, as much for his own comfort as hers. At five or six years old, she didn't appear to comprehend this violation of the family home.

Cooper raised his rifle in the air and held his left hand up, palm outwards.

'Easy now. There's no need for your wife and children to die. We're only here for you. So why don't you disarm the switch and we can talk about this?'

'You'll find my wife and children willing to die as martyrs, if that be the will of Allah.'

Willard's gun coughed twice, delivering a double tap to the forehead of El Zayyoud's wife, covering the wall in blood and brain matter. The children screamed as their mother's corpse folded to the floor.

'Your wife got her wish,' Willard barked over the children's cries. 'She's a martyr. Are you really certain you want your children to join her in Paradise?'

Uncertainty showed in El Zayyoud's eyes for the first time as he watched his children sob over the body of his wife, her blood soaking into the fabric of their pyjamas. But his distrust of the Templars was clear.

'What proof do I have that you'll keep your word? What's to stop you killing us all if I disarm my vest?'

'Nothing,' Willard replied. 'But it's a possibility, versus a certainty if you detonate that vest. Choice is yours. You have five seconds to decide. Five. Four.'

El Zayyoud looked at the body of his wife and then back to Willard. The ruthlessness of his foes was all too apparent.

'Wait! I disarm.' He reached across slowly with his free hand and disconnected the detonator wire from the vest. He let the trigger slip from his fingers and raised both hands in the air, taking a step back from the children.

Willard pressed a finger to his earpiece and then nodded. He fired another double tap, executing El Zayyoud in the same manner as his wife. A high keening note filled the room as the boy started to sob. His sister sat staring into space, lost in the horror.

'What the fuck!' Cooper snarled. 'He'd surrendered.'

'Mission Control said to terminate him. Something we call chain of command, Templar-Private Cooper. Ten lashes ought to refresh your memory.' Willard opened his comms again. 'Target is neutralised. Area secured. Send in a clean-up squad.'

Cooper knew he was in enough trouble already but couldn't stop himself.

'What about the children, sir?'

Willard, reminded of their presence, glanced at the grieving children.

'They'll be taken to a re-education camp. Taught to be good Christians. We're not monsters.'

Cooper thought differently, but a warning look from Jackson told him to drop it. He slung his rifle over his shoulder, squatted down and took hold of the girl. She screamed as he pulled her away from her mother. He tried to hush her as he deposited her on the bed. She glared at him and scuttled back, grabbing hold of a pillow and hugging it to her chest, bloody hands and limbs leaving a trail of prints in her wake. The son pulled away angrily and spat out a stream of invective that required no translation when Cooper tried to repeat the procedure with him. He didn't hold out much hope for the boy's rehabilitation; psychological torture would only more deeply entrench his hatred.

Pedersen took out his com-unit and snapped a couple of pictures of El Zayyoud's corpse.

'Seriously?'

'Yeah, seriously, Coop. We just bagged the fucker behind President Hamilton's assassination. Damn straight I'm taking some pictures! When we finally get some leave the folks back home will be treating us like the goddamn heroes we are.'

'That sounds suspiciously like pride,' Willard said. He held out his hand. 'Give me the com-unit, son.'

Pederson stared petulantly at his commanding officer and then capitulated. Willard deleted the images and handed the com-unit back. He looked round the room, making sure each man met his gaze in turn.

'We're Christian soldiers. We serve His will. Never forget that. Now move out. Clean-up squad will handle it from here.'

Cooper was the last to leave. The image of El Zayyoud's son kneeling in his father's blood burned itself into his retinas. El Zayyoud might have bankrolled and planned Hamilton's assassination, but he certainly hadn't pulled the trigger. The identity of the shooter remained suspiciously absent from both media and military reports. He shook his head to clear it. For now, his focus had to be on staying alive long enough to make it back home.

The night air was cool, a sluggish breeze carrying the scent of pine. Cooper stopped to look round the garden; with its turpentine trees and flower beds it was an oasis of calm divorced from the violence inside the house. Willard had paused a couple of metres ahead, finger once again pressed to his earpiece as he received further instruction. Jackson and Pedersen were already at the breach in the wall, the night's action seemingly already forgotten.

The explosion threw Cooper to the ground. He rolled onto his back, ears ringing, as he watched smoke and flames billow from the shattered front of the house. Willard was also staring at the house, his expression unreadable. He reached up and pulled a sliver of glass from his cheek, stared at the bead of crimson on its point.

'Huh. Guess the boy really was ready to be a martyr.'

CHAPTER 5

TV21 Interview Transcript #1: Jefferson Lynch in conversation with former RSA Captain Connor Stephens via satellite uplink from an undisclosed location.

Jefferson Lynch: Captain Stephens, thank you for agreeing to speak with me this evening. I'm certain it will be an enlightening interview for TV21 subscribers.

Connor Stephens: It's just plain ol' Connor now – I left my rank and my affiliation to the RSA behind when I left Syria and that life.

JL: Of course, my mistake. But up until six weeks ago you were on active duty with the Third Infantry Division in the Daraa Governorate of Syria?

CS: That's correct, Jefferson. Our original deployment was in Israel eight months previously, in the wake of the Templar beach landings at Palmachim and Tel Aviv. With Jerusalem under siege, we were brought in to assist Israeli forces with administering the captured territories.

JL: A police action?

CS: Of a sort. The infrastructure was a mess — twenty-five years of underinvestment and neglect by the Caliphate, then the damage inflicted by our military strikes. Engineering corps were working twenty-four-seven to restore power, running water and comms. The fear was of fifth columnists and suicide bombers in the Arab civilian population seeking to damage those efforts.

JL: And did they? Attack you, I mean.

CS: See, that's the damnedest thing. Intel counted the civilian population prior to the invasion at just south of six million. In the four months I was in country I reckon we were lucky to have encountered twenty thousand. To begin with we just thought they were biding their time — plotting, preparing, planning. We'd deployed FASCAM and CROWS along our defensive perimeters and hunter-killer drones constantly patrolled the area. Abdul had good reason to keep his head down, y'know? So I didn't read too much into it.

JL: So what changed? Why did you start to doubt the narrative?

CS: Narrative? That's a good word. It was the change in narrative. All of a sudden, the civilians had taken refuge in Jerusalem or fled south to Egypt, we had to remember that the borders with Jordan and Syria were porous. That's the sort of talk people make up when they're trying to talk themselves out of something they don't want to believe. But when you started to look at the official figures — two hundred thousand airlifted out of Jerusalem during the ceasefire, another three quarters of a million across the Egyptian border. Well, they just didn't stack up. At the last official count there were a million and a half refugees in resettlement camps in Israel, which leaves about three and a half million civilians unaccounted for. Did they all make it to Jordan and Syria? Where did they get the vehicles and fuel? Why did none of our satellites track these convoys? The more you drill down into the details and required logistics, the more impossible it becomes.

JL: Let me stop you there a second. Because, if I'm hearing you right, what you're telling me leads to a frightening conclusion. For the avoidance of any doubt, I'll just come straight out with it. You're accusing the Religious States of America of one of the largest acts of genocide in modern history?

CS [lengthy pause, followed by a dispirited sigh]: Truth is, I can't prove a thing. I doubt anyone can. They're too thorough for that. But I know what I saw, and the math don't add up. You, yourself, recorded and broadcast Colonel Tyler calling in an airstrike on a refugee column to erase a war crime committed by the men under his command. Was he the only one? I doubt it. And who knows everything that happened once the Israelis began resettling their lands? Three and a half million is a big number — maybe impossibly big. But there's no doubt in my mind that hundreds of thousands of Caliphate civilians were made to disappear within months of the Templars capturing Jerusalem. The detail might be lacking, but that doesn't make it any less of a fact, whatever Fox wants to tell the folks back home.

JL: I see. So, having reached this conclusion, did you raise it with your superiors or any of the NGOs, such as the Red Crescent? From what you've said, it had to be on your mind, right?

CS: You have to remember the timeline here. Much of what I've said only became clear after we left Israel. We might not have been on the front line, but there was a war going on. That shit keeps you occupied. Anyway, the Knesset invoked the Law of Return again and with the IDF strengthened and the nano-virus to secure their borders, we got the order to bug out. The Caliphate was on the run and the campaign was progressing through Syria and Jordan. Once again, we were deployed to administer the newly captured territories.

JL: And you saw more of the same in Syria? Unexplained disappearances?

CS: No. What we saw was worse in many ways. The civilians who weren't killed in the airstrikes or ground fighting were basically abandoned. Left without food, shelter, or clean drinking water, disease picking off those who didn't die of starvation first. We were putting in infrastructure, but none of it was for the relief of the civilian population. Everything was fenced off, defended, use of lethal force sanctioned to protect our assets. It's like they wanted the population to turn feral, to feed upon itself. That way, they'd have no chance of organising against us. See, our supply lines were getting too long to defend, our forces stretched too thin. It was this or the mobilisation of thousands more troops – possibly the reintroduction of the draft. That was never going to fly back home. Easier by far just to bomb the country flat and turn it into a parking lot.

JL: But surely there was some sort of pushback? What you're saying is monstrous. Inhuman. They might not have been white or Christian, but these are women, children, the elderly and the infirm we're talking about. Goddamn human beings! Are you seriously telling me that not one of the swine out there lifted so much as a finger to help them? Tell me you at least voiced a protest.

[Transcript interrupted as Stephens breaks down and starts to sob. We hear a cigarette being lit and a long inhale follows.]

JL: Do you need to take a break?

CS [faint at first, but growing louder]: No. Let's get this done. It's why I agreed to this interview. It didn't sit right with a lot of the men – seeing children starving, women being raped and murdered, the dead and dying left in the street. I took it to my CO and he shut me down, told me to follow my orders and make sure the men under me did the same. I said I wanted to make a formal complaint. He told me if I did, he'd see I was stripped of my commission and spent the next five years in a military stockade. So, yes, I buckled. But I was far from the only one disturbed and disgusted by what the top brass was sanctioning. We weren't all going to walk by on the other side.

It started with individuals smuggling a bit of food here, some medicine there. A drop in the ocean, I know, but it grew into an informal network as we learned who we could trust. Trouble was our efforts started to get noticed. A corporal under my command, Billings, a good family man, got picked up by the Military Police. They charged him with theft of RSA property – MREs and antibiotics – delivered a public punishment beating and sentenced him to thirty days in the stockade. It escalated rapidly from there. Eventually a young kid from the motor pool was caught attempting to drive a young woman and her two-year-old daughter to the coast. A ship had been organised – probably destined for Turkey, which shows how desperate they were if life in an internment camp was preferable to staying put. The kid was made and the MPs followed him, intending to close down the operation. Turns out the captain and first mate of the ship were found to be armed, most likely for self-defence as there are pirates operating in the Med. Anyway, the weapons and munitions they'd got were so antiquated firing them would pose a serious threat to life and limb. Doesn't matter, they handed them over without a fight – they got classed as insurgents and the kid was charged with aiding and abetting the enemy. The court martial was super-fast and he was up in front of a firing squad three days later. All because he wanted to help some terrified girl and her child. I knew then I had to get out, and get out quick.

JL: So you decided to desert?

CS: Sounds bad when you say it like that, but as far as I'm concerned I ain't guilty of no dereliction of duty. I joined the army to serve and protect my country. Now, I got no beef with what's happening with the Caliphate. Far as I'm concerned, those mutts deserve everything they got coming to them. Not just for what they've done to us and the Israelis, but for all the shit they've done to their own people. So the broader mission I get. But what was happening to the civilians? There was no clear and present danger. No threat at all. We should have been helping them. Demonstrating the values America stands for. How else are we ever going to convince them democracy is the way forward? Instead, we proved ourselves no better than the Caliphate. Maybe worse, seeing as we're Christians. So I made plans for my own exit. Forged my CO's signature on some papers of transit, stocked up a JLTV and lit out south through Jordan. Been travelling ever since. Can't really say more about it than that.

JL: You believe your life to be in danger?

CS: I know my life is in danger. You called me a deserter — the official classification is absent without leave, but I've also been declared an apostate and an Islamist sympathiser. The government has placed a bounty on my head. Pays more if I'm alive, but dead isn't exactly chump change. Probably going to be on the run until the end of my days, however long that is. Not that I'm looking for sympathy. Compared to what I've seen, my life ain't so bad. Some might see it as fair penance, given all I let slide. Could be right at that. I don't know for sure. But what I do know is that someone has to speak for those who no longer can. How else will the American people learn about what's being done in their name and the name of their God? I'm trusting you with my truth, Mr Lynch. Don't let me down. And don't dishonour the dead or fail those still living. Because you won't find any absolution for that kind of sin. Believe me, I know.

JL: You have my word. I won't let you or them down.

Transcript Ends

Six months of broadcasting for TV21 and what did Lynch have to show for it? Nada. Zilch. Bupkis. Public opinion in the RSA showed little or no sign of turning against the war. There was the occasional muttering from Europa City regarding the destruction of cultural sites and civilian casualties, but the arms exports continued. Even the Muslim countries of the African Tech Corps remained content to put profit before the prophet. In short, he was pissing against the wind. He needed something bigger, a story that would cut through to the public at large.

The old republic had comprised fifty states, some twenty-nine of which now formed the Religious States of America. The secessionists had bombed the remaining twenty-one states into submission during the civil war of

2049, reducing them to a largely agrarian existence. At least that was the surface projection. Rumour had it they were neither as submissive nor as pastoral as they appeared. That same rumour went under the name of the Free America movement; a resistance dedicated to reuniting and restoring America to its founding values.

A notification pinged on Lynch's com-unit; the search algorithm had completed some five hours and fifty-three minutes after he initiated it. He scrolled through the results, deleting the noise and flagging those that warranted further investigation. Free America: it sounded like a joke, but the evidence was mounting that this was something more than a group of keyboard warriors initiating flame wars. The money trail wound its way through shell companies and dummy corporations to arrive in the accounts of Europa City arms manufactories and the African Tech Corps, the outputs of which made their way to Canada.

Lynch tapped an embedded document and a video started to play. The night-vision satellite imagery showed a cargo barge docking on the Pennsylvanian shore of Lake Erie. Resolution was low but Lynch had seen enough military vehicles during his time with the Templars to recognise the profiles of JLTVs and APCs. An unmistakeable preparation for war. But who was leading it? Some of the money was emanating out of North Africa, which meant Free America had to be active on the continent. Somewhere, there was someone he could talk to.

Lynch might have been butting against indifference for six months, but that hadn't prevented him from cultivating sources. He flicked through his contacts. Morry Landau was typical of the Casablanca underclass; a grifter, a two-bit hustler, always looking for an angle to exploit, everything from cybernauts to arms trafficking. In respect of the latter, he often acted as an intermediate between the tech corps and the kind of customer whose name did not appear on any invoice.

Lynch hit dial and the face of a dark-skinned man of

middle years with several days' beard growth popped up on his screen.

'Morry, how's it going?'

Morry stared at Lynch's face in return.

'Jesus! What happened to you? Actually, never mind. Wouldn't want to give the impression I give a fuck. What can I do for you?'

'Free America.' Lynch let the words hang.

'That some kind of special offer?'

'Don't crack wise. This is me you're talking to.'

'Say I do know something. What's your interest?'

'I'm looking for an introduction. Our aims might be mutually beneficial.'

Morry sucked at a hollow tooth. Decision made, he said, 'You know Rick's Café?'

'Horrible tourist trap on Sour Jdid, riffs off some ancient movie?'

'That's the place. Be there tomorrow night at eight. If my contact's interested in you, he'll make himself known. And Lynch, that's another one you owe me. Time's coming when you're going to have to balance the books.'

The connection ended. Lynch looked over to where Tazi was sitting on the sofa sipping a water. Somehow he didn't think his CPO would be best pleased about the arrangement. He stood up. Might as well bite the bullet.

CHAPTER 6

The old-fashioned neon sign above the heavy wooden doors said 'Rick's Café Americain'. Lynch pushed his way through the door, forcing Tazi to step quickly after him. The restaurant's interior was a homage to another, more civilised age, with curved arches, a sculpted bar, balconies and balustrades. The walls were covered with *tadelakt*, intricate geometric tile patterns accenting the fireplaces and the risers of the central stairway. Lynch had visited before, drawn by the reference to his homeland, and while he remained impressed by the beauty of its traditional Moroccan craftsmanship, the theatrical trappings, as he'd indicated to Morry, galled him.

A figure detached itself from the bar; a man of middle height, dressed in a white tuxedo jacket, crisp white shirt and black bow tie. He wore his dark hair slicked back, a faded scar perpendicular to his top lip lending a stiffness to his mouth, from the corner of which dangled a cigarette. He stopped directly in front of Lynch.

'Of all the gin joints in all the towns in all world, he walks into mine.'

Lynch shook his head. 'It was kinda funny the first time, but I don't get it.' He barged through the hologram, making it flicker and glitch.

'You mean you've never seen the film? It's a mid-twentieth-century classic.'

'And here we are, almost in the twenty-second. So you'll forgive my lack of appreciation for ancient movies.'

Tazi shook her head and stepped round the hologram, which shrugged and made its way over to the piano on the far side of the bar, where the piano player greeted it with, 'You want me to play the song, boss?'

'Yeah, I want you to play the song.'

She caught up with Lynch just as he was ordering a beer with a whiskey chaser. 'You forgotten what you were told about ordering food and drink in public?'

'Nope. I heard you well enough. But I know these swine – poisoning me won't make enough of a statement for the folks back home. You having one?'

Tazi declined and Lynch tapped for his drinks. He downed the whiskey before picking up the beer and starting towards a corner table. Tazi caught hold of his good arm and steered him towards a more central table with a view of the exits. They sat either side of the brass table lamp, its beaded fringe reflecting the light in multiple colours at varying angles.

'I don't like it. This informant of yours could be setting you up.'

'You said that already. An' I already told you – no story ever waltzed up to a journalist sitting in his apartment.'

Lynch took a mouthful of beer. He knew it was her job, but Tazi's constant vigilance was jangling his nerves. His com-unit read 20:05. He looked round the bar, trying to spot any obvious contenders, and came up empty. Maybe Morry was right; he was overestimating his value to the resistance. He'd give it another beer, maybe two, before cutting his losses.

Their heads turned in unison as the door opened to admit a stocky figure with long hair and a bushy beard, dressed in cargo trousers, boots and a tight-fitting T-shirt.

He ignored the hologram's greeting and marched across to the bar, where the barman directed him to Lynch's table. Lynch saw Tazi's hand drop to her boot as the man approached.

The stranger thrust out a hand in greeting.

'Hank Russell. I'm a big fan of your work, Mr Lynch.'

Lynch backed away from the proffered hand and looked to Tazi for instruction. The CPO pointed a hand-held scanner at Russell and checked the readout.

'All right. You can sit. But I want both hands where I can see them.'

'Thank you.' Russell did as she said, apparently used to such precautions.

'Nice to hear an American accent,' Lynch said. 'Midwest?'

'Nebraska. Born and bred.'

'Uh-huh. Well, while it's always a pleasure to meet a fan, I get the feeling you're here for more than an autograph. What can I do for you?'

'Our mutual friend implied it was more a case of what you might be willing to do for us.'

'That rather depends on who "us" is.'

'Dreamers. Or should I say, people who share a common dream – the American one. Is that good enough for you?'

'Still kind of vague to be honest. But it looks like we do share a common goal. One I'd like to help with – cover your struggle, get the story out. For which I'm going to need access to the prime movers within the Free America movement.'

Russell's expression stiffened.

'I'm afraid that would require a level of trust that presently doesn't exist between us.'

'Goddamn it!' Lynch spat. 'I exposed that Templar psycho, Colonel Tyler, for wiping out a refugee column – barely made it out with my life. Plus, I've spent the last six months highlighting more of the same. What more proof do you need we're on the same side?'

'You were recruited by CIA Operations Officer Matthew Hannah?'

'"Blackmailed" is the word you're looking for. Gave me a choice between twenty years' federal time for drug smuggling or becoming a war correspondent.'

'And that,' Russell said, tapping his finger on the table, 'is exactly the sort of thing that doesn't do your credibility any favours. I knew Hannah back in the day when we were still batting for the same team. Even then, he was a devious sonofabitch, willing to play the long game. None of his agents would stand a chance of getting close to Free America. But a man like you, a critic and known agitator, apparently marked for death, might just make it.'

'I'd forgotten just how paranoid most of you spooks are. You really believe they'd flush Tyler's career down the pan just to set me up with a cover?'

'Our sources indicate the colonel's political aspirations far outweighed his devotion to God, which would have made sacrificing him an easy call. That said, he never struck me as the type to commit suicide. Maybe you can shed a little light on that?'

It was Lynch's turn to smile coldly.

'That would require a level of trust between us we've yet to attain. But here's the thing; if you really thought I was some sort of spy you wouldn't have bothered coming this evening. How about you stop pussyfooting around and tell me what it is you want from me. What exactly can I do to earn this much vaunted trust of yours?'

'Why don't we do just that.' Russell looked at Tazi. 'I'm going to put my hand, *slowly*, into my right pocket. All right?'

At Tazi's nod, he took out a white noise generator and placed it on the table.

'It's taken a long time to build the resistance and we can't afford to jeopardise it. No one, whatever their apparent bona fides, is above suspicion. So, with Captain Tazi's permission, I'm going to place a data-disc on the table.'

'Captain Tazi?' Lynch shot an inquiring glance at the CPO.

'Didn't your protector tell you? Prior to starting up RPS she served for five years with the Royal Moroccan Army. Decorated twice, I believe?'

Tazi's eyes narrowed as she silently reappraised Russell. Finally, she said, 'The disc?'

Lynch tried to keep his expression neutral as Russell placed the disc on the table, but it piqued his curiosity.

'You want to convince us you're for real? Broadcast the contents of this disc on TV21. But once you do, there's no turning back.'

Russell stood, pocketed the white noise generator and headed towards the exit.

Lynch looked across the table at Tazi.

'What do you think?'

'Without sounding too much like Russell, I think this could be some sort of elaborate double-bluff to draw you out or discredit you with false information. By your own admission, Morry Landau is the sort of low-life that would sell you out to the highest bidder.'

'Can't deny that's a possibility.' Lynch chewed his lip. 'But at the same time, it can't hurt to view the data. See if it's even half as explosive as Russell claims.'

Lynch reached for the disc, but Tazi was faster. She ran the scanner across it and confirmed it was negative for toxins and explosives. Even so, she placed it in one of the pockets of her tactical vest.

'All right. Finish your beer and we'll go back to your apartment and see what's on this mysterious disc.'

CHAPTER 7

Walker watched the vein throb in Hannah's temple. As he let the invective wash over him he wondered if the CIA's newest deputy director was about to stroke out. The thought made him nervous and he broke eye contact, looking off to the side.

Shelving lined three of the walls, giving the room a claustrophobic quality. Of all the offices in Langley, Hannah's was unique, with its reams of hard copy files – because paper couldn't be hacked and once you burned it the data was unrecoverable. As true as this was, such an eccentricity would not have been tolerated in a lesser agent. But no one could deny that Matt Hannah got results, or that he currently had the ear of the president. He was not a man to make an enemy of, so Walker kept his mouth shut as he listened to why his use of a drone strike was a poor choice and doomed to failure.

Finally seeing a gap, Walker said, 'With respect, sir, Lynch got lucky. He won't next time.'

'Was it luck?' Hannah steepled his fingers and fixed Walker with a basilisk stare. 'You served with Lynch.'

'He was assigned to my unit, yes, but we didn't spend much time together,' Walker explained, sounding more defensive than he intended. 'When he wasn't at Tyler's beck and call, he hung out with Cooper, Mackinlay, even the Israeli, Katz.'

'Ah, yes. Templar-Private Cooper, the last man standing from that little group. We're keeping an eye on him in case he's picked up any bad habits from Lynch. As to Jefferson Lynch himself.' Hannah stabbed out with his forefinger. 'You're to handle it in person this time. Your flight to Mohammed the Fifth International leaves at oh-six hundred tomorrow. There'll be a submarine waiting off the coast for your extraction. If it goes wrong we will, of course, deny all and any knowledge of you.'

'I still don't see why we're going to so much trouble over some redneck loser. The man's a drunk, a nobody. He can't hurt us.'

Hannah permitted himself a tight smile. 'And that, Joe, is the reason you're sitting on the other side of the desk.'

The deputy director picked up a file and started to leaf through it; Walker took the hint and stood. The quicker he put Lynch in the ground and could move on to a more important target, the happier he would be.

Walker paused outside the office and pinched the bridge of his nose in response to the beginning of a tension headache. A year ago, when Hannah had recruited him during his convalescence at Akrotiri Air Base, his role had seemed far clearer: eliminate problems. But his induction at Langley had featured interminable lectures on geopolitics and history, with a specific focus on the Middle East and its relationship with the Greater Russian Collective and the remnants of China and Pakistan. Walker had battled his way through them, viewing the texts as obstacles to overcome between tradecraft, surveillance and countersurveillance training. If the lectures had taught him nothing else it was that the only good Islamist was a dead one. This business of setting up one faction to face off against another invariably ended with them turning on you. Better to kill them all and let God sort it out. That's what his former brothers were doing out in Syria: making the world a better place one dead Abdul at a time. Perhaps it wasn't too late to go back? First, he had to complete this mission.

He made his way to the main open-plan office and sat down at his desk. A thumbprint and retinal scan unlocked his terminal. His fingers stabbed at the keyboard in a series of angry motions as he called up the latest intel on Lynch, who had been discharged from the hospital with minor injuries. Walker shook his head. That man really did have the Devil's luck.

Walker's com-unit pinged and the screen lit up with the notification of his flight details. He would be travelling under the name of Simon Enderby, a Canadian engineering student interviewing for an internship with the Alami Tech Corps. His hotel was booked under a different identity, Jon van Dijk, a Europa City national. Each came with an appropriate driver's licence and passport. He opened the attached biographical material and started to read, committing the details to memory.

CHAPTER 8

Hopkins turned up the collar of her suit jacket in an attempt at warding off the rain. The granite walls of the Panopticon's Outer-Circle contrasted sharply with the surrounding green of the lawn. But it was the Watchtower that drew the eye; six storeys of alabaster marble at the top of which sat the Central Office, providing the president with a 360-degree view. Work on a replacement for the White House had commenced in 2051 when the capitol was officially transferred to Richmond, with President Woody Lyndhurst taking up residence in 2054 at the beginning of his second term. The architectural style was simple to the point of austere, functionality taking precedence over aesthetics in a building designed to convey power.

A pair of secret service agents stood one either side of the steel entrance door. The older and more senior agent inclined his head in a slight nod as Hopkins approached.

'How are you today, Stuart?'

'I'm fine, Ms Hopkins.'

Stuart held up his hand as she stepped forward. Hopkins took a deep breath and exhaled, releasing her irritation. She had accessed the Panopticon almost every day for the last six months and without fail they went through the same pantomime. She produced her ID card and handed it to Stuart, who made a show of checking the photo before handing the card back and ushering her towards the biometric scanner. Fingerprints and facial scan verified, the door swished open, granting access to a curving corridor.

Hopkins followed the corridor to the right, moving in an anti-clockwise direction past the door of the Cabinet and Situation rooms to arrive at the Lyndhurst Room. A second biometric scan granted her access. The room beyond was keystone shaped, the walls narrowing towards the opposite end. Primarily used for press conferences, it contained a microphone-lined podium behind which Woody Lyndhurst stared down from his portrait on the wall, a pair of furled Cross and Stars flags, one either side, framing the former president. Lyndhurst had the beard of an Old Testament prophet and the country he had help found was one of wrath and vengeance, opposed to love and forgiveness. A nation where a woman either had to be exceptional or, Hopkins smiled bitterly to herself, extremely devious to get anywhere near the levers of power.

At the far end of the room she used her pass to summon the elevator; the Lyndhurst Room provided the official access point to the Watchtower. Hopkins pressed the button for the sixth floor and swiped open her com-unit. She checked her meeting notifications and sent out a stock response to the Panopticon's press office. The current press corps left a lot to be desired, comprising kids still wet behind the ears or jaded hacks, long since past their sell-by date. Her lip curled in distaste; at least there were no mavericks like Jefferson Lynch. That fucker really was the gift that kept on giving. The elevator door pinged open.

Hopkins knocked and entered the Central Office without waiting for a response. Gerrard stood with his back to her, staring out of the armoured window at the buildings below. He turned slowly and muttered a greeting, his attention clearly focused elsewhere.

'I take it you haven't forgotten we've a live broadcast scheduled in thirty minutes? Time to tell the world we've eliminated El Zayyoud and avenged President Hamilton.'

Gerrard nodded absently. 'Is he here?'

'Is who here?'

'Vanderbilt,' Gerrard snapped. 'Who else? That old bastard won't have forgotten us dragging him before a Senate inquiry. Instead of stepping down he's tightening his hold on power, meeting regularly with Bishop Gibson and Bishop Connors. If he gets the full weight of the Church behind the Templars we could be in real trouble. Shit, I wouldn't put it past him to have been behind what happened to Tyler.'

'Now you're just being paranoid.'

'I'm not so sure. Why isn't Hannah watching Vanderbilt? The ungrateful shit seems to have forgotten that I made deputy director of the Agency.'

'You need to focus, Charles. Have you read through the speech I sent you?'

'There you go again. Treating me as though I'm some rank amateur.'

'I think nothing of the sort. But we might want to hold off announcing further troop deployments – it's playing badly in the focus groups.'

'I've read the reports, Susanna. But there's no point having the Caliphate on the run if we don't capitalise on it.'

'I get where you're coming from with that, but we also need to consider the midterms. On the subject of which, I'm going to seek the nomination for Virginia.'

'A five-term senator like Paul Rodgers will be a tough act to follow.' Gerrard's eyes bored into Hopkins. 'You wouldn't happen to know who leaked his predilection for young boys to the press?'

Hopkins smiled coldly. 'As Bishop Gibson is apt to remind us, sodomy is a sin.'

'As are adultery and fornication.'

'Touché, Charles. But seeing as you're hardly without

sin, I take it I can rely on your full support?'

A knock at the door saved Gerrard from having to answer. He called out 'enter' and a make-up artist appeared to prepare him for his broadcast.

Hopkins was of a mind to send the girl away, but she had scheduled the broadcast herself. She would just have to work on Gerrard another time.

'Twenty-five minutes to broadcast. Make sure you read through the speech again.'

'You're not staying to watch?'

'I have to prepare a statement for the press about the destruction of the Umayyad Mosque, remember? Computer error ought to suffice. Should quieten down the sabre-rattling from Europa City and the African Tech Corps.'

Hopkins nodded to Gerrard, secure in the knowledge that the presence of the make-up girl made it impossible for him to reply to her subtle rebuke. But her mood was dour as she swept from the room; she was tired of cleaning up after Gerrard. Targeting religious and historic sites might play well with the grassroots support back home, but they couldn't afford the international condemnation. If Europa City followed through on its threat to impose sanctions the war machine would stutter to a halt. Why did all the men in her life have a pathological desire to break shit? Tyler might have been a vicious thug, but in many respects that was his job. Gerrard, though, ought to know better. He was right about one thing: Grand Master Vanderbilt had undoubtedly played a part in Tyler's untimely demise. But there was no sense in fuelling his paranoia. She would speak to Hannah instead and find a way to draw Vanderbilt's fangs.

Hopkins nodded absently to one of the staffers, stepping round him as he exited the elevator. The control panel lit up in response to her thumbprint, displaying the options appropriate to her security clearance, and she selected her office on the fourth floor. She examined her reflection in the elevator's mirrored walls as it descended, and smoothed down the lines of her skirt, which stopped a modest six inches below her knees, revealing plain stockings. Her make-up was subtle but flawless, foundation with a hint of blusher to highlight her cheekbones, and a light gloss on the lips. It was the look of a professional and competent woman, one who wanted to be taken seriously. But in the swamp of Richmond politics a woman had to work twice as hard as a man to earn a quarter of the respect. Sometimes, she wondered if it was worth all the pain. Ambition was indeed a cruel master.

Hopkins sat at her desk and swiped on her terminal. The half-composed press release stared balefully back at her. The excuses were just that, lacking conviction or any sense of remorse. Damn Gerrard. It could wait. She opened another document. A decade of lobbying on the Hill had made her a lot of enemies, but it had also given her the dirt on many of them. Gerrard's endorsement was all well and good, but she was going to need more political muscle to reach the Senate. She scanned the list of names, looking for a suitable candidate, then hit dial on her com-unit.

'What the hell do you want?' Gerschwitz snarled.

'Now, David, is that any way to greet an old friend?'

'You're not a friend. You're a viper. A particularly poisonous one at that.'

'True,' Hopkins conceded, 'and if you don't want bit, you better listen up. I'll be announcing my candidacy for the Senate next week. I expect your full backing.'

'Fine. Just don't go expecting any miracles.'

'What's that supposed to mean?'

'You're not exactly Miss Congeniality.'

There was a click as the call was terminated. Hopkins stared at her com-unit and then dropped it on the desk with a shrug. She could live with that.

CHAPTER 9

Cooper swung the M60 on its mount, angling it down towards a line of Caliphate soldiers below. The ammunition belt rattled through the gun as he depressed the trigger, M13 links pinging on the cabin floor as it sent out a steady stream of death. He felt numb as he watched the enemy combatants twist and turn under the impact of the DU flechettes, which were encased in a plastic sabot loaded into a standard 7.62 x 51mm case. Designed primarily for armour, the flechettes reached velocities in excess of 4,000 fps, punching through human flesh to exit in a shower of blood and bone fragments. On the opposite side of the SB Defiant XV attack helicopter Pedersen's M60 spat out a similar rain of destruction as the AI piloted them across the Caliphate front lines. Behind them, the ruins of Damascus stretched back to a horizon dominated by Mount Qasioun. It was here, in a series of complex entrenchments, that the city's defenders would make their final stand. Casualty projections for a ground assault were high and so the Templar's Combat Aviation Brigade had once more taken to the skies to pave the way.

The Defiant banked sharply away and upwards, accelerating to its maximum speed of 365 kph. Cooper swung himself in from the door and gripped his lanyard where it attached to the frame above his head. The loading drone swung out on its rail opposite, its mechanical arms feeding a fresh ammunition belt into the M60. He felt the vibration through the soles of his boots as the Defiant launched the first two of its complement of sixteen Hellfire missiles. A second and third pair followed at two-second intervals. Then the chain gun rattled to life, a five-second burst firing fifty 30mm rounds. The High Command called it shock and awe, but to Cooper it felt more like murder. He looked sideways at the stiff-backed figure of Colonel Willard, who in turn looked out of the cockpit window, monitoring the destruction below. The console in front of Willard displayed real-time telemetry from the other five attack helicopters, overlaid across satellite images of the Caliphate defences. Counters totalled each round and missile as it was fired, followed by its projected impact on the enemy's strength. Unlike his disgraced predecessor, Willard was bereft of any gung-ho desire to get his boots on the ground. The mission objective was to take the Caliphate stronghold and he was committed to accomplishing that goal in the most efficient manner possible.

The Defiant's nose dipped as it decelerated towards the ground and Cooper automatically swung back to the ready position. He initiated the live satellite feed on his HUD and spotted an enemy NSTV as it emerged from behind the cover of a ruined building. Armour plating covered the windscreen and hood of the heavily modified Toyota Hilux, but it was the DShK heavy machine gun mounted on the flat bed that caught his attention as the operator trained its distinctive 'spider web' ring sights on the Defiant. As superannuated as the weapon was, it didn't make it any less dangerous. As if to prove the point, a .50 calibre round punched through the fuselage above his head, showering the cabin with shrapnel. Cooper ignored the pain as a piece of white-hot metal ripped open his right cheek, and returned fire, pivoting the M60 round to target the NSTV from the rear as the helicopter flew past. His first burst tore through the gunner, propelling him over the Hilux's cab and depositing his spreadeagled body across the hood. The next burst ripped through the cab itself. The ensuing explosion lifted the vehicle into the air and deposited it on its roof, leaving its wheels to spin ineffectually in the air.

'Hey, Coop! You all right, man?'

'Yeah, just a flesh wound,' Cooper replied to Pedersen, feeling the warm wetness that soaked the neck of his tunic for the first time. His hand shook as he fumbled a field dressing from his tactical vest and applied it to his cheek. For all the horrors he had witnessed, Cooper had emerged physically unscathed until now. The wound was an unwelcome reminder of his own mortality. He hoped it wasn't a presage of the future.

'Sharpen up, soldier!'

'Yes, sir!'

Muscle memory guided Cooper's hands as he checked the ammunition feed to his weapon. He scanned the satellite stream and selected a fresh target on the ground as the Defiant turned in for another attack. Pedersen's M60 chattered in unison with his own as they strafed the Caliphate trench below, tearing up sandbags and sending the enemy diving for cover. The last of the ammunition belt fed through Cooper's gun as the copter banked sharply again, circling upwards.

Cooper felt as much as heard the *whumph-whumph* as another pair of Hellfire missiles sped away from the Defiant. They struck the side of Mount Qasioun, initiating an avalanche of rock and scree that swept away trees, shrubs and Caliphate emplacements with cold neutrality. Explosions from their sister attack helicopters produced similar effects, the squadron acting in concert to obliterate an entire flank of the mountain.

Willard shook his head tersely as an amber warning light flashed on the console. He toggled on comms.

'Chorus of Vengeance, this is Choirmaster. All attack

craft are to return to base for resupply.'

The colonel finally turned his back on the destruction below and faced his crew.

'Good shooting today, boys. Abdul is learning the hard way not to mess with the RS of A. Keep this up and it just might all be over by Christmas.'

Pedersen responded with an enthusiastic fist pump. Cooper kept his own counsel as he stared at the arid landscape below. He didn't need to turn round to know Willard had his eyes fixed on him. The colonel had been decidedly cool since their run-in over El Zayyoud. Cooper felt the lash marks on his back twinge in sympathy at the memory, a reminder that he could not afford to show any weakness or engender doubt in the minds of his brothers if he wanted to make it out of this alive. He swung himself round into the cabin.

'Christmas, eh? I'd sure prefer my ma's cooking to MREs.'

'God willing, you will get your wish.' Willard locked eyes with Cooper. 'Although I doubt He will be able to spare all of His soldiers.'

Cooper unclipped his lanyard from his vest and jumped down to the deck of the aircraft carrier. The Defiants were on a forty-minute turnaround for refuelling and rearmament, and Willard had let the medical officer know he had a soldier coming in for treatment. Cooper spotted him, a tall figure in a white tunic, standing on the far side of the deck next to a trestle table.

The MO checked his pad. 'TP Cooper, shrapnel wound?'

Cooper nodded and the doctor put aside his pad and opened the case on the table. Without warning, he reached up and tore the dressing from Cooper's face. Cooper stifled a curse.

'Quit grousing. I've had bigger cuts shaving.'

Cooper gritted his teeth as the MO irrigated the wound with saline solution. His nitrile-clad fingers probed the edges of the laceration.

'Yes, nothing to worry about. Soon have you good as new.'

True to his word, the MO closed the wound with skin glue and applied a fresh dressing. He picked up a needle-gun from the case and fired the antibiotics through Cooper's uniform tunic and into his right shoulder. Cooper rubbed his arm.

'That's us done here. Get moving. Chop chop!'

Cooper took the hint and made his way inside the carrier. He passed along the corridor with its engraved crucifix on one side and the all-seeing eye of God on the other, designed to survive anything short of the ship's destruction. Reaching the first set of stairs, he descended, turning right at the bottom. Here, the carrier's design had been modified to suit the spiritual requirements of the Order; the compact chapel was followed by six penitents' cells, where errant brothers could spend time in prayer and reflection. The door to the gymnasium stood open, the whipping post at odds with the vaulting horse and parallel bars. Cooper felt a phantom pain between his shoulders and hurried on. Arrows pointed the way to the galley and he increased his pace, boots ringing on the chequer plate floor.

Cooper nodded to the crew members of the other Defiants as he navigated between the tables to reach the one where Pedersen sat alone.

Pedersen pointed to one of the pair of steaming mugs.

'Coffee. Black. No sugar.'

Cooper nodded his thanks and picked up the mug. The coffee scalded his tongue, but he took a second mouthful regardless, enjoying the kick of the caffeine. Pedersen wrapped both hands round his own mug and blew on the surface. The steam formed a sheen on his swarthy skin. If Cooper was honest, he didn't much care for the man, but other than Sergeant Jackson he was the last of his own intake, the others having been redeployed while he and Pedersen were on punishment duty in Jerusalem. Pedersen had hit the beach at Palmachim with him. Been there on that fateful day of the refugee massacre. Waded through gore on the streets of Jerusalem to wrest it from Caliphate control. That surely had to count for something. Just what, Cooper wasn't certain. And did it really matter in the grand scheme of things?

Pedersen, in common with the rest of the men in the galley, looked unperturbed by what had just taken place. Was it a lack of imagination or intellectual capacity that allowed his brothers to carry out their orders by rote? Perhaps, but Cooper was under no illusions as to his own intellect. His instructors had drilled it into him time and time again that the Caliphate was their sworn enemy. The Templars' holy mission was to destroy the enemy in the name of the one true God. It seemed simple and true enough until you were faced with taking a man's life; taking everything away from him before he took it away from you. But what if his brothers were right and he was somehow defective, an aberration? Damn Lynch and his questions! The crazy fucker had infected his thinking and there was no cure for it.

He checked the time on his com-unit: twenty minutes until the next assault. Pedersen sat calmly drinking his coffee, enjoying a break from duty. Cooper's coffee now tasted bitter. If only he could click his heels together and be home, 'cause he sure as shit wasn't in Arkansas.

'Word has it Ismail himself is leading the insurgents,' Pedersen said, a hint of awe creeping into his voice.

'Marshal Ismail?'

'Ain't that what I just said? Intel says he assumed command after we put down al-Qurayshi in Jerusalem.'

'He's the new caliph?'

'Not in name, but certainly in everything else that counts.' Pedersen glanced furtively around and lowered his voice. 'Gonna be a tough nut to crack. Back in seventy-three he led the counterattack on Tel Aviv – drove our forces back into the sea after drawing them out with a feint. Ordered the wounded put to the sword – pure medieval shit.'

'Yeah, I remember Sergeant Jackson talking about that. Said the Caliphate would have been driven out of Saudi Arabia in less than a year, but for Ismail. Took closer to four in the end, and not for want of trying to kill him. Thought they'd gotten close once or twice with drone strikes, but they turned to be decoys. Kept his command post mobile and his circle small, deliberately firing out disinformation. If he's really at Mount Qasioun you can be sure we only know because he wants us to know.'

'Or maybe he's finally slipped up. Happens to everyone eventually. One thing you can be sure of, if he's there Willard will want his scalp. And you know what that means...'

'Yeah. We're the hammer he's going to use to crack that nut.'

'Kneel!'

The Templars obeyed the command as one, dropping to their knees and placing the palms of their right hands over their hearts. Colonel Willard copied their actions, but where his men bowed their heads, he raised his own towards the heavens, his voice loud and clear as he recited the prayer before battle.

'Lord, we beseech thee in the name of thy son, Jesus Christ, to bestow your blessing on this, our most holy and solemn undertaking. May you strengthen our resolve that our arms will not weaken against the heathen; that we be victorious over him and all his evil works. Not for us, my lord, not for us, but to your name give the glory. Amen!'

The Templars chorused the final amen and rose, peeling off into their assigned units for the assault. Sergeant Jackson reached out and gripped Cooper's right arm just above the elbow. Cooper returned the grip, with a quick squeeze. Jackson might fully believe in the mission, but he possessed a moral compass Cooper often found lacking in the other Templars. His presence quieted Cooper's doubts.

'Good to see you, son.'

'And you, Sarge. Guess we're ready to rock 'n' roll?'

'Yeah. Time to kick Abdul's butt again.'

Cooper pulled open the driver's door of the JLTV. It, and the rest of the fleet, were the fast-attack version with larger wheels and a jacked-up rear axle with improved suspension. He climbed inside and started the JLTV, its souped-up e-turbo engine delivering 616 horsepower. It was a beast of a machine compared with the standard transport model and Cooper felt a guilty pleasure in driving it.

Jackson clambered into the front passenger seat while Pedersen, Goodman and Martinez boarded the rear compartment of the vehicle, the latter visibly bouncing with barely restrained energy. Cooper felt wary of Tyler's former adjutant: he had the air of a man with something to prove since being reassigned to regular combat duty. Goodman had recently been promoted to corporal, a role he did not seem fully comfortable with. But, as the Syrian campaign became increasingly bitter, it was clear his combat skills were more valued than his role as a translator: dead men, after all, tell no tales.

Jackson signalled to move out and Cooper put the transmission in drive. The other twelve JLTVs rolled forward in an arrow formation with Willard's command vehicle at its apex. They jolted across a landscape pocked and cratered like the moon, rolling up collapsed walls like ramps and briefly launching themselves skyward as they sped towards Mount Qasioun. Against the odds, ragged pockets of Caliphate resistance emerged from dugouts, shell holes and tumbledown buildings. Tracer rounds arced towards the Templar convoy, most sparking harmlessly off the JLTVs' armour. But at least one found its mark; the third JLTV at the right of the formation bumped into its neighbour before slewing to a halt. Cooper initiated the CROWS and the automated turret atop the JLTV began spitting out .50 calibre rounds, targeting via infrared and motion sensors. The rear-view cam showed the stricken JLTV starting up again and accelerating back into formation.

Cooper checked the countdown on the dash display and eased up on the accelerator. The railguns fired on cue, arcing over the Templar convoy to rain destruction on the Caliphate entrenchments at the foot of the mountain. Cooper eased off the power further, allowing time for the railguns to recharge and fire a second salvo. Rock, plascrete, steel and body parts were thrown up into the air to fall as gory precipitation. A secondary chain of explosions followed as a munitions dump went up, an oily black cloud mushrooming into the sky. The CROWS continued to pick off the dogged survivors, impervious to pleas or gestures of surrender. At his swearing in, following Hamilton's assassination, President Gerrard had promised there would be no quarter given. The Caliphate was to be pursued in every theatre of war with extreme prejudice. The CROWS higher AI functionality and threat analysis had been disabled, resulting in them denuding the landscape of life. Moral implications aside, Templar casualties were down and Gerrard's approval rating up.

Cooper stopped the JLTV at the foot of the mountain; the railgun bombardment and preceding airstrikes had left the terrain too broken and unstable to traverse. From this point on it would be a deadly game of hide and seek with the surviving insurgents, hunting them down through the series of caves dug into the mountain.

Willard's voice sounded over the comms.

'Weapons hot, boys. And make sure your cams capture images of all Caliphate dead, just in case we bag any celebrities. Okay, let's get this done!'

'Fuckin' A!' Martinez snarled as he jumped from the JLTV.

Cooper followed Jackson's more cautious lead, lowering his goggles, initiating the HUD and synching it to his motion detector. They fanned out, moving gingerly across the rock fragments and scree, weapons at the ready. The air was still, but heavy with the acrid smell of high explosive. Something turned under Cooper's foot and he looked down at a severed forearm. Time was he would have retched, but by now he'd seen too much for the human detritus of war to affect him.

'There!' Martinez's assault rifle chattered, throwing the plump body of a rabbit high into the air.

'Yeah, reckon he was pointing towards Mecca. Must have been a Muslim bunny.'

'Fuck you, Pedersen!'

Sergeant Jackson waved them to silence and pointed to the half-collapsed mouth of a cave. Cooper went to infrared and followed Jackson into its maw, with Pedersen watching their six. The floor angled up steeply while the ceiling dropped, forcing them to proceed at a crouch. It was as silent as a tomb and Cooper suspected that was exactly what it had become for its Caliphate defenders. Suspicion became fact seconds later when he encountered the first in a series of Caliphate casualties. The body lay curled against the wall where the shock wave had thrown it. A blast powerful enough to propel a body through the air killed by rupturing the lungs, spraying blood into the alveoli, leaving no room for that all important life-giving air. Cooper turned the body over with his foot. The facial recognition software chimed negative. He moved on.

The tunnel opened into a large chamber, toolmarks on the wall indicating it had been extended by human hands. Food and munitions crates lay scattered across the floor, spilling their contents. Cooper pictured a frantic search for supplies as the Templar missiles impacted the mountain. But where had the insurgents fled? He spotted scuff marks on the ground, ending in a stack of boxes pushed against the wall. Passing his hand up and down the edge, he felt the faint movement of air.

'Sarge! Got something here.'

Jackson held up his hand as Cooper made to slide back the crates and he froze in position. The sergeant squatted down and Cooper followed his line of sight to where a monofilament wire snaked off into the darkness. Jackson traced the wire along the side of the crate to the point it disappeared through a narrow gap. He shook his head and stood up.

'Fall back,' Jackson ordered. He pointed to the ceiling at the mouth of the tunnel they had entered by. 'Coop. Pedersen. I want charges up there. Abdul wants a tomb; we'll give him one.'

Cooper opened his belt pouch and extracted a block of C4. He pressed it into the roof of the tunnel and inserted a detonator. Six paces down the tunnel, Pedersen repeated the procedure and signalled to Jackson. The sergeant waved them off down the tunnel, following behind.

Cooper paused at the entrance to the tunnel and confirmed his sensor readings were clear. He emerged blinking into the light and retreated another twenty metres, where he turned and covered Pedersen's exit. Jackson appeared five seconds later, his rifle slung over his shoulder, a radio detonator in his hand. His head tilted back as he examined the cracked face of the mountain. He took half a dozen paces back and pressed the detonator.

Dust and smoked billowed from the tunnel in the wake of the muffled explosion. A deafening crack sounded as a slab of rock sheared off the mountain face and Jackson took another set of hurried steps back as it crashed into the ground, sealing the tunnel behind tonnes of stone.

'Don't think you'll be rolling that away in three days' time, motherfuckers.'

CHAPTER 10

T V21 Interview Transcript #2: Jefferson Lynch in conversation with Aluf Mishne Shimon Baruch of the Israel Defense Forces via satellite link from Jerusalem.

Jefferson Lynch: Colonel, firstly, I'd like to thank you for agreeing to this interview. I'm sure you're a busy man, with many responsibilities.

Shimon Baruch: True, there is much to do in order to protect and defend our borders, but I also feel it is important to set the record straight. As is the case throughout so much of history, foul and untrue rumours are circulating about the state of Israel and the intentions of our government. As you were witness first-hand to the liberation of Jerusalem before your ... hasty departure, who better than yourself to test the veracity of my words?

JL: Thank you for that vote of confidence, Colonel. Bearing that in mind, perhaps we should start with the elephant, or should that be the molecule, in the room. You freely admit to the deployment of a targeted nano-virus against Caliphate troops in Jerusalem? A form of weapon explicitly proscribed under the terms of the North–West Frontier Accord.

SB: Is that what you journalists call a leading question, Mr Lynch? You were there. You saw the result of the weapon. The Knesset does not deny the safe deployment of such a weapon.

JL: 'Safe deployment' meaning the literal liquidation of almost two hundred men in less than a minute?

SB: The Accord you speak of primarily deals with the indiscriminate use of such weapons against civilians and the possibility of a runaway reaction, leading to an extinction level event. The weapon used was range- and time-limited, rendering such events impossible. More pertinently, its deployment saved many thousands of lives — Christian, Jewish and Muslim — as without it, the fighting would have continued for many weeks, if not months.

JL: Say the world is willing to accept that defence — the use of a banned weapon in order to save lives. The question must be asked: do you have more of these weapons? And if so, under what circumstances are you willing to use them?

SB: Israel has a right to defend itself.

JL: With respect, Colonel, that's not an answer.

SB: It is as much of an answer as I am able to give.

JL: Guess we're going to have to take that as a yes. Moving on, satellite jamming technology has now been in place over Israel for six months, rendering it opaque to observers.

SB: A security measure. We do not wish to be spied on, by our enemies or our friends.

JL: And does that fear of being spied on extend to UN inspectors? Or is there some other reason they have been barred from entering Israel?

SB: You refer to the rumours of concentration camps, yes?

JL: Isn't the official term 'resettlement camps'? Shanty towns for those unwilling or unable to return to their former homes in the Caliphate.

SB: That is precisely what they are, Mr Lynch, although I object to the use of the word 'shanty'. Yes, these are prefab structures, but they are fully equipped with sanitation, running water, electricity and a plentiful supply of food.

JL: And communications?

SB: That, I'm afraid, has not been possible on security grounds. Residents, however, are entitled to have messages sent on their behalf.

JL [mumbled]: That's mighty white of you.

SB: I'm sorry, I did not catch that, Mr Lynch. Would you please repeat.

JL: Must be the connection. Surely you can understand how it looks to the outside world? No satellite imagery. No inspections. No first-hand communications. It's all well and good citing security, but with the best will in the world, it looks like you have something to hide.

SB: I assure you and your subscribers that we are hiding nothing. Vital defence work is currently taking place to ensure there can never be a repeat of the tragedy of '63, during which time we cannot risk any information falling into the hands of our enemies. This has meant operating at the highest security level. But rest assured, from next month, UN and NGO inspectors will be allowed access to the camps.

JL: They will, huh?

SB: You sound surprised? I would have thought, after your reporting in Jerusalem, you'd have realised we're not monsters. A great wrong has been done to our people — one of many throughout history. But we refuse to repay it in kind, whatever propaganda the antisemites might spread.

JL: The intention of this interview is to establish the facts, not spread lies. If all is as you say, Colonel, I'll ensure my subscribers are among the first to know.

SB: I'd expect nothing less from a man of your ... integrity. Now, if you'll excuse me, I do indeed have other matters to attend to.

JL: Of course. And thank you again for your time, Colonel. It's been illuminating.

Transcript Ends

Lynch tapped the ash off his cigarette into an overflowing ashtray, disturbing the empty bourbon bottle and the dirty glass next to his datapad. A low whistle escaped his lips as he contemplated what appeared to be a copy of a classified CIA document authorising the assassination of President Hamilton and his replacement by Gerrard, seen as a safer pair of hands for furthering American interests. Exactly how much of a smoking gun the file was would depend on whether he could verify it as genuine. But for Lynch's money it looked the part. Or maybe that was the whole point, to play to his prejudices. Either way, Russell was right; the contents were dynamite.

Lynch stubbed out his cigarette and scooped his datapad into his satchel.

'I'm heading to the station to see the news editor.'

Tazi appeared from the kitchen and barred his way to the door.

'Wouldn't it be safer to just email the file?'

'Can't risk it – the file's too sensitive to risk it being intercepted. Besides, if I know that old stoat Berkani, he'll take some convincing to run the story.'

'In that case I'll accompany you.'

Lynch gave an indifferent shrug to disguise his relief and let Tazi get the door. He locked the apartment and followed her down to the underground garage, where she had left the Lincoln. The doors clicked open at her approach and Lynch bundled himself into the passenger seat and belted himself in. As the car drove off, he took out the data-disc and stared at it. Could something seemingly so small and unimportant really be the key to bringing down the Gerrard administration?

The car took an unexpected left turn, more of Tazi's evasive manoeuvres. He looked over, intending to protest, impatient to reach the TV21 offices as swiftly as possible, but Tazi's expression brooked no argument. He wondered if he had overreacted in engaging a CPO, wondered if his enemies would content themselves with one attempt on his life. Then he looked down at the disc, thought about its contents, and knew the RSA wasn't about to forgive and forget. Its short and brutal history provided plenty of examples.

Tazi pulled the Lincoln up onto the sidewalk and stopped directly opposite the entrance to the office. Lynch's door opened of its own accord and he unclipped his seatbelt. In the time it took for him to unfold his limbs, Tazi had sprinted round the front of the vehicle. Her pistol was in her hand, held discreetly against her left thigh, trigger finger flat against the slide. She motioned Lynch towards the entrance with her eyes.

Tazi followed close behind, tailgating him when he used his ID badge and retinal scan to open the door. The security guard looked up and waved to Lynch as he crossed to the elevators, seemingly oblivious to his shadow. Lynch made a mental note to speak to Berkani about the useless fat fuck. Tazi all but pushed him into the elevator, apparently sensing the risk of a confrontation.

The elevator indicator seemed to move with impossible slowness as the carriage ascended to the sixth floor. Lynch felt Tazi's hand on his arm as she attempted to ground him.

He took a deep breath and shook out his arms as the elevator doors finally hissed open. He covered the distance to the editor's office in a couple of long strides and rapped smartly on the door with his knuckles.

Malik Berkani looked up from his screen as Lynch barged in, a note of annoyance flickering across his face. Lynch, deciding it best not to give him the opportunity to remonstrate, slapped the disc down on the desk.

'Read what's on here before you say anything. I guarantee you won't be disappointed.'

Berkani, used to Lynch's mercurial moods, inserted the disc into his pad. His eyes widened as he caught sight of Tazi standing behind and slightly to Lynch's left.

'Who the hell is she and what's she doing in my office? In case you've forgotten, this is meant to be a secure building.'

'She's probably all that's standing between you being my employer and having to pay out on my death-in-service benefits. Or did the explosion in the street a couple of days back escape your notice?'

Berkani tutted but his reply remained unspoken as he took in the contents of the newly opened document. He skimmed through it quickly, letting out a low whistle. But experience had long since taught him that anything that looked too good to be true probably was.

'It's one thing to claim the CIA was behind President Hamilton's assassination, but unless your source can prove it, it's just another crazy conspiracy theory.'

'He didn't strike me as the type to go on record. But it's a moot point. We both know the RSA will deny it, whatever provenance we find. Best course of action is to publish and be damned. Put the bastards on the back foot. The more they deny it, the more people will believe the truth of it.'

Berkani shook his head. 'Legal won't accept that kind of risk. If it's not verified, it doesn't run. End of story.'

'Seriously? This is dynamite. Exactly the kind of exposé you've been hounding me for. You can't just dismiss it out of hand. Not when it's the very shit you hired me to find.'

'You've been a journalist and a broadcaster long enough to know how this works – there isn't a news network in the whole of North Africa that will risk bankruptcy by running that story as is.' Berkani waved his hand. 'Go off, do some due diligence, and we'll talk again if you find anything.'

Lynch held out his hand for the disc and Berkani ejected it from his pad. Lynch's knuckles whitened as he clenched his fingers round the disc.

'I thought you had more balls. More vision. Guess I was wrong.'

Berkani leaned back in his chair and folded his arms.

'And I thought you were a professional. On the subject of which, you owe me a broadcast for tomorrow. Don't be late, or I may have to reassess your contract.'

Lynch gritted his teeth as he resisted the urge to swing for Berkani. He needed him for now and the swine knew it, so he nodded and turned on his heel. He felt Tazi's hand on his shoulder, subtle pressure once again pushing him forward, the CPO's duty extending to protecting him from himself.

Lynch's anger built steadily all the way back to the car. Russell had made it clear that access to Free America depended on him broadcasting the document, but he knew Berkani well enough to know the editor wouldn't back down. If Berkani wouldn't sanction it, he'd just have to go through the back door. Whatever ICE TV21 had in place protecting their systems, it surely wasn't in the same league as the mil-spec Black ICE he'd hacked to broadcast the truth about Colonel Tyler.

Tazi turned to face Lynch, blocking his way to the car.

'I hope you're not about to do anything stupid.'

'What makes you think I might be?'

'Because you're smiling, and not in a comforting way.'

'Guess I'm going to have to work on that.'

CHAPTER 11

T he cave was almost forty metres below the surface but it still shook in response to the explosions above, depositing a rain of dust that dropped through the holo-map. Of the three men present, two looked fearfully towards the ceiling while the third man's attention remained focused on the projected aerial map. He studied it intently for a few seconds before pointing to a warren of streets at the heart of Damascus.

'Here. This is where we will challenge the American infidels. As with the other captured districts, they must expend resources to hold on to gains. We will bleed them with hit-and-fade tactics. Make them pay for each square foot in blood. With their lines of supply already stretched, this will slow them to a crawl.'

Silence followed Marshal Ismail's announcement and he looked to his two colleagues; both were in their late forties, the shorter, more compact one bore the insignia of a lieutenant general, the other that of a brigadier general.

'You disagree?'

The shorter man looked to his companion and rocked on his heels.

'No, but I see no plan for victory. I hear talk of delay and hold, but the reality is Caliphate territory shrinks daily. Surely this cannot be the will of Allah?'

'It is not for man to question the will of Allah. You know this, Ahmad.'

'Apologies, Marshal.' Ahmad bowed his head. 'But it is not easy to see our glorious Caliphate so oppressed by the infidels. They've taken Jerusalem and given it back to their Jewish lapdogs. Destroyed the glory of Al Aqsa Mosque, and martyred Caliph Abu Ahmad al-Nasr al-Qurayshi in the same cowardly attack. They lie. They kill. They spread the word of their false god with impunity. How can this be so?'

'We live in challenging times, of that there can be no doubt. But now is not the time for our faith to weaken.' Ismail turned to his other subordinate, who up until now had remained silent. 'And you, Carim, old friend. Do you also doubt the wisdom of our course of action?'

'No, you are the most gifted of our commanders, and a worthy successor to our beloved caliph, may he dwell for eternity in Paradise. But I do share our brother's frustration. We need to strike back at the Americans on their home soil. Bring death and terror directly to their lands. Make their people suffer as ours have suffered. They should not be allowed to sleep soundly in their beds while our women lament and our children wail.'

Ismail switched off the holo-map, preferring not to step through it, and reached out to rest his hand on Carim's shoulder.

'In time, I truly believe the Americans will bring these things on themselves. But for now, I counsel patience. The world watches and it is not blind. Our enemy is cunning. You know as well as I that we had nothing to do with President Hamilton's assassination. This was a classic false flag operation, designed to stir up support for the Americans' continued aggression against Islam. El Zayyoud was a man of deep faith, but he was no jihadist. It would have been an easy matter for the CIA to hire a cybernaut from Europa City or North Africa to falsify his financial records and produce their so-called smoking gun.'

'Then why do we not tell the world?' Carim snarled.

'Because the world is not ready to listen. I do not ask for your patience for no reason. Our intelligence reports discord, both within the Religious States and outside of it in the supposedly subjugated territories of the former United States. Rest assured, we are whispering words in the right ears, diverting funds as appropriate. The infidels are not the only ones who can plot and scheme. Soon, they will have to look to their own shores and we will be ready to sweep them back into the waters of the Mediterranean. We are playing the long game here. But let me assure you that our final victory is coming.'

Another missile strike shook the cave, sending down a fresh rain of dust and pebbles. Lieutenant General Ahmad removed his olive kepi and shook the red sand from it.

'I think they're getting closer.'

Ismail nodded his agreement. 'Come. We shall move to the lower levels and continue our discussion on the defence of the city.'

The marshal reached down and turned the iron ring set into a hatch in the floor. A vein stood out on his temple as he pulled back on the ring, his subordinates knowing better than to offer assistance. The hatch swung ponderously upwards, locking into position at ninety degrees. Ismail fumbled around the inside lip of the hatch and a harsh white light fluoresced to life, illuminating the rungs of a ladder fixed to the wall. He motioned Ahmad and Carim forward, allowing them both to descend before him while a steady stream of debris fell from the ceiling.

Ismail pulled the hatch closed and, gripping the outside of the ladder with his feet and hands, slid rapidly to the bottom. The tunnel at its base was large enough for him to stand upright and he followed its gradual downward slope for fifty metres before it opened into a spherical chamber with another two tunnels leading off from it. Ahmad and Carim were already seated at the trestle table in the centre of the room. Ismail sat opposite them and once more projected the holo-map from his com-unit. He felt the faintest of tremors as the bombardment continued above and looked towards one of the exits. The Americans thought they had successfully entombed their enemies, but the mountain was like a rabbit warren with multiple exits, its chambers and tunnels hewn out of the rock over the decades by successive generations of fighters. Ismail knew the ordnance currently being deployed would, at most, collapse some of the upper levels. Detonation of a MOAB would be a different story. Fortunately, the proximity of Damascus and its civilian population was likely to curtail such a move, with the Americans still recovering from the bad PR generated by the railgun bombardment of Jerusalem. Still, they were fanatics, and one could never be too careful of such men. He offered up a silent prayer to Allah and bent once more over the map.

'The old quarter of the city is a maze of winding streets and derelict houses. As I said previously, guerrilla tactics will serve us well in this environment.' Ismail looked to his subordinates and received curt nods in response. 'Good. We are agreed. Now, before we offer up our prayers for victory, let us discuss Operation Lahab. Ahmad, you have selected some suitable targets?'

'Yes, Marshal, we've mapped various patrol routes. The Americans are arrogant – not expecting any opposition, they run patrols on a regular basis. It will be easy to ambush one.'

'Good. But remember, this is not about revenge. We need prisoners. It is vital that the world sees these Templars are not the invincible gods the Americans make them out to be. We will prove they are just men. Men who can be humbled.'

CHAPTER 12

Cooper looked out of the window of the JLTV as it jolted its way through the streets of the now subjugated Damascus. The devastation was almost total, with three in four buildings reduced to rubble, twisted lengths of rebar reaching imploringly towards the sky. Service squads were working round the clock to keep the roads clear, fighting a losing battle against the ongoing collapse of shattered apartment blocks and shops. Clouds of flies buzzed above the pools of raw sewage that oozed from the shattered drains. The stench permeated the JLTV's cabin, overwhelming the environmental scrubbers. Not just effluent, but the now familiar sickly-sweet odour of rotting flesh. A stick-thin man picked through the ruins, searching for scraps of food and clothing; a gang of feral youths hovered nearby, seemingly ready to rob him of anything he might find. He ignored both youths and the various bodies bloated with decomposition gasses. Disease would swiftly follow, adding to the effects of starvation and cold. A fresh round of misery brought to the civilian population by the RS of A.

Cooper tore his gaze away and turned it on his colleagues instead, searching for some trace of empathy or a sign that they grasped the magnitude of the humanitarian crisis unfolding around them. Martinez kept his attention focused on the road ahead as Cooper continued to thread the vehicle along its patrol route. Pedersen sat furiously chewing gum while he ran a whetstone along the edges of his knife. Only Jackson met and held Cooper's gaze, his expression resigned.

'We're going to step in and help, right?'

Jackson shook his head. 'Our orders are to secure the area and carry on to the next Caliphate stronghold – Tadmur.'

'We can't just leave these people to starve, Sarge. We do that, we're no better than the Caliphate! Hell, we're worse.'

Pedersen's lip curled in a sneer. 'Guess they should have thought about the consequences of supporting the Caliphate.'

'Are you going to sit there and tell me you honestly believe they had a choice? You've seen the shit they do to civilians. Punishment beatings, public floggings, amputations and beheadings.'

'Who cares? Far as I'm concerned, Abdul has it coming – they shouldn't have murdered the president. But what can you expect from a bunch of savages who worship a false god? So why don't you shut that stupid mouth of yours and let the rest of us be?'

Cooper lapsed into silence. He knew from bitter experience this was an argument he would never win. He recalled his own indoctrination during basic training, an attempt to forge him into an instrument of God dedicated to ending the scourge of the Caliphate. For a time, he had almost been onboard with it, until the horrors of war had lifted the scales from his eyes. The brotherhood he had shared with his comrades had dwindled away since the siege of Jerusalem, leaving him feeling isolated and exposed. With hindsight, he might have been better off throwing in his lot with Lynch. But the thought of never being able to see his family again was too much to bear. And yet, with all leave cancelled, was he really any better off? It might be months or even years before he saw them again. Hell, with both sides fighting the war on increasingly brutal terms, he might not live to see them at all. With comms locked down except for essential military traffic, he couldn't even get a message through to them, tell them how much he loved and missed them.

At least they were safe back home and the money he was sending making a difference, as evidenced by the last message he had received, shortly before President Hamilton's assassination.

Cooper must have read it a hundred times by now: when he closed his eyes, he could see the text on the screen. His father had received his first course of nano-therapy for his arthritis and was responding well. Shania was due to take up an admin post at the Jonesboro Sheriff's Office. Dale and Wade were receiving after-school tuition to improve their grades. As for his mother, who had written the letter, he could sense her relief at no longer having to budget every dollar, and her joy at seeing her children's prospects improve. He could also tell she was proud of him, but fearful for him, too. Cooper wished he could carry some of that weight for her, but recognised he was far from the master of his own fate.

Of his own burdens, the Route 1 massacre weighed ever more heavily upon him. Muslim or not, he was certain those people had had hopes and dreams just like his own family. After all, they were fleeing a war zone in the uncertain hope of a better life elsewhere. But he and Mackinlay had ended those four lives; five, if you counted the woman's unborn baby. Mackinlay had panicked and opened fire, Cooper joining in for fear of making another mistake and endangering his comrades. Another wrong decision. But, unlike the MILES simulation, the dead hadn't got up, dusted themselves off and walked away.

If Mackinlay had harboured any doubts beyond those he claimed not to have, a Caliphate bullet had put an end to them during the final assault on Jerusalem. Cooper wondered if he had indeed ascended to the heavens, as Chaplain-Commander Du Pont continually preached: the just reward of a good soldier of Christ. Perhaps Du Pont, the Pope and the rest had got it wrong and Mac was burning in Hell instead. The more Cooper saw of the war the more he thought it likely that Mac and the rest of the dead, Muslim, Jew or Christian, had simply ended. And yet he still prayed morning, noon and night, duties permitting, even though he thought no one was listening. For who else could he appeal to for forgiveness? Certainly not the dead.

Jackson put a finger to his ear and nodded. 'Unit Six has come under heavy fire and needs assistance. Cooper, hit it!'

Cooper, jarred back to the present, spun the JLTV round as the nav-comp locked onto their comrades' GPS signal. A dead end loomed ahead, the road choked with rubble, and he hit the brakes before throwing the JLTV into reverse, doubling back to a previous junction. Twice more they found the road north blocked, forcing them to detour to the west in a long curving arc, finally approaching the target zone from the north. Cooper hit the brakes again in response to a makeshift barricade of broken furniture, then gunned the engine, crashing through into the square beyond in a shower of wood and glass fragments.

The blazing wreck of Unit Six's JLTV lay on its side. Cooper approached it cautiously, slewing to the side in response to a sudden burst of tracer fire that continued to drive them to the left, the glowing rounds throwing up clods of earth. He saw the tarp covering on the road too late to avoid it and the steering wheel juddered in his hands as the JLTV's wheels dropped into the concealed ditch.

The engine howled as Cooper attempted to reverse, the spinning wheels throwing up a cloud of dirt and debris.

'Try forward instead!' Jackson barked.

Cooper's hand froze on the shift as a slight figure stepped out from behind the cover of the wrecked JLTV, raised an RPG to its shoulder and fired.

CHAPTER 13

Cooper threw himself clear of the JLTV as the rocket struck. Superheated air and flames washed over him as he rolled away. He shook his head to clear it and saw Jackson staggering past, flames billowing from the rear of his vest. The sergeant dropped to his knees and Cooper leapt on him, pushing him down and rolling him in the dirt to beat out the flames. He felt the impact of bullets striking his body armour as he grabbed Jackson's MOLLE straps and dragged him into the cover of their wrecked JLTV.

Jackson moaned in pain as Cooper lay him on his stomach. Having no time to assess the extent of the burns, he grabbed a couple of pen injectors from his medical pouch and stabbed them into Jackson's thigh, delivering a cocktail of opioids and amphetamines. Shooting him up with a speedball might be medically dubious, but he needed Jackson conscious if they were to have any hope of fighting their way clear.

The drugs kicked in quickly and the sergeant opened his eyes.

'Pedersen, Martinez?'

Cooper shook his head. 'Tango Uniform.' He ducked instinctively in response to the rattle of small-arms fire against the JLTV.

'Sitrep.'

'Two hostiles on either side of the square, plus the kid with the RPG. Whichever way we move, we're hemmed in. Our assault rifles are still inside the JLTV, so it's sidearms only.' Cooper pointed to the pulsing light on his vest. 'I've activated the distress beacon, but...' He left the sentence unfinished. Both men knew that anyone responding would be more likely to recover their bodies than effect a rescue.

'Mighty convenient that our friends out there have managed to target four of the operatives responsible for killing El Zayyoud.'

'But how could they know? That information could only come from ... our guys.'

'Exactly. Could be someone's decided to do a little housecleaning after what happened to Tyler.'

Cooper thought it a stretch, a product of paranoia. But then again, as the saying went, being paranoid didn't mean they weren't out to get you. Ice formed in his gut as he recalled Tyler pointing his pistol at Lynch in the wake of the broadcast exposing him for ordering an air strike on a refugee column. He heard Tyler order him to step aside, telling him with Lynch gone there would be no one to contradict their version of events. But Cooper, having been instrumental in those events, couldn't let it go. There had been that terrible moment when he felt sure his CO would shoot him dead before taking out Lynch, but Jackson had come up behind Tyler, forced his gun to his head and made him pull the trigger. With Tyler facing disgrace it had been easy to spin the story of his suicide, particularly with Lynch in the wind. The truth, however, had a habit of surfacing. Was that motive enough to want them dead? Certainly. But Cooper suspected some deeper motive, rooted in internal politics. Now, however, was not the time to debate it.

Cooper drew his SIG Sauer M19, set it to fire a three-round burst and racked back the slide. He looked at Jackson and saw agreement in his eyes; their only hope was to try and blast their way out.

Jackson used hand signals to indicate they should move to the rear of the JLTV and attack from either side. Cooper belly-crawled into position on the left and waited for Jackson to reach his mark. The sergeant drew himself up into a crouch and held up his hand. Cooper, seeing Jackson tilt his head, strained to hear over the crackle of flames. Was he imagining it? No. He heard it again; the dull slap of an equipment pouch hitting a body as someone crept forward. Their attackers, possibly believing them to be dead or incapacitated, had grown bold enough to investigate. Cooper nodded his understanding.

Cooper readied his pistol as Jackson ran down a three, two, one count on his fingers. The Templars stepped out from cover in unison. Cooper snapped off a burst, not so much concerned with hitting his target as gaining the psychological advantage. The startled Caliphate soldier attempted to return fire, his shots going wide. Cooper's second burst took him high in the chest, lifting him off his feet, by which point Cooper was already turning in response to an angry scream. His third burst hit the soldier with the RPG centre mass. He completed his turn to the right to discover Jackson standing over the body of the third insurgent. The sergeant kicked the assault rifle away from his hand and put a double-tap into his head.

Cooper moved on to his own marks. He stood over his first target and froze. The boy lying on the ground was thirteen years of age at most. Feeling Jackson's eyes on him, he fired the double-tap and moved on to the next. The sharp, shallow breaths that punctuated his groans warned Cooper that their third opponent was still alive.

Cooper moved the boy's weapon away and squatted down; another child soldier, about twelve years old this time. The boy's eyes were wide with fear and pain as he struggled to breathe through punctured lungs that were slowly filling with blood. Cooper squatted down, cradled the boy's head in his lap and took his left hand. Death had stripped the child of his hatred and his sense of other. Now, during his last moments, he wanted nothing more than the comfort of another human being. It didn't matter that he wore the uniform of a sworn enemy. His fingers tightened round Cooper's own; each breath a wet gurgle, faster and shallower than the last. The death rattle came a few seconds later. Cooper had heard it often enough to recognise it as final. He drew the boy's eyelids closed and laid his head gently on the ground. What was it Lynch had said? Some mother's son. He blinked back treacherous tears, born as much of rage as sorrow at finding himself forced to fight and kill children.

Cooper heard the grunt and turned to see Jackson fall to his knees. He reached the sergeant in time to see his eyes roll back into his head as he crumpled to the ground. He checked frantically for a pulse, found none, and forced himself to be calm and check again. It was there, weak and thready, but there.

'Don't you dare die on me now, you bastard!'

Cooper delivered a slap. Jackson groaned in response but failed to regain consciousness. He hit him again, hoping the pain would cut through the shock.

'Damn you, Sarge, stay with me! Hold on a few more minutes, help's coming. Just hang in there.'

CHAPTER 14

T*V21 Interview Transcript #3: Jefferson Lynch in conversation with Marshal Abu Salman Ismail via satellite link from Damascus Refugee Camp 7.*

Jefferson Lynch: Marshal Ismail, you were witness to the First Templar Division's Combat Aviation Brigade's attack on the Umayyad Mosque of Damascus?

Marshal Ismail: I was. And it is only by the will of Allah that I was not martyred that day while I was at prayer. One hundred and seventeen of the faithful were not so fortunate.

JL: It's hard to escape the parallel with the assassination of Caliph Abu Ahmad al-Nasr al-Qurayshi via a drone strike on Al-Aqsa Mosque. Given you are the Caliphate's military and, to a large extent, spiritual leader, do you believe yourself to have been the primary target?

MI: I don't profess to know what is in the minds of the American infidels. But this is only the latest in a series of attacks on historic and religious sites.

JL: You're calling this a war crime? A deliberate act of cultural vandalism by the RS government?

MI: I fail to see how it could be viewed in any other light. It was an unprovoked attack on a place of worship.

JL: According to the Central Office press corps this was a tragic accident, the result of a computer error. I take it you dispute that statement?

MI: As I alluded to earlier, the destruction of one mosque is unfortunate. Nine begins to look like a deliberate and sustained campaign of terror. And that is only those within Syria. Similar 'accidents' have occurred in Jordan and Lebanon. Are we really expected to believe this is a result of a rogue batch of AIs? If so, the RSA should demand a refund from the African Tech Corps.

JL: You also allege the targeting of schools and hospitals.

MI: Once again, there is no allegation – only hard, cold statistics. The Americans are waging total war against Islam. They claim it is only radical Islam, the Islamists, that they seek to defeat, but they kill women and children indiscriminately, both directly with weapons and indirectly through starvation and the denial of medicines and aid. This, they do in the name of Christ. Theirs is an ideological war, driven by the desire to wipe the Muslim people from the face of the earth.

JL: But isn't that what the RSA says of the Islamic Caliphate – that they commit their crimes in the names of Allah? That they seek the destruction of the Christian faith? Aren't we talking about two sides of the same coin here? Religious fundamentalism perverts the teachings of both Christ and Allah.

MI: Like many Westerners, you confuse the adherence to Sharia law with radicalism. Who is the real aggressor here? The Americans cite the bombing in Austin and the assassination of President Hamilton as justification for their actions, but show me a clear and undisputed link to the Caliphate. You can't. Because one does not exist.

JL: Are you saying these are false flag operations designed to stir up hatred against the Caliphate?

MI: That is precisely what I'm saying, Mr Lynch. Were they justified in assisting the Israelites to reclaim Palestine? Well, I'm sure you'll agree that is a complicated question concerning a long-disputed territory with right and wrong on both sides, although I think the Jews must take much of the blame. But what justification is there for the invasion of Syria, for arming and assisting rebel factions in Jordan and Lebanon? There is a clear agenda of forced regime change; first to isolate the Caliphate and then to destroy it. The Israelites commit atrocities and then scream at the world that they have the right to defend themselves. But what of the Caliphate? Don't we have that same right in the face of naked aggression?

JL: Perhaps. But the question on the lips of the rest of the world as it looks on is: where does this end? Are we seeing a repeat of the First World War, with powerful factions locked in a brutal war of attrition? Will the winner be the last Christian or Muslim soldier left standing? Do you see yourself as playing, for example, von Hindenburg to Grand Master Vanderbilt's Haig?

MI: I don't think that comparison holds. The goal of the Allied Forces was to prevent German expansion. Here, the end game is the eradication of the Caliphate. We have been driven mercilessly from Saudi Arabia, the land you call Israel, and now the RSA seeks to remove us from Syria and Jordan. We are not fighting to conquer, merely to survive. With stakes so high, our only viable strategy is to inflict as much damage on the enemy as possible. Whatever the cost.

JL: That's surely a zero-sum game for either side?

MI: For the families of the fallen and the innocents caught in the crossfire, most certainly. But what of those feeding the war machine? Continued conflict — a state of perpetual war — is in their best interest. Regardless of what the Caliphate wants, the corporations will never let the Religious States lay down their arms. Unless wiser heads prevail, I fear it is the fate of our two peoples to be continuously at one another's throats.

JL: If people do nothing that will probably be the case. But the will of the people should neither be discounted nor underestimated. The old American republic was founded on that principle, and I believe it can be embraced once more.

MI: I thought the purview of a journalist was to deal in facts, not romance?

JL [bitter laughter]: Guess you got me there. But returning to the issue: the man who routed the Templars at Tel Aviv surely has some strategy to defend the Caliphate against American aggression?

MI: If I do, I'm hardly going to discuss military strategy live on air. But if history has taught us nothing else, it is that wars are rarely won through strength of arms alone. My decision to grant you an interview must have surely triggered some curiosity, Mr Lynch. You must have asked yourself: what's in it for me? The answer is that I'm trusting you, and similar news channels, to get the truth out to the wider world. You are my advocate in the court of public opinion. America is a net importer of food, consumer goods and arms. Where diplomacy fails, the weight of sanctions must be brought to bear. But in the meantime, our armies will continue to defend the faithful. Allah willing, we will prevail.

JL: I'm not sure I share your faith in my abilities, Marshal Ismail. But I feel that weight and I'll do my best to carry it, because some day this lousy war has got to end.

MI: It must. It is to be hoped that enlightened individuals such as you and I will live to see that day.

Transcript Ends

Lynch closed the door behind him and strode toward the chair in front of Berkani's desk. His editor looked up and glowered at him.

'Did I say you could sit?'

Lynch shrugged and sat anyway, earning himself another glare. Experience had long since taught him that being peremptorily summoned to an editor's office never ended well. He folded his arms defensively across his chest and counted down in his head: three, two, one…

'What the fuck was that?'

Lynch arched an eyebrow. 'Come again, boss?'

'Don't play stupid with me, Lynch. Your interview, and I use that word advisedly, with Marshal Ismail. Where was your impartiality, your examination of the facts?'

'I thought you'd be pleased to see my countrymen depicted in a bad light.'

'I could get any mutt off the streets of Casablanca to bad-mouth the RSA, but that doesn't advance the cause. You were supposed to verify Ismail's allegations – not get all misty eyed about an America that hasn't existed for forty years!' Berkani rolled his eyes and pulled at his beard. 'Damn it, man, you're better than this. What's going on in that big brain of yours?'

'You mean other than being targeted by a drone attack?'

'I already offered you leave. You were the one who wanted to keep working. Wasn't it your sacred duty to report the truth regardless of the danger, or some such shit?'

'Think that might have been the booze on top of the painkillers.'

'Do yourself a favour and take a day or two off. Your next broadcast isn't until the end of the week. Stick with the facts – there's enough of them out there – and we can maybe, I say maybe, use the Ismail piece as support. Now, do us both a favour and get out of my sight before I change my mind.'

Lynch scraped back his chair and sprang upright. His

hands twitched open and closed as he hovered, uncertain, searching for a reply. Berkani let him off the hook by swivelling his chair to the side to look at one of the screens in the curving array that surrounded him. Lynch nodded, seemingly to himself, and made for the door.

Tazi stood waiting for him in the main office. As essential as a CPO might be, he still found her presence unsettling. He'd spent the better part of a year in the company of the Templars, but Tazi's energy was different. There was something in the way she carried herself that signalled danger.

Tazi snapped her fingers.

'Hey! You zoning out on me?'

'Sorry. Just thinking about my next article.'

'Bossman wasn't happy?'

'What makes you say that?'

'In the short time I've known you, I've never seen you move so fast. Like someone lit a fire under you.'

'Yeah? Just remember, if someone does light a fire it's your job to put it out.'

Tazi snapped off a mock salute and pointed Lynch towards the elevator. He followed her direction, swiping open his com-unit as he walked. He scrolled to 'orders' and hit repeat, ordering four hundred cigarettes and two bottles of barrel strength uncut bourbon.

Lynch let out a yell of protest as Tazi snatched his com-unit.

'Don't tell me you're ordering online in your own name on an unencrypted app?'

'How the hell else am I going to keep myself in smokes and whiskey?'

Tazi cancelled the order and handed back the com-unit.

'Not like this. I'll make arrangements. But if you ask me, you ought to cut back on the booze.'

'Good thing I'm not asking you, then.'

'Suit yourself. My job is to protect you from external threats. Any harm you do to yourself is your own affair.'

'Does that mean I can drive?'

'Not in your wildest, Lynch.'

The elevator door pinged open and Lynch stepped inside. He had been lying earlier, but now he focused his thoughts on his next article. He needed to get Berkani off his back. The documents Russell had provided were proof of the dirty war being waged by the Gerrard administration. Tyler's death had allowed them to roll out the old 'one bad apple' excuse, but Lynch knew the rot penetrated right to the heart. Why did Berkani have to be so goddamn pig-headed about releasing the data?

CHAPTER 15

Walker tried to ignore the rattling of the antiquated air-con unit as he concentrated on his screen. Morocco was depressingly similar to Israel: dry, dusty and dead. For a city keen to leverage the tourist dollar, Casablanca remained stuck in the early part of the century. It had taken him less than five minutes to break into the city's surveillance cams and locate Lynch. Since then, he had spent the last three days following him round the city. His CPO knew her stuff, changing the route daily, balancing a high degree of collateral damage against situations so crowded she might not see danger approaching.

Intrigued, he had pulled her file: Alia Tazi, age 23, born Casablanca Municipal Hospital October 13, 2066. Enlisted in the Royal Moroccan Army officer training programme April 2083, graduated October 2083 with the rank of sub-lieutenant. Applied and accepted to Second Paratroop Brigade January 2085, received her 'wings' August 2085 with the rank of lieutenant. Promoted to captain July 2087. Resigned her commission November 2088. Formed Red Phoenix Security February 2089, which was where things got interesting.

The origins of its start-up capital were murky, bouncing

through various offshore accounts. Tazi was suspected of being involved in two high-profile assassinations, eliminating the CEO and CFO of the Elhassan Tech Corp. While no formal charges were brought, it looked as though Tazi's decision to leave the army might have been the path of least resistance. In a little over a year, she had built up a significant client base, protecting the sort of individuals she might previously have been happy to terminate. Penance, or simple financial calculus? Whichever way you looked at it, she was a skilled adversary who made the execution of his sanction more difficult.

'Keep it simple' was a maxim drilled into the Templars, and one reinforced by the Agency. A short-range sniper shot offered a simple solution to target elimination. Walker kicked off a route analysis, overlaying each day, searching for a subconscious pattern or a point close to the TV21 offices that Lynch passed through every time. He checked his com-unit; still no messages from Hannah, but after Lynch's latest broadcast his handler's silence was unlikely to last. He split his screen, bringing up the footage. Lynch's lips moved silently but Walker had previously committed the words to memory, the journalist declaring America to be a rogue state, the proof of which he would shortly deliver. Bluster or something more? He shook his head, annoyed with himself for overthinking it. That was the problem with dealing with media parasites like Lynch, who were convinced of their intellectual superiority. Cooper and Mackinlay might not have seen it, but Walker had. The way Lynch peppered his interviews with pitfalls while looking down his nose at you. He pretended to care, to be interested in your thoughts and opinions, while scavenging for copy he could convert into clicks and approval ratings. Walker almost felt sorry for him. After all, what was he at the end of the day? A man without faith, without hope, desperate to display his mediocre talents to the world. Just like Walker's old teachers and college lecturers. If those self-important fools could see him now, they'd realise how wrong they had been about him.

A beep from his datapad informed him the analysis was complete. He scrolled through the results, confirming what he had already surmised. It took Lynch an average of 4.7 seconds to swipe in and complete the retinal scan required to access the building. There would be no greater or more reliable window of opportunity.

Walker stood and stretched the kinks out of his muscles. He retrieved a bubble pack from the bedside table, pressed out a couple of pills and washed the frenzy down with a mouthful of cold coffee. He crossed to the built-in wardrobe, slid back the door and removed the floor tiles to reveal a concealed floor safe. The compartment was accessed via a thumbprint and retinal scan. Walker retrieved the twelve-by-sixteen-inch case from inside. The case contained the disassembled parts of a Remington 800 Covert Urban Sniper Rifle, chambered for a .338 Lapua Magnum round. He removed each component from its compartment and cleaned it before placing it on the bed, finishing with the ten-round magazine. Satisfied all was in order, Walker assembled the rifle and checked the action before breaking it down again. By then the stims had kicked in, bringing with them a familiar cold clarity. The adjacent office block would provide a suitable vantage point from which to take the shot. All he needed to do was arrange access.

Walker parked the van ten metres from the office block adjacent to the TV21 studio. He pulled on a trucker cap, shading his eyes, and checked his reflection in the rear-view mirror. An unfamiliar face with brown eyes, shoulder-length black hair and matching beard stared back at him. He winked at himself and exited the vehicle, stopping to pull back the side door and retrieve a large metal toolbox.

The receptionist started guiltily in response to Walker clearing his throat and pushed her com-unit off to the side.

He held up his ID card, identifying him as Henri Gilot, an employee of Ajax Field Services. The company logo and surname matched those printed on the right breast of his overalls.

'Can I help you?'

Walker flashed her his com-unit, displaying a generic work order. 'I've a maintenance request for Kadiri Tech Corps. Fungal spores in the air-con.'

The receptionist checked her screen. 'Are you certain? I don't have anything logged.'

'Emergency call out. Black mould. Nasty stuff. Once it gets into the system it can travel through the entire building in no time at all. Get that in your lungs,' he took a sharp intake of breath, 'well, let's just say it ain't pretty.'

'It's really that serious?'

Walker nodded.

'All right. I guess you better deal with it. Kadiri is on the fourth floor.'

She handed Walker a swipe card and pointed to the elevator on the other side of reception. Walker snapped off a jaunty salute and picked up the toolbox. He didn't need to look round to know the receptionist had gone back to staring at her com-unit. Feeling generous, he gave her a fifteen per cent chance of being able to provide the authorities with a useable description of himself.

The elevator opened onto a short corridor, the far end of which was blocked with a security door. Walker swiped his pass, but the indicator LED remained red. He stabbed his thumb against the intercom button instead.

'Yes, can I help you?'

'I need to speak to the manager.'

'Speaking. Please identify yourself.'

'Henri Gilot, Ajax Field Services. I'm here to carry out an emergency purge of the air-con. Fungal infection. I need you to clear the office.'

'Nobody informed me. This is most irregular.'

Walker made a show of checking his com-unit. 'Request

was filed by a Mr Bennani,' Walker advised, giving the name of the building services manager.

'Very well. How long will it take?'

'About two hours. Guess everyone is going for an early lunch.'

Walker's quip met with dead air, but the sensor LED flashed green and he heard the maglock release. As he pushed open the door an automated message advised employees to save their work, lock their stations and exit the building. He walked with confidence, turning side on or stepping aside to let the departing workers pass as he made his way to the compressor room.

Walker gave it five minutes before peering round the edge of the door. The office was empty. He squatted down, opened the toolbox and removed the top tray of tools to reveal the parts of the CUSR. Muscle memory took over from conscious thought as he assembled the rifle, inserted the magazine and pulled back the bolt to chamber a round. His com-unit was still tapped into the city's surveillance cams and he zoned in on the Lincoln as it slowed for a stop light. Traffic conditions put it ten minutes out from the office: perfect timing.

Walker selected the glass cutter from the tray of tools and shouldered the rifle. He crossed the office to the windows and walked back and forth until he found the best view of the entrance to the TV21 studios: a steep angle but almost directly in line. The sucker squelched as he attached it to the glass, spinning the arm with its cutting head in a clockwise direction. Escaping argon hissed as he lifted the circle of glass free and placed it to the side. His com-unit displayed Lynch's ETA as three minutes. He slid the rifle barrel with its suppressor through the aperture.

Walker's world shrank down to the crosshairs framed by the scope. He sighted the office door, the card reader seemingly close enough for him to reach out and touch, and waited.

His com-unit beeped a warning that the Lincoln had

arrived. Walker ignored it and continued to cover the door; confident his prey would come to him. Lynch's torso filled the scope as he fumbled with the ID card on its lanyard. Walker tracked slightly to the left, aiming for Lynch's heart. As he took up first pressure on the trigger, Tazi stepped in front of Lynch. A problem, but not insurmountable. If he couldn't shoot round her, he would shoot through her. His finger pulled back on the trigger.

The top of Tazi's shoulder exploded in a spray of blood, the bullet travelling on to its target. Lynch slammed against the door and slid slowly downwards.

CHAPTER 16

Lynch held up his shirt and stared at the indentation; grateful that Tazi insisted he wear a nano-weave fabric, and equally grateful she had taken most of the force out of the high-velocity round. He dropped the shirt into his lap and shifted awkwardly in the chair. In common with police interview rooms across the world, the furnishings were designed for functionality over comfort.

Lieutenant Hirsch regarded him impassively across the table. It came again, that nagging suspicion that he should know the kid from somewhere. Lynch shook his head to clear it. Tried to gauge if he was about to find himself helping the police with their enquiries. 'Voluntary attendance,' Hirsh had said, but Lynch had the impression that could change swiftly enough if his answers weren't to the lieutenant's liking.

Hirsch pointed to Lynch's shirt. 'Guess you've Tazi to thank for that.'

'Damn straight!'

'Way I see it, that's twice you've got lucky. Don't suppose you're ready to see sense and abandon this fool crusade of yours? In case it's escaped your notice, it's not just your life on the line.'

'I get that. I really do. But whoever this mutt is, they're not going to stop, regardless of what action I take or don't take. Goddamn it! What kind of world are we living in if we let a rogue state frighten us into silence? The RSA is sanctioning agents to carry out terrorist acts on foreign soil. Isn't it the National Brigade's duty to hunt down this would-be assassin? Or does justice and doing the right thing come second to the realpolitik of maintaining diplomatic relations with the RSA?'

Hirsch broke eye contact. 'Look, I can't promise anything, but I'll take it up with Commandant Idrissi, see if I can at least get a squad car assigned to watch your apartment. Meantime, there's someone here wants to see you.'

A knock sounded on the door and it swung open to admit Tazi. She looked pale but otherwise remarkably healthy for someone who had just stopped a bullet. Seeing Lynch's confusion, she smiled.

'Nanotech – rebuilt the tissue in minutes.'

Lynch looked at his own injured arm, which he was still favouring after removing the sling.

'How come I didn't get that shit?'

'Guess you should have taken out better health insurance.'

Lynch nodded, not trusting himself to speak due to a sudden constriction in his throat. Ever since Hannah had dragged him kicking and screaming into this godawful war, he'd been reliant on the kindness of strangers to save his ass. Of course, he only had himself to blame for that. With an addict's logic, it seemed perfectly sensible to try to smuggle four kilos of cocaine into the States. The CIA spook had made the choice bet23ween covering the war and twenty years in the pen a no-brainer. Lynch might not be a villain, but he was certainly no hero. And yet people seemed to see some worth in him, or at least in his work. It made him uncomfortable.

'I'm glad you're … okay.'

'That makes two of us. I must apologise. Clearly, I underestimated the threat to your life. Rest assured; I won't make that mistake again.'

'Thanks, but that won't be necessary. As the lieutenant here has pointed out, I've already put enough people in danger.'

'I rather think that's my choice, don't you? Particularly when the reputation of Red Phoenix is at stake.'

Lynch turned to Hirsch. 'Can she do that?'

The lieutenant shrugged. 'Not my jurisdiction.'

'All right. Here's an easier one for you. Am I free to go?'

'You always were, Mr Lynch. We're merely trying to ascertain the circumstances of this latest attempt on your life.'

'The powers that be in the RSA want me dead. It ain't nothing more complicated than that. Only question is what you and your bosses are going to do about it.'

Lynch stood up and pulled on his shirt, the nano-weave rose petal pattern shimmering and bending the light as he buttoned it up. He flexed the fingers of his right hand experimentally, felt the residual weakness and wondered just how long his luck would hold out.

'If you're ready, Lynch? Tazi asked. 'The car's waiting outside.'

They completed the journey back to Lynch's apartment in silence, the journalist staring out of the passenger side window, seeing danger lurking in every shadow. Tazi had advised him to avoid going back – he was clearly under surveillance – but Lynch insisted. He couldn't abandon the data-disc, not when its broadcast remained his only hope of contacting the leaders of the Free America movement.

Tazi had just finished parking up when Lynch's com-unit buzzed. The caller display said 'unknown number'. He noticed a treacherous tremble in his hand as he accepted the call.

Russell's voice had a high, accusatory note as it crackled from the speaker.

'I thought you had integrity, Lynch. Thought you cared about making a difference. Why the fuck haven't you broadcast what I gave you?'

'I'm fine, thanks for asking.'

'Fuck you, Lynch. Answer the damn question!'

'My editor wants proof the document is genuine. Don't suppose you'd care to give me that?'

'Who am I talking to? I thought it was Jefferson Lynch, not some pussy who needs an editor and a network behind him. You should broadcast it and be damned, just like you did with that fascist prick, Tyler. The American public needs to hear the truth.'

'Difference is, I knew for a fact that data was genuine, having witnessed and recorded it myself. And I don't want any more collateral.'

'Damn it, man, don't go weak sister on me now. My associates and I took a huge risk getting that file to you. Don't let us down.'

'I'm working on it, all right...' Lynch's voice trailed off as the sound of pounding footsteps followed by a loud bang burst from his com-unit. He heard shouts, automatic gunfire and screaming. The line went dead.

'Shit. Looks like things are heading south.'

Lynch turned and sprinted towards the elevator, his reservations about provenance forgotten. He ignored Tazi's shout of protest. If Russell had been compromised the disc was of even greater importance. Five minutes. Ten at most. Was that so much to ask for? Once he'd broadcast the contents of the disc, he'd be happy for her to spirit him to a place of safety.

CHAPTER 17

Vanderbilt studied Gibson as he tilted back his glass and swallowed the Veuve Clicquot with seemingly scant appreciation. White flecks of flesh glinted amid the silver of his beard. Gibson, like many of the Church's hardliners, was a grubby parvenu, the strength and unbending rigidity of his faith having elevated him far beyond his social class. But those same humble origins meant he had the ear of the people, forcing Vanderbilt to indulge the Bishop of the Catholic Diocese of Richmond. Here was a man for whom wealth meant ostentation. Vanderbilt had first felt the bishop's shock and then his disdain as he looked round the dining room, taking in the Shaker table, chairs and sideboard. Where Vanderbilt appreciated the elegance of simplicity, Gibson saw only the rude and the crude. Revolutions, it seemed, made for strange bedfellows.

Vanderbilt's adjutant, Lachlan, moved unobtrusively about the table, clearing the salvers with their broken lobster shells, silver crackers and long forks, and stacking them on a hostess trolley. He topped up Gibson's glass, noted Vanderbilt's subtle nod and retired to the kitchen.

Gibson patted his belly. 'You keep a most excellent

table, Grand Master.'

'By God's grace, your Excellency.'

'Indeed. All transpires by His will and under His watchful eye. Speaking of which, your victory in Damascus and the elimination of the heretic, El Zayyoud, must be most pleasing to the good Lord.'

Vanderbilt, seeing Gibson seeking validation of his compliment, replied, 'I am but His humble servant.' He composed his features and sought to inject the necessary gravitas into his voice as he continued. 'We might be winning the battles against the Caliphate, but I fear we are losing the war for America's soul. Gerrard is not a true believer. The same must be said of the majority of Congress. They set a poor moral example for the public, particularly now that Jezebel of a press secretary has announced she's standing for Congress. There are those in the military who believe it's time for the Church to take a more active role in governing this great nation of ours. If you follow my meaning?'

Bishop Gibson lapsed into what he intended to be taken for a thoughtful silence. But he was no poker player. Vanderbilt watched the emotions flit across his face: fear at openly discussing treachery superseded by his naked lust for power.

'Our new republic is still young. Teething problems are to be expected. A firmer hand on the tiller to steer us through these turbulent times might, as you suggest, be necessary. Perhaps even desirable.'

Vanderbilt relaxed, satisfied the bishop was onboard. 'As you say, Your Excellency. As to the means: provided our Syrian campaign progresses according to plan, we will be able to withdraw the bulk of Templar forces, leaving conventional military personnel in charge. Combined with this year's intake, that will provide sufficient troops to make the necessary arrests and declare a state of emergency.'

'I see,' Gibson said, the hint of fear again showing in his eyes. 'And what charges do you intend to bring against

President Gerrard?'

'Apostasy, for one – we both know he's not a fit spiritual leader – and treason for a second. I've yet to prove it, but I strongly suspect his involvement in the removal of his predecessor. Not that I mourn Hamilton's passing, but he was still our rightfully elected president. We must maintain standards and order, lest chaos engulf us.'

'Indeed, Grand Master.' Gibson drained his glass. 'Is there any more wine left?'

Vanderbilt stood and reached over to pour the wine himself, forcing a smile even while wincing internally at the waste of a good vintage.

'I can count on your support, and, by extension, that of the Church?'

'While I wish otherwise, it would appear that I must bear the burden of leadership for the good of the people. But.' Gibson raised a blunt forefinger. 'We shall only govern for as long as it takes to put a freshly elected government in place.'

'Of course, Your Excellency.'

Vanderbilt poured a modest measure of wine into his own glass and raised it in a toast. 'To service.'

Bishop Gibson returned the toast and drained the contents of his glass. Vanderbilt poured the last of the wine into Gibson's glass, noting the bishop's flushed complexion. He hoped God wouldn't see fit to call the bishop to His side before their plans came to fruition.

The Grand Master fitted his earpiece and started the playback. Gibson's voice sounded loud and clear; Vanderbilt's insurance should his new partner develop cold feet. As that conspirator of long ago remarked: we must hang together or surely we shall hang separately.

'What do you make of our new ally?' Vanderbilt asked Lachlan.

'Greedy, venal. But most of all, ambitious, sir. He sees

the opportunity to elevate himself to the status of a divinely appointed ruler. He can be depended on only for as long as he can do so without risk to himself.'

'Which is why we should keep a close eye on him. Meantime, we must return to the daily grind. What are my appointments for tomorrow?'

Lachlan took out his com-unit and studied the screen. 'Just the one, sir – a meeting with the President, Secretary of Defense, and the Chairman of the Joint Chiefs of Staff at ten to discuss the assault on Tadmur.'

'Ah, yes. Kordowski and Morrison.' Vanderbilt steepled his fingers. 'Kordowski has got some grit, but Morrison … Morrison might well prove to be the weak link.'

'Sir?'

'Thinking aloud, is all. It may be profitable to do a little fishing tomorrow. Determine how aligned our conspirators truly are.'

'I see. If that's all, sir?'

'Indeed, Lachlan. I shall see you in the morning.'

'God willing.'

Lachlan's delivery was deadpan. So much so, that Vanderbilt wondered if his adjutant was mocking him. If he were, it was so subtle as to be unproveable. He shook his head to clear it as Lachlan closed the study door quietly behind him, leaving the Grand Master in the dim glow of a single table lamp.

Vanderbilt placed his earpiece on the table and stretched out his limbs before standing. He crossed to the desk, picked up his com-unit and did the arithmetic: just after midnight in Richmond would be 7am in Syria. A dull stab of pain spread through his right shoulder as he sat; the echo of a thirty-year-old wound. The X-rays showed nothing, but he remained convinced some fragment of the Caliphate bullet must be lurking in his flesh. Or maybe it was God's subtle reminder of his mortality.

Vanderbilt initiated an encrypted call, which was picked up on the second ring. Colonel James Willard appeared on the screen; clean-shaven and with a crewcut, the hardness in his eyes gave the lie to his otherwise youthful features. What he lacked in strategic planning compared to Tyler, he more than compensated for with loyalty.

'Colonel Willard, you have news for me?'

'Yes, Grand Master. I regret to inform you that we've suffered casualties as a result of insurgent guerrilla action. Eight Templars killed in action, including Pedersen and Martinez. Sergeant Jackson was badly burned in the same attack. We've evacuated him to Akrotiri Air Base for treatment. Templar-Private Cooper has returned to normal duty.'

'I'm sensing a "but" here.'

'Probably nothing, Grand Master. He had to be disciplined following the El Zayyoud operation. I fear his faith is wavering. That kind of doubt can spread like a disease. But he undoubtedly saved Sergeant Jackson's life.'

'A concern, yes,' Vanderbilt conceded, 'but sometimes we must trust in the Lord.'

'Sir?'

'Pull him from frontline duties and assign him to sector patrol. A less combat-oriented role will allow him time to consider his position. With God's grace, he'll remember his duty.'

'And if he doesn't?'

'We shall cross that bridge when we come to it. God speed, Colonel.'

CHAPTER 18

Cooper ignored the pain in his knees. He had been kneeling on the hard earth of the tabernacle floor for almost two hours, his line of sight fixed on the Bible that rested atop the small altar. A stand-mounted crucifix sat behind it, and behind that the baucent, the Templar battle flag; the red cross pattée on black and white horizontal bars. Cooper would be the first to admit that he had never held any great religious conviction. But what little he possessed had shrunk even further throughout the Syrian campaign, with its seemingly endless sequence of horrors. The tabernacle, however, offered a rare opportunity for solitude, providing a space for contemplation and prayer. Or so he'd thought.

Cooper felt a hand on his shoulder and the voice that spoke next belonged to Chaplain-Commander Du Pont.

'Are you praying for Sergeant Jackson?' The Chaplain-Commander continued without waiting for a response. 'His wounds are grievous, but I don't believe the good Lord is ready to receive our brother just yet.'

Cooper hesitated, but the guilt sat like a weight on his chest. He needed to be free of it.

'They were children.'

'Who were?'

'The insurgents who ambushed the JLTV. I swear, one of them was lucky to be ten years old. What kind of god permits something as messed up as that?'

'Remember, God gave us free will. Some use that to create beautiful works of art, or to build great cathedrals to His honour and glory. Others use it for evil, especially the heathens. You mustn't reproach yourself for killing those children – evildoers put them in harm's way to try and weaken your resolve. Thankfully neither yourself nor Sergeant Jackson were found wanting in your moment of trial.'

'That might be true, but it doesn't make me feel any better about it.'

'If all duty were easy, my son, then every man would be a saint.' The Chaplain-Commander knelt beside Cooper. 'Come, let us pray together, so the Lord may ease your soul and strengthen your conviction.'

Cooper bowed his head and said the words, but they offered no respite from his guilt. Fear gripped him. Fear of never getting back to America and of never seeing his family again. Fear of losing control and of what he might do in such a circumstance. He pictured himself striding into the mess tent, assault rifle on full auto, and gunning down his sworn brothers. Imagined the looks of shock, betrayal and pain as the bullets struck home, spraying crimson through the air and across the tables. Saw the bodies face down in their meals or sprawled on the floor, individual bloody pools spreading slowly out and merging. On and on, sparing no man; drawing his pistol when the rifle clicked empty, and finishing the wounded with his knife when his pistol ran dry. He would finally be the physical embodiment of the wrath of God they had trained him to be. A scythe cutting through humanity without mercy.

Du Pont concluded the prayer. 'Amen.'

The silence stretched awkwardly until Cooper realised what the chaplain-commander had said and echoed it back to him. Du Pont placed his hand back on Cooper's shoulder and pushed down to assist himself in rising.

'As the story of Thomas tells us, it is easy to disbelieve that which we have not seen personally. But blessed are those who have faith without the proof of personal experience. When all around you appears dark, find the light in the justness of our cause. I will pray for you, Brother Cooper.'

Cooper clasped his hands together and closed his eyes, but it was no use. The little equilibrium he had found was gone, destroyed by notions of honour and duty. He stood and dusted off the knees of his combat trousers. His stomach grumbled but he ignored it, his bloody vision still fresh in his mind, and decided to return to his tent.

The setting sun greeted Cooper as he pushed back the flap of the tabernacle and he stopped for a moment to admire the deep red glow that lit up the horizon. Witnessing the beauty of nature was the closest he ever felt to God. The *thrum* of the generators kicking in was followed a few seconds later by the harsh glare of spotlights, both within the camp and mounted along the perimeter fence. Cooper exhaled noisily through his nose and kicked a pebble across the trampled-down dirt. He walked along the fence line, staring at the already darkening rocks and sand. The temperature dipped with the sun and he rolled down the sleeves of his tunic as the hairs rose on his forearms. He tried hard not to hate the Arabs and their religion, but he had seen enough desert to last a lifetime. Baked by day. Frozen by night. Surely no one lived out here by choice?

His route took him past the latrines, the smell of chemicals not quite masking the stench of shit. Something else they didn't tell you in the recruiting pamphlets. He bowed his head and walked on, patting the grille of the first in a series of JLTVs. Tomorrow they would load up and ride for Tadmur, the latest town to be wrested back from the Caliphate; or, more accurately, bombed into submission. Isaac 'Vicious' Vaughn would have been proud: they had finally done away with the outmoded concept of civilians and embraced his philosophy of total war. The world looked on and … said nothing.

Cooper identified his tent from the number stencilled on its side. He unzipped the flap, ducked inside and closed it behind him. Reaching up, he tapped the light hanging from its apex and it fluoresced to life, bathing the tent in a harsh white glow. A rummage through his backpack turned up a couple of protein bars, which he washed down with tepid water from his canteen, promising himself a decent breakfast in the morning. Too early for bed; he unlaced his boots and laid himself out on his sleeping bag, propping himself up against his backpack. He grabbed his com-unit and scrolled through the various messages he had composed during the lockdown. The ones to his sister, his brothers and his parents would eventually be sent when the comms embargo was lifted. Then there were the ones he wrote to Lynch; really a dialogue with himself.

Dear Jefferson,

Hope you made it clear and are busy setting the world to rights? We're on comms lockdown, so no news in or out, but I find it hard to imagine you being able to stay quiet for long.

Don't say 'I told you so' but you were right about this lousy war. I've tried my best to leave but they won't let me. Maybe once we push the Caliphate back to Iraq they'll finally agree to my discharge. But there always seems to be another campaign, another critical mission objective. I'm trying as hard as I can to avoid being eaten by this war, to hold on to the good in me. I don't mind telling you, it's more difficult than I thought it'd be. Sometimes it really is kill or be killed. And I don't mind admitting I want to live. Want to see my family again. Is that so bad?

Tyler was a brute, but I don't think he hated the Arabs. People and objectives were of use to him or they weren't. It might have been cold, but at least it was understandable. His replacement, Willard, scares me more than Tyler ever did. He's like some kind of living weapon: High Command point him at a target and he fires and keeps firing until it's eliminated. No questions. No remorse. It's effective. But where does it end? We've pushed the Caliphate back through Lebanon, Jordan and Syria, but who or what fills the vacuum left behind?

The towns, villages and cities are largely ruins, without power, fresh water or functioning hospitals and schools. People are starving, disease is everywhere, and we walk on by. How can we expect democracy to take root in such conditions? The strong are already preying on the weak, forming into tribal gangs. They'll unify under some warlord or other, who will point the blame firmly at us, and we're back to square one. I used to think you were crazy. Hell, you are crazy, but that don't mean you ain't right. It's all about the military-industrial complex, producing a never-ending war to feed the arms industry.

I feel so small, so helpless. It's like a nightmare I can't wake up from. You might have been a drunken pain in the ass, but at least you knew how to make sense of it all. I wish you were here. Cracking wise and bitching. Walking the line.

Yours,
Billy Ray

CHAPTER 19

Walker froze the screen. The electronic watermark of the CIA seal with its left-facing American eagle's head was clearly visible on the document, as was the director's name. Both were easy to fake and no proof of provenance, but that hardly mattered in the context of the document's contents: the authorisation of a false flag operation to assassinate President Hamilton. Even the possibility of it being true would seriously undermine their justification for attacking the Caliphate.

Walker didn't need to look at his com-unit to know the incoming call was from Deputy Directory Hannah.

'That's twice you've fucked up now – I won't tolerate a third time. You're to take Lynch out regardless of the collateral. The Moroccans will bump their gums a bit, but they won't make too big a stink about it with a new trade deal hanging in the balance.'

'If that's how you want it played, sir, I got no problem with that. Just make sure my extraction is ready.'

Walker finished connecting the detonator and sat back on his heels to examine his work. The case contained six kilos of C4 wired to an electronic detonator, its receiver triggered from his com-unit. No timers, no tilt switches, no dummy detonators; a crude device designed to deliver a crude result. But sometimes that was all you needed.

Walker swiped open his datapad and opened the surveillance cam feeds. Lynch remained in his apartment, accompanied by Alia Tazi. He widened his search to scan the surrounding blocks but discovered no sign of additional support from Red Phoenix Security, the CPO apparently confident she could handle a direct assault on the apartment. Perhaps she could. But Walker didn't intend on going toe-to-toe with her just to answer the question. He called up the building schematics and examined the sub-basement parking garage. A series of reinforced plascrete pillars supported the accommodation floors above, the loss of two or three of which should be sufficient to bring the building down. Still, better to be thorough. He opened the simulation software and modelled several explosions, varying the direction and position of the blast, identifying the north-east corner as the optimum placement.

Commandant Idrissi appeared to be staring at a point six inches above Hirsch's head. With his obviously dyed black hair and doughy features, it would be easy to mistake Idrissi as soft, perhaps even comical, but Hirsch knew his commanding officer possessed a sharp intellect, coupled with an unbending attitude to procedure. Idrissi also viewed foreigners with deep suspicion and Hirsch found himself tolerated on account of his ability as a detective and, in a force riddled by corruption, one of the few officers known to be incorruptible. But Hirsch knew he was pushing their working relationship to its limits.

'Surely we can spare one car, sir?'

'The issue is not one of resource or budget, but of policy. I thought I made myself abundantly clear last we spoke. Apparently not. The National Brigade's remit is to investigate terrorism, organised and white-collar crime. We're not paid to babysit mad dog foreigners who are intent on antagonising their own government. You advised Jefferson Lynch to cease broadcasting for his own protection. It's not your concern, or anyone else's in this department for that matter, if he chooses to ignore that advice.'

'If it were only Lynch's life at stake I might be inclined to agree. But the Americans have clearly demonstrated they don't care who else gets hurt or killed in their pursuit of Lynch.'

'Correct me if I'm wrong, Lieutenant, but last I checked the only person other than Lynch to be injured during these attempts was Alia Tazi, a private security contractor, and as such one step removed from a mercenary. Other than that, there's been some property damage – that's what insurance is for.'

'And you're willing to gamble the next attempt won't result in fatalities?'

'I doubt the Americans would be so foolish. They know the rules of the game and have been playing it too long to make such a miscalculation. I think we've wasted enough time discussing this. Frankly, your journalist should count himself lucky we haven't put him on a flight back home. Believe me, there are plenty in government who are minded to do so.'

'Very good, sir.'

Hirsch held Idrissi's stare, daring him to make something more of it. Disappointment vied with relief when his commander waved a hand towards the door in dismissal. Hirsch pulled the door open with unnecessary force and made his way to his desk on the opposite side of the open-plan office.

The National Brigade was situated on the upper floor of the Police Prefecture between the Brahim Rouhani and Mohamed Zerktouni boulevards. Thirty years ago, its shining ziggurat was raised as a symbol of power, but a reaction to the coastal salt air had transformed most of its marble white plascrete to a leprous grey riddled with cracks. Now its decaying edifice, like many who worked there, had seen better days. Symbols, Hirsch reflected, were important.

He sat heavily in his chair and drummed his fingers on the desk. Idrissi was right; he had warned Lynch. What more could be do? And there it was, like a barb in his heart: Lynch's accusation that he was allowing the rule of law to become subservient to political necessity. Almost like he knew which button to push. But Lynch couldn't possibly know; that was too farfetched. Probably nothing more than the instincts that made him a good journalist, knowing where to apply pressure to get the story.

Hirsch took out his com-unit. He looked from its screen to Idrissi's office door and back again. Stupid, even dangerous, given his past, but you had to have a code. He'd broken his once before and it had brought him and those around him nothing but pain. He opened a channel to a patrol car before he could change his mind.

'Hey, Rickhard! This a social call, or is there something we can do for you?'

'You know me too well, Faissal. You boys anywhere near Sidi Mohamed Ben Abdellah?'

'About a K out, but our patrol doesn't pass directly by.'

'Change of plan. I want surveillance on the King Hassan apartment block. We have reason to believe an attempt will be made on the life of one of the residents, Jefferson Lynch, apartment seven-twenty-four.'

'You got some details on that, Lieutenant?'

'Negative at this time. I'm sending you a com-number for Alia Tazi, she's a Red Phoenix CPO. I want you to tie her into your comms.'

'A civilian?'

'I know it's irregular, but you have my authorisation. And Faissal, whoever these guys are, they're dangerous. Be careful.'

'Don't worry, we got it covered.'

Hirsch dropped his com-unit on the desk and rubbed his eyes. A lead weight seemed to have settled in his gut, the presentiment of doom. Exactly whose was yet to be revealed.

Walker made his way down to the street, the gunmetal case gripped in his left hand. He walked past the garish shopfronts, selling spices, rugs and electronic consumer goods, and took up position next to the parking bays. Five minutes later he spotted an approaching Dacia SUV, a couple of years old but otherwise unremarkable. The driver, her head covered with a hijab, parked up and exited. She opened the rear door and collected a pair of shopping bags from the seat. Walker switched on the signal jammer as she turned and plipped the locks, preventing them from closing, and cloning the key's frequency. He watched her walk along the street, pausing to check a melon for ripeness, before disappearing inside a grocery store.

Walker synched his com-unit to the vehicle's dash display and pulled out into the road. He brought up the cams inside Lynch's apartment block and confirmed no movement in its corridors or entrance vestibule. *I got you now, you bastard.*

Walker turned into the street and drove past the King Hassan, looking for a parking space. Blue and red lights flashed as he passed a side street and he heard the *whoop-whoop* of a siren. A second later a white car marked with the red and green diagonal stripes of the *Sûreté Nationale* pulled out behind him and signalled for him to pull over. He looked up and down the street, saw it otherwise deserted, and complied.

The first cop, a middle-aged man with a notable paunch, hefted himself out of the passenger seat and strolled down the sidewalk. Walker lowered his window in response.

'Is there a problem, officer?'

'Routine ID check, sir. Please turn off your engine and

step out of the vehicle.'

Walker killed the engine and checked the Glock tucked into back of his jeans. He smiled as he closed the SUV's door behind him, his eyes flitting from the cop to his partner, who had exited the patrol car and was in the process of lighting a cigarette.

'Licence?'

Walker patted down his pockets. 'Got it here somewhere. Ah, here it is.'

The silenced pistol coughed twice, drilling two neat holes in the cop's chest. Walker pivoted and put two rounds into the heart of the second cop as he threw aside his cigarette and fumbled with the retaining strap on his holster.

CHAPTER 20

Lynch killed the uplink to his implant and tucked the data-disc into his leather satchel. His cracking of the TV21 ICE had been crude, with no time to cover his tracks, but his relationship with Berkani was well and truly shot anyway. He had lit the blue touch paper now and there could be no turning back. President Gerrard's cronies would be coming for him, just as they had apparently come for Russell. The ex-spook appeared capable of looking out for himself, but Lynch couldn't shake a sense of misgiving. Or the nagging suspicion he had failed to protect his source, ridiculous as that might seem.

He looked over at Tazi, saw she was still studying her com-unit.

'What the hell are you playing at? We need to go – said it yourself that it was a bad idea coming back here. For once I agree. The bastards are closing in. I can feel it!'

'Try to relax, Lynch. That's what they want – to scare you, make you expose yourself. I need to check the route to the safe house is clear. Once there, I can sort out the logistics of smuggling you out of the city. The trick will be staying clear of the RSA spy satellites.'

'That's easy for you to say,' Lynch muttered under his

breath.

Lynch crossed to the island in the centre of the open-plan living space and cracked open a bottle of bourbon. He looked through the detritus of unwashed crockery for a clean glass, gave up and took a long pull from the bottle. A second search located his cigarettes and he lit up, blowing smoke towards the slow rotation of the ceiling fan. He had never been good at waiting; even less so at allowing other people to make decisions for him. But with no contacts and no money, he was reliant on Tazi arranging transport and logistical support.

'Shit! Move, move!'

Lynch looked up in time for Tazi to thrust the grab bag she had prepared for him into his hands.

'We got incoming,' she explained. 'Single assailant. He's taken out the cops and is heading for the basement.'

Lynch allowed Tazi to hustle him out of the apartment. When he made for the elevators, she pulled him past and directed him towards the fire exit. He pushed through the door and hit the stairs running, taking two or three steps at a time and using the handrail to spin himself about the intermediate landing and onto the next flight. Two flights per storey, seven storeys up, Lynch did the maths as he descended. The breath rasped in his lungs and a wave of dizziness stole over him, the result of having sustained himself over the last three days on a diet of cigarettes and alcohol. What he'd give for a little meth right now. He pressed on, vaguely aware of Tazi somewhere behind him, covering their inglorious retreat.

The door to the underground parking garage loomed in front of him and he turned to see Tazi clear the stairs, gun held out in a two-handed grip in front of her. She held up a hand, signalling him to wait. Lynch bent over and braced his hands on his thighs as he fought to draw breath into his lungs. He watched Tazi open the door and scope out the garage before motioning him forward. The lights of the Lincoln blinked on and he heard the motor power up as they approached.

'Back seat,' Tazi instructed. 'Lie down on the floor.'

Lynch obeyed her instructions, pulling the door closed behind him as the car sped towards the exit ramp. The automatic barrier started to rise slowly. Too slowly. Lynch felt the impact and heard the crack as the car crashed through, its rear end fishtailing as Tazi swung it hard onto the street. The rolling, thunderous boom of an explosion followed their exit and Lynch looked out of the back window in time to see a long tongue of flame and a billowing cloud of smoke and debris chase after them. The apartment block dwindled into the distance as Tazi accelerated away, but Lynch saw it shiver and shake as the bottom floor disintegrated, watched glass, plascrete and steel tumble to earth, entombing who knew how many innocents.

'Holy Mother of God,' Lynch breathed.

'Keep your damn head down! We got company.'

Lynch risked another glance and saw an SUV pull out into the traffic, shouldering another car aside. He ignored Tazi's imprecations to get down and clipped in his seatbelt instead.

'Can't this tank of yours go any faster?'

Tazi ignored him and hit accept as an incoming call flashed up on her com-unit.

'Tazi, Hirsch. What the fuck is going on? We've got reports of an explosion. Unit Twenty-One isn't answering.'

'Sorry, Rikki, but your boys are dead. Have eyes on a single Tango. He took out your guys before blowing up the King Hassan.'

'The Americans wouldn't be so foolish, eh?'

'What?'

'Speaking to myself. What's your situation?'

'We're heading north on Brahim Roudani. Being pursued by a red Dacia Elite, registration five-seven-five-three-one-*kāf*-one-one.'

'I'll get an APB out on it. Hang tight.'

'Like we have any other choice.'

Lynch heard the motor whine as Tazi pushed the car to its limits, but the SUV remained stubbornly on their tail. Tazi checked her mirrors and pulled the car out into the leftmost lane, a goods lorry's horn sounding loudly as she pulled out in front of it.

'Hold tight!'

Before he could ask why, Tazi rammed the Lincoln into the central reservation. Metal screeched and sparks flew as the weight of the car carried it through the crash barrier and onto the adjacent lane. A cacophony of horns sounded as the Lincoln continued against the flow of traffic.

'Are you fucking insane?'

'Relax. I know what I'm doing.'

'Didn't Custer say that to his men right before the Battle of Little Bighorn?'

Lynch closed his eyes and then opened them again. After all he'd been through, might as well look death in the face. The Lincoln swerved left, left again, and then back to the right as Tazi jinked in and out of the traffic, forcing other vehicles to brake and swerve to avoid her. Metal crumpled and glass shattered as she left a series of collisions and pileups in their wake. He looked out the passenger side window and saw the SUV keeping pace with them on the other side of the crash barrier. An oncoming truck suddenly blocked the view ahead. Tazi wrenched the wheel to the left and the Lincoln slewed across the road. The door mirror whistled past as the truck caught it. And then there was a clear patch of road ahead across all four lanes. Tazi triggered the handbrake and the Lincoln spun round with a screech of burning rubber. She kicked the car back into gear as the SUV shot past, now travelling in the opposite direction. Lynch released a breath he hadn't realised he was holding.

'Maybe you're not so crazy after all.'

'Don't start celebrating yet. He'll be able to exit and follow us in a klick or so. Reckon I've bought us a minute or two at best and drawn a fuckload of attention in the process.'

As if to illustrate her point a pair of patrol cars merged from the police access ramp, sirens wailing and lights flashing. Tazi pressed down on the accelerator, the front wheel grinding against the metal of the buckled driver's side wing. One of the patrol cars closed the distance while the other fell back to escort an incoming ambulance. The pursuing SUV swerved past the ambulance and police car with seeming ease.

Tazi was good. But was she good enough?

A warning to pull over and surrender blasted from the patrol car's speakers, repeating in French, Arabic and English. Lynch could tell by the set of Tazi's shoulders that she had no intention of complying. She checked the nav screen and took the exit for Félix Houphouët-Boigny. He hoped she had a plan.

The Lincoln shuddered as Tazi nosed a jeep out of the way, turning onto des Almohades. She accelerated again, overtaking and cutting back in as the patrol car took up position less than two car lengths behind them, the SUV hard on its tail.

'What are they holding back for?'

'That.' Tazi pointed through the windscreen at pair of police officers deploying a spike strip across the road.

She kept going as the patrol car skidded to a halt behind them. The Lincoln's tyres hissed and popped as they ran over the spikes, Tazi fighting to retain control. Lynch's stomach lurched as the rear end spun out, turning the car 180 degrees. Sparks flew from the wheel rims as the Lincoln ground to halt, coming to rest outside the door of Rick's Café. The SUV careered past them, crashing to a halt against the central reservation, smoke billowing from its engine. The wail of fast-approaching sirens filled the air.

Tazi released Lynch's seatbelt and pulled him from the wrecked car. She pushed him towards the café as Lynch's would-be assassin clambered from the SUV and took aim with an assault rifle. A burst of rounds splintered the heavy wooden door above Lynch's head as Tazi pushed him through and down. She turned and snapped off a couple of shots of her own, forcing the gunman to duck.

Lynch dragged himself over to the window and looked out. Tazi and his attacker were standing five metres apart, weapons aimed at each other. Overhead, a cloud scudded momentarily across the sun, giving Lynch his first clear look at the man who had so ruthlessly pursued him.

'Walker!'

CHAPTER 21

Lynch pushed open the door and stepped out onto the street. He had never been close to Walker, put off by the reek of a true believer. The kid was only here because Mackinlay had risked his neck to bring him in after he was shot in the leg at Palmachim. It was a favour he had declined to return when Mackinlay bought it during the final assault on Jerusalem. Afterwards, he had been happy to accept Hannah's offer of a job, which said all you needed to know about the kid, in Lynch's opinion. But if there was even the slightest chance that he could put an end to this madness before more lives were lost then he had to take it.

'Lynch!' Tazi hissed. 'Get your crazy ass back inside.'

Walker chuckled mirthlessly. 'You better listen to the li'l lady, Jefferson.'

'You're a long way from Langley, Walker. How's life with the Agency working out for you?'

'Well enough, since you ask. I've found a better way to serve my country, something a traitor like you wouldn't understand.'

'If by serving your country you mean killing innocents, you're goddamn right I'll never understand.'

Walker inclined his head his head in response to the

approaching sirens. He kept his rifle steady as he retreated into the shadows. Tazi fired off a couple of shots in his direction and shoved Lynch back inside the café.

A crowd of customers and staff milled about the bar in confusion. Lynch felt their growing fear as they saw the pistol in Tazi's hand and connected it with the recent crashes and gunfire, and the rapidly closing police sirens. All eyes were on them as the people in the bar tried to work out if they were in the presence of criminals or terrorists, and what those options meant for their own survivability. Lynch knew they were seconds from mass panic, an ugly situation that would end badly for all concerned.

Tazi pointed her gun at the floor. Her voice was calm but authoritative when she spoke.

'I need you all to exit the building through the front doors. The police are coming and will ensure your safety.'

A blonde-haired woman in a black trouser suit drew herself up to her full height and smoothed down her lapels. She crossed the floor, her dignity undermined by a visible tremble in her shoulders.

'Cara Fitzgerald, general manager. What guarantee do I have that you're telling the truth?'

'None. But would you prefer to take your chances in here with us, or outside?'

Fitzgerald's lips formed a moue, her disgust almost great enough to succeed in forming a wrinkle in her perfect brow. But duty superseded any afront to her social dignity. She crooked a finger towards the bar and a tall, thin man with a head of black curls detached himself with a swish of his tailcoat.

'Jacque, would please escort our guests from the premises.'

The head waiter nodded and rounded up two of the waiting staff to assist with the evacuation. Lynch watched Tazi watching the customers, alert to the danger of some have-a-go hero. A large florid-faced man looked the type, but the mousy woman holding tightly to his right arm kept him in check. The lunch crowd on a Wednesday was fortunately light and Lynch counted eight guests, three waiting staff, a cook and the kitchen porter.

Fitzgerald hovered, unwilling to abandon her responsibility. Tazi motioned her to leave with a jerk of her head.

'It's a café, not a ship. Nobody expects you to go down with it.'

Fitzgerald looked set to argue and then she saw Lynch.

'You're that journalist from TV21. The one who spouts all that nonsense about the RSA.'

'One man's gibberish is another man's truth.'

'I always thought you looked like a criminal. It's in the eyes. One can tell.'

'Then I suggest you do as my partner with the gun says and leave.'

Fitzgerald sniffed her disdain and pushed through the heavy wooden doors. Tazi grabbed the wrought-iron handle, pulled it shut and turned the key.

Outside, they heard the squelch of a police megaphone.

'Armed police. Kneel down with your hands clasped upon your head.'

Tazi was already moving, dragging the nearest table towards the door. A brass table lamp toppled to the floor, scattering glass beads in all directions.

'Don't just stand there, Lynch, give me a hand. It won't take the cops long to figure out we're still inside.'

Lynch helped her with the table and turned it on its side, jamming the top against the door. He looked round and selected a smaller circular one, while Tazi stacked a couple of the ornately carved wooden chairs. The result looked more like an obstacle course than a serious barricade. He moved one of the slats of the vertical blinds with a finger and peeked outside. Parked police cruisers had blockaded the road either side of the café, while an ARV sat facing it. Uniformed officers were escorting the last of the customers beyond the blockade. He spotted an officer with captain's braid on his uniform talking to the driver of the ARV, a hopeful sign they intended to open negotiations before opening fire.

Bemused, Lynch made his way to the bar and lifted the countertop. He searched the shelves for a few moments before fetching down a bottle of Chivas Regal 18 Year Old and pouring himself a couple of fingers. Lynch swirled it in the glass, took a sniff and then knocked it back. He smacked his lips appreciatively and poured another.

'So, what's the plan here? With Walker gone, surely it makes sense to take our chances with the cops?'

Tazi shook her head. 'You've lived here long enough to know the regular cops are so crooked they have to be screwed into their trousers. You'll be lucky to last the day in so-called protective custody. You need to get out of here and out of the city.'

'I presume you have some sort of plan for that?'

Tazi elbowed Lynch out of the way and tapped a button on the console next to the cash register. The Bogart hologram flickered to life, looked round itself and turned to Lynch.

'Of all the gin joints in all the towns in all the world …'

'Computer, freeze program.'

Tazi walked round the hologram, examining it closely. High-end tech, possibly Bamako or maybe Sfax. Definitely one of the Big Three. She checked the ceiling, looking for the emitters and lasers that provided the object and reference waves; the coverage was good throughout the bar and restaurant area.

'I fail to see what use this guy is going to be. Are we going to aggravate the cops into submission?'

'No. You are.' Tazi shut off the hologram. 'Come to the centre of the floor. That's it.' She turned on the console's imaging cameras. 'Good. Now, turn in a slow circle. And back the other way. Now walk to the bar and back again.' Tazi checked the scans. 'Yeah, that ought to do it.'

'Do what?'

Tazi motioned him over to the console and pointed Lynch to the screen, which was displaying a 3D image of Humphrey Bogart. She tapped a couple of keys and the image stripped down to a wireframe.

'What are you, Lynch? Six foot two, six three? One eighty pounds?'

'Six three and a hundred and ninety.'

The wireframe stretched and slimmed down as Tazi entered the details. She hit another key and skin tone started at the crown and worked its way down the digital mannequin, creating a sexless image with no nipples or genitalia. Further keystrokes brought in his rose petal shirt, combat trousers and work boots. The image rotated slowly as she checked the details. Satisfied, she linked her com-unit to the console, navigated to the TV21 site and downloaded Lynch's broadcast archive.

'Need to synthesise your voice and get a better range of expressions,' Tazi explained in response to Lynch's raised eyebrow.

The imaging software worked away in the background as Tazi typed in a range of responses. It wouldn't stand up to a great deal of scrutiny, but it ought to do the job. The completed icon flashed on the screen and she keyed on the projectors.

Lynch's doppelganger appeared beside the piano. It took out a cigarette, lit up and blew smoke towards the ceiling. 'Goddamn, I need a drink.' It walked towards the bar with a jerky, flailing of limbs.

'I don't walk like that,' Lynch protested. 'Do I?'

Ignoring him, Tazi brought up the building schematics and pointed out the cellar loading hatch in the basement.

'That's your exit right there.'

'Surely SWAT will be crawling all over the place by now?'

'That's where Lieutenant Hirsch comes into play. I'll open negotiations with the cops with your hologram on display while Hirsch redeploys the team by the cellar.'

'And then what? I run for the rest of my life?'

'If need be. This way your life will be measured in weeks or months, perhaps even years. Stay here and it's going to be hours. That much I can guarantee you.'

Tazi removed the pistol from its holster on her right hip. She handed the SIG Compact to him grip first.

'I take it you know how to use one of these?'

Lynch nodded.

'Then synch your com-unit to mine and wait in the cellar for my signal.'

'Would it make any difference if I said this is a bad idea?'

'No.'

'That's what I thought.'

CHAPTER 22

Hopkins found the Watchtower's briefing room claustrophobic at the best of times; a windowless, airless bunker far below ground. Now, the air was ripe with testosterone as Grand Master Vanderbilt and President Gerrard each sought to test the limits of the other's influence and power. Morrison looked particularly uncomfortable with the display, fiddling with his datapad, but the Secretary of Defense had been showing increasing signs of squeamishness as the reality of their conspiracy sank in. Or perhaps it was simple jealousy? Like herself, he had taken his share of the risk for no reward, while Gerrard became president and appointed Kordowski VP in his stead.

She looked at the former Chairman of the Joint Chiefs of Staff. Grey hair, grey eyes, saturnine expression; a seemingly unremarkable man. But behind those hooded eyes the wheels of calculation were in motion as he tallied the strengths and weaknesses of the two greatest sources of authority in the country and their ability to either block or assist his ambition. Yet another man, in a seemingly endless succession, who wanted to be president. How pathetic. And yet, if she were honest, didn't she, against the tide of public opinion and the weight of recent history, covet that office for herself? Someone had to end the perpetual cycle of war in the Middle East.

In almost a century of conflict they had never truly defeated the Islamists. There were times, as now, that they were forced to retreat, to shave off their beards and hide within the puppet democracies the West installed in their place. But they always came back, stronger and more determined, regardless of how much money or many lives the RSA spent in its chimerical pursuit of victory. There had to be a better way.

Hopkins gave herself a mental shake and tuned back into the conversation. Vanderbilt was speaking in the slow, deliberate and slightly exasperated tone of a man forced to state the obvious.

'I can assure you, Mr President, that the campaign is progressing according to plan. Templar forces have captured Tadmur and Caliphate troops are in full retreat. Satellite images show the remnants massing near Aleppo, where we expect them to make a final stand. In short, we are on the cusp of a historic victory.'

'Excellent.' Gerrard smiled. 'Next stop Baghdad.'

'That, I'm afraid, would be premature. Our forces and lines of supply are already stretched to breaking point. Pressing on into Iraq would leave them perilously exposed to a Caliphate counterattack. Marshal Ismail has been quiet so far, but while he has refused to lay claim to the title of caliph out of respect for his predecessor, his capability as a military strategist is in no doubt. It would be prudent to reinforce and resupply our troops in Syria and Jordan while gathering intel. Such a strategy will also afford the opportunity to recall Templar forces to the RSA for some R and R. After all, my men have been in the vanguard of the campaign since the first beach landing in Israel eighteen months ago.'

'Isn't that precisely why we spent all that money on training and equipping your Templars in the first place?

From where I'm sitting, it makes no sense to withdraw our finest troops from theatre.'

'I can assure you that Templar forces remain dedicated to the cause of defeating the Caliphate. The task they were created for. When the time comes to expand our operations into Iraq they will not be found wanting. But my men need rest if they are to maintain optimum efficiency. At the end of the day, they are still human and psychological reports show they are under great stress. We would be foolish to engage the Caliphate with a blunted weapon.'

'Fine.' Gerrard conceded with ill grace. 'We'll see about rotating Templar forces at the end of the current offensive.' He held up an admonishing finger. 'But a skeleton command force is to remain in situ at all times to oversee operations in Syria.'

'Of course, Mr President. Thank you for your understanding.'

The Grand Master stood and nodded his farewell. A shiver ran down Hopkins' spine as she watched him leave. Thaddeus Vanderbilt was not a man to forgive and forget. He had lost considerable face when summoned to appear before the Senate inquiry into the death of Mohamed al-Hashimi, the commander of the Caliphate's Jerusalem Guard. That he was being scapegoated for Colonel Tyler's failure must have been particularly galling, especially when it was suggested he should step down in favour of Tyler. But then Tyler had conveniently shot himself. Hopkins felt an emptiness where she supposed she should feel loss or regret at the death of her former lover. Tyler had been a means to an end, her control over him an indirect means of accessing the power otherwise denied her. Now she was forced to hitch herself to Gerrard's less stable and more unpredictable wagon.

'Sweep the room, Morrison,' Gerrard ordered.

'I already swept it before the meeting.'

'And I'm telling you to sweep it again.'

Morrison scraped back his chair and took out a handheld

scanner. He ran it over the desk, the walls, ceilings and door of the briefing room before scanning Gerrard, Hopkins and Kordowski. Finally, he passed the scanner to Gerrard and allowed the president to scan him.

'See? Still no listening devices.'

Gerrard grunted and placed the scanner on the table. He tapped at his console, initiating a com-link with the deputy director of the CIA.

Hannah leaned back in his chair, deliberately pulling his face back from the camera.

There's someone else who benefitted almost immediately from their treachery, Hopkins thought bitterly.

'I take it you caught all that, Matt?'

'Yes, sir. From a military standpoint, Vanderbilt's request is sound.'

'I sense a "but" here.'

'More an intuition. As you know, surveillance has failed to throw up anything of interest. But following his latest meeting with Vanderbilt, Bishop Gibson has stepped up his criticism of Congress generally, and yourself and Hopkins in particular. I believe the expression he used was "the moral vacuity at the heart of government".'

'Is that enough to arrest Gibson for sedition?'

'At a stretch, perhaps, but I'd counsel against it. Such a move might well prove to be the spark that ignites a larger conflagration. There are better ways of undermining the bishop's authority and neutralising the threat posed by his followers.'

'Ways, from your tone, I'd be better off not asking about.'

'Precisely.'

'In which case I'll leave it in your capable hands, Deputy Director.'

Gerrard closed the link and turned to Hopkins.

'Keep your ear to the ground on this. Whatever happens, I want the fallout contained.'

'It would help if I knew what sort of contingency to plan

for.'

'Plan for the worst. The deputy director isn't known for his subtlety.'

Hopkins nodded her agreement while seething internally. Gerrard was setting her up to fail by assigning her a nebulous task. General misogyny, or a more subtle powerplay? Endorsing her run for the Senate with one hand while undermining her credibility with the other? The latter, if true, implied he felt sufficiently threatened by her to avoid any overt action. She had been hoping to keep Gerschwitz's support in reserve, but it looked like she might have to deploy him sooner than anticipated.

CHAPTER 23

Broken glass crunched under Cooper's boot. He turned his head to the left and took in the row of boarded-up shopfronts, their walls pockmarked with bullet holes. Infrared and motion sensors detected no life larger than a rat, but they were numerous. Beside him, Goodman shifted his grip on his assault rifle as he scanned the opposite side of the street. This was Tadmur, but it could just as easily have been Damascus, and before that Jerusalem, the differences in architecture and climate reduced to the unvarying sights and smells of war. The smell in particular permeated Cooper's uniform, hair and skin, refused to be washed away. A potent mix of smoke, high-explosive, human excrement and the sickly-sweet cloying odour of rotting flesh. Burial detachments had collected the visible corpses, bulldozing them into mass graves. But that still left hundreds more to rot, buried under rubble, lying in cellars and backrooms that they dared not enter for fear of boobytraps. Out of sight but most definitely not out of mind.

The *whup-whup* of rotors drew Cooper's attention aloft. It was one of the regular transporters, carrying relief troops, supplies and equipment. The skies were full of them as the

RSA sought to consolidate its gains. A heavier bass rumble signalled the approach of one of the big transporters, a Sikorsky CH-59K. It was slung with a prefab plascrete fortification, ready to be dropped into the barricade they were constructing around the city. Someone, somewhere, was making a lot of money out of the war. But wasn't that always the case? Hell, he was beginning to sound like his old pal Donny, believing the war to be one big conspiracy. He knuckled his eyes, hoping to somehow magically scrub the atrocities he had witnessed from his mind. With each passing day the gap between the Templars and the Caliphate seemed to narrow, always supposing there had been a difference to begin with. If he'd had the presence of mind to ask himself that before he enlisted, he wouldn't be in this mess. Good old hindsight.

Goodman held up his hand to signal he wanted to stop. He looked round and shook his head ruefully.

'You know, I didn't think we'd stop until we reached Baghdad – the old blitzkrieg philosophy.'

'If Tyler was still running the show you'd probably be right. But Willard does exactly what he's told. Textbook soldiering. Guess the brass are happier with that – they don't like surprises.'

Goodman set off again and Cooper fell into step with him, reminding himself they were still in enemy territory, regardless of what his HUD showed or didn't show. The fighting had been heavier here, every third or fourth building reduced to rubble, like jagged stumps in a mouth full of rotting teeth. He eyed the surrounding flat roofs, paying particular attention to air-con units and water tanks, spots where a sniper might lurk.

Goodman looked sideways at Cooper.

'It was you and Sergeant Jackson who found Tyler's body. Y'know, I didn't peg the colonel as the suicide type. Lynch's broadcast was harsh, but...'

Cooper shrugged. 'Who's to say what goes through a man's mind when he sees everything that he's worked for about to go down the drain?'

'No. I just don't see it. Not Tyler. Fucker was meaner than a rattlesnake and twice as dangerous when backed into a corner.'

'He certainly had his moments. No denying that. Hey,' Cooper said, changing the subject, 'you reckon there's any truth in the rumour we're going to be shipped home for some R and R once the city is secure? Not like they need all of us to man the barricades.'

'I hope so, man. First thing I'm gonna do is lie me down on a real bed and sleep till I can't sleep no more. Then I'm going take me a long hot bath. Soak this war right out of me. Know what I mean? There's this little diner, Rosie's, about a klick from where I live. They do these waffles with maple syrup and the crispiest bacon – stack those bad boys up with butter melting on top. Man, you think you've had waffles and bacon before? Trust me, not until you've had Rosie's. Gonna have me one of those specials every morning. See if I don't. Then I'm gonna…'

Cooper let Goodman's waffle rhapsody wash over him. They had turned off the main drag into a side street, its surface little more than a dirt track. It was eerily quiet, even compared with the rest of the city, the shutters on the windows fastened tight. The hairs on the back of his neck rose in response to an unknown but definite danger. Something was off. He held up his hand and signalled Goodman to stop while he scanned the area. Sensors showed zero movement, not even the ubiquitous rats. Scared off by a bigger predator?

Impatient, Goodman started to retrace his steps, intending to return to the main thoroughfare. Something clicked beneath his foot and he froze. Cooper met his gaze and together they looked down to see the outline of the landmine beneath his boot.

CHAPTER 24

L ynch shifted his weight from one leg to the other, trying to ease the cramp in his muscles as he squatted by the cellar loading hatch. He ran a hand over his scalp and down to his neck, wiping away the sweat.

Tazi's voice sounded clear in his ear as she negotiated with the SWAT commander. Every so often he heard his own voice, strident, often nonsensical, as his holographic doppelganger played its part. He fought the urge to rush upstairs and reveal himself. Bad enough the girl had taken a bullet for him without getting herself jammed up with the cops. But her warning not to trust them rang true, which made depending on Hirsch all the more difficult.

He'd only met the lieutenant a couple of times and still couldn't shake the suspicion that he knew him from somewhere. More pertinently, why would Hirsch put his neck on the line for him? Was the world finally waking up to the dangers of the RSA and its military adventurism? It seemed an outlandish hope, but it was all Lynch had to cling to. To do otherwise made everything he had done worthless.

Not that it prevented him from torturing himself, imagining a version of the world where he had erased the evidence of the refugee massacre instead of broadcasting it.

In that reality Tyler was still alive, leading his troops all the way to Baghdad and victory while Lynch did the chat show circuit, regaling his hosts, and by extension the American public, with his daring exploits.

But sooner or later the weight of the lies would have crushed him. Always supposing he didn't meet with an accident first. The Agency didn't leave loose ends. Much as this reality might suck, Tazi was right: it was the only one in which he had any hope of a future. He heard her voice now, strident and imperial.

'I've told you already – I will only negotiate with Commandant Idrissi.'

'I'm not sure that's possible at this time,' the SWAT commander replied. 'Let me see what I can do.'

Lynch heard the officer's retreating steps as he marched away from the café. Smart girl, playing for time. But two could play that game and the SWAT commander didn't sound like a dummy. Sweat stung Lynch's eyes and he wiped his brow with his shirt sleeve. Overhead, an ancient air-con unit rattled and wheezed. How could it be so goddamn hot? Fear sweat.

The silence stretched and Lynch's nerves stretched with it. Shots fired. A potential terrorist attack in progress. Idrissi should have been straight on the com. He wanted to yell at Tazi to cut her losses and run before the cops brought the hammer down. He maybe would have if Hirsch hadn't beaten him to it.

The lieutenant's voice crackled over the comms: 'Idrissi isn't coming, the SWAT team are preparing for a breach – you need to get out now!'

Tazi's response was calm, resolute. 'If I move, they'll know we're on to them and attack straight away. Only way this works is if I stay.'

'Goddamn it,' Lynch swore. 'I'm not leaving you!' He hauled open the cellar door to find Tazi blocking his exit.

'Said I'd get you out, Lynch. Don't make a liar of me.'

His concern must have been visible, as her expression

softened a fraction.

'Don't worry. I got this. Now go before I change my mind and hand you over – earn myself a tidy sum.'

Lynch nodded, not trusting himself to speak. A precious couple of seconds ticked by as he stared at the now-closed door before finally turning away. He crossed to the loading hatch, opened it a crack and peered out. Two uniformed officers stood beside their patrol car, watching the rear of the building. No way round them, which meant going through them. He pulled back the slide on his pistol and raised it to take aim. His finger reached first pressure on the trigger and stopped. He couldn't do it; killing them was cold-blooded murder, regardless of how much danger his life was in. Particularly when he had no way of knowing if they were dirty or just doing as they were told. The line between the two could be thin enough, but that didn't matter.

A burst of static heralded an incoming message on the police comms channel. 'Ten seventy-two, Boulevard Emile Zola. Repeat Ten seventy-two, Boulevard Emile Zola.'

The officers, jolted out of their complacency, looked unsure as to whether they should respond or not. Hirsch's arrival in an unmarked car with a concealed siren wailing behind the grille added to their confusion. They stared at him as he parked up and exited the vehicle, flashing them his badge.

'Don't worry, I got this – they need all the help they can get with the riot on Emile Zola. Gang of punks jacked up on chrome – worst I've seen.'

The cops shared a look and clambered into their car. They hit the lights and siren and screeched away, leaving the stink of burning rubber in their wake. Hirsch shook his head, bemused.

Lynch tucked the pistol in the waistband of his trousers and pushed open the loading hatch. He trotted round the front of Hirsch's car and opened the passenger door. As he hauled on the seatbelt Hirsh looked at him askance.

'Where's Tazi?'

'Holding the fort to cover our escape.'

Hirsch swore under his breath. 'I don't like it.'

'Can't say I do either. But...'

Both men turned in response to the detonation of a flash-bang. It was followed almost immediately by the chatter of automatic fire. Hirsch put the car in drive and pulled away fast.

CHAPTER 25

Cooper examined the earth carefully before kneeling, making sure there were no adjacent mines. He slid his knife from its sheath and used the point to carefully scrape the earth from the top of the mine, exposing the pressure plate.

'What the fuck do you think you're doing? Stop playing the hero and get your crazy ass to safety! I'll jump for it once you're clear. If I'm lucky, it'll only take a leg off. You detonate it with us on top – it'll kill us both!'

'Shut the fuck up, Pete. I need to concentrate. And keep your damn foot still!'

The mine looked like it was based on the old M14, geriatric but effective. Cooper cleared away more earth and saw the plate had been rotated into the armed position, the 'A' aligned with an arrow on the main body of the mine. By all accounts the spring should have driven the firing pin into the detonator. Corrosion must have jammed it, but removing the pressure could just as easily free it.

'Need something to cushion the mechanism.'

'Never a can of expanding foam when you need it.' Goodman laughed bitterly.

'No, but...'

Cooper ripped open his medical pouch and pulled out a sachet of blood coagulant. He tore open the top and then used his knife to lever up the edge of the pressure plate.

'Here goes nothing.'

Cooper winced as he sliced open his left palm. He clenched his fist, squeezing as much blood as he could into the detonation mechanism. The blood fizzed, popped and expanded as he added the coagulant, forming a crust in seconds. He prodded it experimentally with the tip of his knife and found it unyielding.

'This will either work or it won't,' Goodman said. 'You've done your bit, Coop. No point both of us buying it.'

Cooper couldn't argue with that. He carefully retreated to a safe distance, following his previous path. Goodman nodded that he was ready and Cooper nodded back. He held his breath as Goodman stepped clear of the mine.

Goodman started to laugh. It had a high-pitched hysterical edge to it; relief giving way to mania. Cooper saw the danger.

'Take a moment, Pete. Just breathe. We good? Cool. Now, I want you to follow my footsteps back to me. That's it. Take it nice and easy. No need to hurry.'

Goodman traversed step by step until he joined Cooper in the safety of the main thoroughfare. He'd beaten the odds, pure and simple, and he knew it.

'That was some quick thinking, Coop! I should have been toast. I owe you. Anything you need, just say the word. I mean it. Anything.'

'Forget it. You would have done the same. Brothers. Right?'

While he tried to downplay it, Cooper couldn't quite suppress the pride he felt. He'd taken charge of the situation and probably saved Goodman's life. Fighting the Caliphate, there had been precious little of late that felt like a victory and even less to feel good about. For once, he'd been the right man in the right place.

Goodman opened his own medical pouch. 'Here, let me see that.' He irrigated the wound on Cooper's palm before spraying it with a combined antiseptic and synthetic skin.

Cooper flexed it experimentally; some tightness but otherwise good. He tapped his com-unit.

'Gethsemane, Alpha-niner, copy.'

'Copy Alpha-niner.'

'Zero on my GPS – we need a mine clearance unit.'

'Confirmed, Alpha-niner. Hold your position. Gethsemane out.'

Cooper looked round, scanning for some form of cover while they waited for their support. The boarded-up shopfronts offered little by way of protection, so he fell back to a point where he had direct line of sight into the mined lane and a view in either direction of the main street.

Goodman shifted from foot to foot, trying to dissipate the adrenalin. His edginess transferred itself to Cooper, who found himself turning at every half-heard sound. Tadmur might be in Templar hands, but the insurgents were far from defeated. Maintaining position made them vulnerable.

Cooper's rifle swung up in response to the whine of an approaching vehicle. It dropped a second later as the support JLTV with its RSA markings came into view. The driver gave him the thumbs up as he halted the vehicle a few metres from the mined street. The rear door opened and a ramp extended to deploy a mine-sweeping drone. A pair of robotic arms dangled from the front of the tracked unit, while its cylindrical turret bristled with video, infrared and X-ray lenses.

The driver hopped down from the JLTV. He waved to Cooper and Goodman as he crossed the road, checking the drone's progress on his datapad. The drone stopped and used its robotic arms to carefully unearth a mine. Various lenses scanned it to determine its condition. A second later it sprayed out foam, encapsulating it. The drone moved on.

The driver held out his hand. 'Gabriel Sanchez.'

Cooper shook it and introduced himself and Goodman.

Sanchez pointed to his datapad; its screen displayed over a dozen mines identified by the drone.

'Looks like we're gonna be here a while.' He took out a pack of cigarettes and offered it round. Cooper declined and Goodman accepted. They lit up and smoked in companionable silence.

'Guess you boys have seen some action since Jerusalem?'

'A little,' Cooper conceded, trying to avoid discussing his combat experience.

'I thought about trying out for the Templars, but it's just too tough.' Sanchez pointed to the JLTV. 'But I still wanted to serve my country, so the Support Battalion seemed like a good fit. I know I'm not in the front line like you guys, and I've got nothing but respect for what you're doing. You guys rock. Kicking Caliphate ass.'

'We each serve how can,' Goodman replied, provoking an embarrassed smile from Sanchez.

Cooper looked down and saw the red dot of a laser sight on his chest. He looked at Goodman and Sanchez and saw that they were similarly targeted.

A voice barked, 'Lay down your weapons and raise your hands.'

Half a dozen insurgents came forward to surround them, emerging from shuttered houses on the mined side street. They wore the olive drab of the Caliphate. It struck Cooper the mines were never meant to detonate; merely to serve as a diversion to keep them in situ, allowing the insurgents to take prisoners. The insurgents split into two groups, one half keeping their weapons trained on the Americans while the others frisked them, removing Cooper and Goodman's sidearms and knives.

'Put your hands behind your backs.'

Cooper felt plastic cut into his wrists as his captor tightened a pair of flex cuffs. A hood was drawn over his head, cutting out the light, and he felt a rope being run between the cuffs, joining him to the other prisoners. A harsh shove on his shoulder set him in motion and he set off in a halting walk.

'Where do you think they're taking us?' Sanchez asked.

'No talking!'

Cooper heard the thud of a rifle stock on flesh, a grunt, and the rope went tight, dragging him to the ground. Hands gripped him beneath the shoulders and hauled him to his feet. They walked on in silence, turning again and again, as though navigating a maze. Cooper tried to picture where they were going, drawing on his memory of the streets, but the pattern made no sense and he suspected they were being made to cut back on themselves in a deliberate attempt to confuse and disorientate. At best, he judged them to be deep within the warren of residential houses to the west of their original position. But the real question that nagged at him was why they had been taken prisoner and not killed outright. Previous attacks by the insurgents had employed textbook guerrilla tactics; hit hard and fast and fade away. Hostage-taking was a new and sinister development. Were they to be tortured for information or brutally executed for propaganda purposes? After all he had been through, Cooper found it hard to believe this was how it would end; that he would never see his family again. Would their last memory of him be of some Caliphate propaganda video as his head was hacked from his shoulders? He couldn't, wouldn't, let that happen. The fact they had been taken alive showed they were wanted for a purpose, and that was something he could exploit in order to escape. Plus, he had Goodman to back him up.

A change in the air informed Cooper that they were now indoors. He could feel carpet or a rug under his feet as his captors guided him; they were passing through an entrance hall, or possibly along a corridor. A tug on the rope brought him up sharp and a moment later a kick to the back of his legs dropped him to his knees. He blinked in response to the light as the hood was removed.

The room he found himself in appeared to be a former office, now stripped of equipment and furniture. Blinds were drawn over the windows, concealing the world outside. Two armed guards stood with weapons trained on them. But it was the man who stood between them that drew Cooper's attention. Tall, whipcord thin, a full head of hair streaked with grey and a beard that fell to his chest. Cooper recognised him immediately from intelligence reports: Marshal Ismail, the de facto leader of the Caliphate since Abu Ahmad al-Nasr al-Qurayshi's assassination during a drone strike on Al-Aqsa Mosque. Prophecy said there would be but five caliphs and in deference to this Marshal Ismail had refused the honorific.

Ismail circled his captives, taking in their unforms, rank and insignia. He came to a halt behind Sanchez and drew his pistol.

'This one is worthless.'

The shot sounded impossibly loud in the confined space of the office. Cooper blinked and shook his head, attempting to clear the blood and brain matter from his eyes.

CHAPTER 26

Hirsch indicated and drifted across into the adjacent lane, taking up position behind one of the huge automatic freight trucks that supplied the city with consumer goods manufactured by the Tech Corps. The speedometer read a steady 60 kph.

Lynch waved his hands impatiently.

'What is this, a Sunday drive? Hit the lights and siren and get us moving!'

'We're driving like this to avoid drawing attention,' Hirsch explained patiently. 'Right about now, my colleagues have probably realised you're not in the café. Tazi will be telling the truth when she says she doesn't know where you are, which means they'll have to search the surveillance cams to pick us up – a speeding car, police or not, will be a red flag.'

'I take it there's plan beyond us driving around and admiring the sights?'

'To get you out of the city. There's a charter flight waiting to take you to Europa City.'

Lynch raised an eyebrow.

'Given the amount of weapons tech they sell the RSA, that's hardly neutral territory.'

'Which is why you'll be landing under an assumed name – I downloaded the documents earlier.'

'For someone who said he couldn't interfere in the affairs of a foreign national, you seem to have gone to a lot of trouble to set this up.'

'Afraid I can't take the credit for that. You've Hank Russell to thank for this.'

'Russell's alive? You've heard from him? When?'

'Three, maybe four hours ago. Why?'

'Shit. He called me after that – sounded like he was under attack. Haven't heard from him since. He could be in trouble or dead. We should go look for him.'

'I don't think so. From what I've heard of this Russell character he can look after himself. And he was pretty clear the priority was getting you out. Don't want to screw up any sacrifice he's made, tearing around half-cocked. Besides which, I'm running a big enough risk here as it is.'

Lynch fell silent, leaving Hirsch to concentrate on his driving. He turned left onto Moulay Youssef and then took the exit for the N11. From here it was a relatively straight thirty klicks to the airport. Traffic was heavy but moving steadily. Hirsch checked the mirrors and moved into the centre lane. Some of the tension appeared to ease out of him. Lynch wished he felt the same.

Realistically, they weren't looking for Hirsch's vehicle. But how long would it be until a review of the surveillance cams showed him picking up Lynch? Or the cops he had diverted failed to find a riot? Most of the cams ran ANPR, making it easy to locate a suspect vehicle, even on a busy highway. Lynch shook the thought away: nothing he said or did would change the outcome. He would either make it out of the city or…

They were on the P3038 now and Lynch could see the gleaming white arch of the main terminal. Hirsch pulled up into a Police Only parking bay outside a squat plascrete office bearing the insignia of the *Sûreté Nationale*'s National Brigade. He motioned Lynch to get out of the vehicle and popped the trunk. Lynch followed him round to the rear and had a holdall thrust into his hands. He looked askance at Hirsch.

'Your look is a little too distinctive. Come on, follow me.'

Hirsch used his ID to swipe into the office. A sensor triggered the lights, revealing two desks lined with a bank of monitors. A pair of doors at the back led off to a small kitchen area and a toilet. The sparse white décor made Lynch think of a hospital or doctor's surgery.

'Satellite office,' Hirsch explained. 'We use it to co-ordinate with airport security.'

Lynch unzipped the holdall and unpacked its contents: brogues, white shirt, knitted silk tie, linen suit, blond wig, contact lenses and a diplomatic pouch.

He held up the wig. 'Really?'

'That shaved dome of yours has to go.'

Lynch pulled on the wig and swept the floppy fringe out of his eyes. The sides were long enough to sweep back and cover the tops of his ears; perfect for hiding the fasteners on his temples for his HUD and scar behind his right ear left by the insertion of his implant. He put the lenses in next, turning his brown eyes blue. So far, so Aryan.

Hirsch thrust the shirt and suit trousers at him. 'If you're shy, go change in the restroom.'

Lynch pulled the SIG Compact from the waistband of his trousers and placed it on the desk, ignoring the look Hirsch gave him as he kicked off his boots. He hesitated over the nano-weave shirt; it had saved his life once already, but its rose petal pattern was neither subtle nor discreet. Hirsch snapped his fingers to speed him up and he popped the fasteners.

When Lynch had finished changing, Hirsch backed him against the whiteboard and captured a headshot on his com-unit. He hit 'send' and received an answering bleep from the diplomatic pouch. Hirsch retrieved a high-end com-unit from the pouch and handed it to Lynch.

'Passport, driver's licence and travel documents are all loaded. Diplomatic clearance or not, you still have to pass through immigration.'

Lynch swiped it open and checked his passport – Hans Beck, Europa City trade attaché.

'And what exactly was my mission here?'

Hirsch shrugged. 'Grain. Textiles. It'll all be the same to the immigration officer.' He walked slowly round Lynch. There was no disguising his height or build, but diplomatic checks tended to be less stringent. All he had to do was make it out of Moroccan airspace.

'Let's go.'

Lynch checked the time on his new com-unit. He willed Russell to appear.

'What are you waiting for?'

Lynch balled his fists. He'd clearly spent too much time with those crazy Templar fucks.

'You don't leave a man behind. We have to go and look for Russell.'

'Don't be giving me that shit, Lynch. Not when we're minutes away from getting you out of the city. In case you've forgotten, half the cops in the city are looking for you. As should I be.'

'I don't care. I'm not going without him. And that's final. You don't want to help? That's fine. I'll do it on my own.'

Hirsch jutted out his chin, but Lynch could see his resolve faltering.

Sure enough: 'And how will you find him without my help?' He took out his com-unit and logged in.

Lynch peered over his shoulder. 'What are you doing?'

'Checking the securi-cams and incident reports. See if anything flags up.' Hirsch scrolled through and rejected the various reports with an impressive rapidity. Finally, he tapped the screen. 'There, reports of shots fired in Mediouna, near the money transfer service off the P-treble-three-zero. Officers investigated, found a blood trail but no victims. Put it down as gang-related.'

'But you don't buy it?'

'Not in that area. There's a first time for everything, of course.' Hirsch resumed his search and uttered a grunt of triumph. He turned his com-unit so Lynch could see the screen; the image was a little fuzzy but the figure in the securi-cam still was recognisable as Russell, the Tasshilat money changing service visible in the background. Timestamp put it twenty minutes before the shots were called in.

'Don't suppose there's any point asking you to sit tight while I check it out?' Hirsch asked. 'No, didn't think so.'

Lynch rolled up his shirt and trousers and stowed them, together with the SIG, in the diplomatic pouch. He led the way back to the car almost at a sprint. He was still fastening his seatbelt when Hirsch sounded his horn and pulled out, cutting off a taxi. The taxi driver responded with a long blast of his own horn as they accelerated away.

Mediouna was a province south-east of downtown Casablanca, about a twenty-minute drive in the current traffic conditions. They turned north-west onto the N9 and barrelled along, threading through the suburbs and reaching the more densely populated city centre via the P3330.

Hirsch parked opposite blue lines on the pavement and triggered the 'On Police Business' holo in the centre of the windscreen. Lynch followed him onto the sidewalk and down a side street lined with dusty-looking palm trees. A stray cat arched its back and hissed from the shade as they turned the corner.

Lynch spotted the Tasshilat sign on the opposite side of the street and darted across. At a little after two in the afternoon it should have been open for business, but the frontage of the money transfer shop was shrouded in gloom. He reached out, tentatively pushed the door and felt it give.

Hirsch appeared at Lynch's shoulder, sidearm drawn.

'You know this is crazy, right?'

'Believe I've something of a reputation on that front.'

Lynch pushed open the door and Hirsch darted inside. He gave the lieutenant a count of ten to clear the room before following him. The footprint of the shop totalled less than six square metres, longer than it was wide. A counter with a fold-back top lined the rear wall, a beaded curtain screening the access to the back rooms. Hirsch kept his pistol drawn as he used his left hand to lift the counter. He raised his foot and paused, before stepping round the dark pool of blood on the floor. A series of maroon splotches formed a trail towards the bead curtain.

'What do you think?' Hirsch asked.

'Come into my parlour...'

Hirsch nodded and Lynch leaned over the counter. He spotted an office chair, listing drunkenly, two of its castors broken, and scooped up a threadbare cushion from its seat. At Hirsch's signal Lynch threw the cushion into the beads, which rattled and shook. Silence fell.

Hirsch cautiously pulled the beads aside, letting through a shaft of light from the open back door beyond. The blood trail continued in that direction. A staircase curved upwards to the right, while a door on the left was identified in Arabic as the toilet. He pushed open the door to reveal a porcelain squat set into the floor, with its attendant hose. From this angle he could see the shop backed onto a courtyard lined with shrubbery, a fountain in the centre. The short chirps of bee-eaters could be heard above the plashing of water.

Hirsch motioned Lynch to follow as he headed into the courtyard. The blood trail petered out in front of the fountain. He scanned around but the trail had gone cold, their wounded quarry apparently having stopped the bleeding. A pair of double doors to the right led back to the main street, with a door on the left most likely providing access to the adjacent property. Fifty-fifty as to which way their man had gone, assuming it was Russell and not one his attackers they were trailing.

Both men turned in unison as they heard a clatter from upstairs. Hirsch signalled Lynch to stay put and headed back into the shop. The pounding of his feet on the wooden stairs resounded through the courtyard.

CHAPTER 27

At Hirsch's shout for help, Lynch made his way back into the shop and up the curving staircase. The stairs opened onto a storage room, the steeply angled walls indicating a loft conversion. Russell was lying on a makeshift bed constructed from cardboard boxes. Hirsch knelt beside him with his hands pressed to his side. Even at a distance Lynch could see the ring of blood-soaked cardboard was slowly expanding. He stepped in closer and saw Russell had cut up his jacket in order to bandage a wound in his right side. The makeshift dressing had held long enough for him to double back into the shop, putting any pursuers off the scent. But it had clearly been a temporary reprieve.

Hirsch tossed Lynch the fob for his car. 'Got a med-kit in the trunk.'

Lynch returned a couple of minutes later, breathing heavily. Wiping the sweat from his forehead he felt the wig, grabbed it and threw it at Hirsch, before hunkering down next to Russell.

Russell's face was deathly pale and covered in sweat. They needed to treat him before he succumbed to shock.

Lynch rummaged through the med-kit and found a

fentanyl pen. He jabbed it into Russell's thigh and watched him drift into unconsciousness.

'Help me turn him.'

'You know what you're doing?' Hirsch asked.

'Do you?'

Conceding the point, Hirsch took hold of Russell's shoulder and hip and rotated him towards Lynch, who examined the wound, using the tip of a pair of scissors to move the blood-sodden fabric.

'Looks like a through-and-through – definite entry and exit wounds. Messy. Lots of blood loss. But if it'd hit anything vital he'd have been dead long before now.'

Lynch used the scissors to cut away Russell's shirt and then irrigated the wound with saline solution. He turned to where Hirsch had spread out the contents of the med-kit on top of one of the boxes opposite. His fingers hovered above a coagulant pack before moving onto a laser suture.

'Hold him steady.'

'You sure about this?'

'Honestly? No. But it's the least-worst option.'

Hirsch pressed Russell's good side into the boxes, eliciting a low moan.

'Don't worry. The amount of fentanyl in his system, I doubt he can feel anything.'

Lynch started to cauterise the entry wound. A smell, not unlike roasting pork, filled the room. His stomach roiled rebelliously and he felt bile rise in his throat. He swallowed it down and concentrated on closing the wound. By the time he started on the exit wound he barely noticed the smell at all. Russell stirred but thankfully remained unconscious. Lynch finished up by applying a spray dressing, the sterile plasticised skin an unnatural pink. He found some antibiotics and administered a shot.

Russell's eyes snapped open and his hand locked round Lynch's wrist with unnatural strength as he gasped out a warning: 'We have to get to the airport before it's too late!' He fumbled for his com-unit, unlocked it with his thumb and gave it to Lynch. 'You need to send the flight instruction to the AI autopilot.' He lapsed back into unconsciousness.

'Somehow I don't think any amount of diplomatic dispensation is going to let us waltz him through the airport in this state.' Lynch snapped his fingers. 'My old clothes are in the diplomatic pouch – shouldn't be too bad a fit. Help me get him downstairs to the toilet. We can wash off the blood.'

Forty-five minutes later they were parked up outside the National Brigade's office at the airport. Russell's colour was better, but his legs were rubber. Lynch took out the quart of bourbon they'd stopped off for and cracked open the cap. He splashed Russell's clothes and wet his lips with the spirit.

'People will excuse a drunk a lot of things. Speaking of which.' Lynch took a long swallow from the bottle. He smacked his lips appreciatively and took a second drink before capping the bottle, which then disappeared inside the diplomatic pouch.

Hirsch pinched the bridge of his nose. 'God help us.'

Lynch tapped Russell gently on the cheek with the palm of his hand until his eyes fluttered open.

'Need you to hold it together for a few minutes. Can you do that?'

Russell nodded and Lynch wrapped his left arm about Russell's waist, took hold of his right hand and helped him to his feet.

'All right. Nice and slow.'

Hirsch led Lynch and Russell into the terminal, past a row of self-check-in terminals towards airport security. Lynch stiffened as an armed police officer walked past with a German shepherd on a choke chain padding along beside him. On this occasion the dog ignored him, the vital difference being he didn't have a giant wedge of cocaine in his luggage. Didn't have any luggage at all, for that matter.

Was it really less than two years ago? It felt like a lifetime. For many of the Templars he had unwillingly accompanied into battle during the campaign to liberate Israel it had literally been a lifetime. But he was still alive and that was all that counted.

Hirsch produced his badge and approached another armed officer standing guard in front of an unmarked door.

The officer squinted at the badge, then looked suspiciously at Lynch and Russell.

'What can I do for you, Lieutenant?'

Hirsch pulled out his com-unit and called up a document.

'Diplomatic clearance. Charter flight waiting in hangar ninety-four.'

Hirsch transferred the document and the officer verified it on his own com-unit, scrutinising Lynch and Russell against their ID photos. Finding nothing untoward, he peeled off his right glove and placed his hand against the sensor pad. The door swung open and he waved them through, closed it behind them.

The corridor ran for thirty metres with doors leading off to either side. Hirsch seemed to know where he was going, so Lynch followed in his wake as he made his way to the second but last door on the right. He produced an ID card and tapped it against the door sensor.

The heat hit Lynch like a physical blow as he stepped out onto the tarmac. At a little after midday, it was forty-five degrees with no wind. Sweat prickled his back and chest as he followed Hirsch towards one of three private hangars. He looked anxiously at Russell, but the heat seemed to have a beneficial effect on the wounded man; head raised, eyes focused.

Hirsch opened his mouth but the roar of one of the big passenger jets blotted out whatever he said. It didn't matter; the middle hangar was clearly marked '94'. Lynch and Russell followed Hirsch into the hangar where a Learjet sat with its cabin door open, ready for boarding.

Hirsch stepped in close and together they manhandled Russell up the steps of the aircraft. Sweat beaded Russell's forehead again as they eased him into one of the seats and reclined it.

Russell waved his arm impatiently. 'We need to get this bird in the air.'

'Reckon that's my cue to leave.' Hirsch shifted uneasily. 'Time I wasn't here.'

'Take it I can't persuade you on a trip back to the motherland?'

'Let's just say my presence in Europa City would bring more heat on you than you can afford and leave it at that.'

It came to Lynch then, suddenly, like a stage magician drawing back the curtain. As a rule, he'd paid little heed to Europa City politics, but one story had caught his attention as it had brought to light shadowy dealings between the city state and the RSA.

'Guess it would that, Detective Duvall. Have to say, you're looking remarkably well – for a dead man.'

Hirsch went pale. But whatever fear or anxiety he felt at his unmasking was quickly shaken off.

'Guess the game's up. How long have you known?'

'I didn't. Not until you confirmed it just now. But it's been nagging at me for a while. Commissioner Sajer's murder was big news in the RSA – I remember the execution. Guess Supreme Councillor Haynes came through on that pardon after all?'

'Something like that,' Hirsch replied. 'Maybe see you around, if you pass back this way again. I'll get the steps and the hangar doors.'

The journalist in Lynch had a hundred questions, but he had to let them go. Russell was right; they needed to get airborne. He transmitted the instructions to the AI and buckled himself into the seat opposite Russell. The Learjet, having received clearance, commenced its taxi. Lynch spotted Hirsch standing to one side as the wingtip cleared the hangar door by inches.

As a rule, the citizens of the RSA were rarely interested in what happened outside its borders, but Sajer's coup in Europa City had cut through. Sajer's motivation in arresting Councillor Haynes for corruption and placing the city under martial law remained unclear. Whatever the reason, it initiated a brutal war between the police and the city's organised crime families, one in which innocent citizens were caught in the crossfire. With the casualties mounting, and Sajer's removal being the only way of ending the conflict, Detective Duvall had killed his mentor for the sake of the city he loved. Lynch had betrayed his own country for much the same reason. History was full of accounts of those who had done evil in hope some greater good would come of it. Few were remembered fondly. But as Duvall/Hirsch had just demonstrated, that kind of idealism was near impossible to shake. Lynch took comfort in that.

Lynch found himself pressed back in his seat as the engines powered up for take-off. Russell drifted in and out of consciousness throughout the climb but appeared to be back in the land of the living by the time they reached cruising altitude.

Lynch shifted uneasily under his gaze. Well, if Russell wouldn't start the conversation, he'd have to do it himself.

'What the hell happened back there?'

'RSA spooks got a lead on me quicker than expected. Must be getting sloppy in my old age – time was, they would never have found me. And even if they had, I would've dropped them both before they got a shot off.'

'Uh-huh. So, what's the plan after we touch down in Europa City?'

'We head to a safehouse where I can get some proper medical treatment – no offence – and recuperate. We can use the downtime to gauge the impact of your last broadcast. Maybe do a follow-up piece.'

'And when do I get to meet the resistance proper?'

'When they, and I, are sure of you.'

'You gotta be yanking my chain here!' Lynch jabbed a

finger towards the wounded man. 'I just saved your ass back there. What more bona fides do you and Free America need? You owe me – for that and the broadcast!'

The muscles bunched in Russell's jaw either through pain or frustration, as he bit out a reply.

'Whatever I owe you doesn't matter a damn. The resistance operates in cells, Lynch. That's how these things work – I get caught, there's only so many I can give up. My vouching for you will only take you so far up the tree. Others will decide if you're in or not. We both know patience isn't your strong suit, but you're going to have to exercise a little.'

Russell slumped back in the chair and closed his eyes. A few seconds later his breathing told Lynch he was asleep. With a scheduled flight time of a little over three hours, Lynch knew he should try and catch some rest himself, but he was still buzzing with adrenalin. Good people had put themselves on the line to get him out of Casablanca and regardless of what Russell said, he wasn't about to sit idly back and wait for others to make their moves. He needed to find out the true aims and ambitions of the Free America movement. And he could only do that by getting to the heart of its leadership.

CHAPTER 28

Walker raised the scope to his eye and scanned the road below. He counted three police cars and a dog handler unit. The dog in question was a gene-edited Rottweiler, standing a good two and a half feet at the shoulder. It strained at the leash, saliva dripping from its bared teeth as it growled its frustration. Not one to be messed with. He moved the scope on, following two officers as they crossed to the entrance of the apartment block and used their override to bypass the security door. Walker shifted his view to the fourth floor and panned right, counting the windows until he reached apartment 4–7, which he had rented under the identity of Jon van Dijk. Presumably, they had identified 'van Dijk' from cam footage, from where it would be a relatively short step to matching his face to that of Simon Enderby, the identity he had used to enter the country. He was well and truly burned.

Walker rocked back on his heels and slipped the scope into an inside pocket. There would be trace DNA in the apartment, but nothing tangible linking the attack to the RSA, and definitely not the Agency. The suspicion would be there, given the target. But in this game, proof was everything.

He scanned through the police frequencies on his com-unit. Lynch was in the wind, his CPO in custody. Much as it galled him, he would have to let it go. Lynch's time would come, but he had to ensure his own liberty first. He slid back from the edge of the roof and crossed to the door that gave access to the building's internal staircase. The stench of urine assailed his nostrils as he made his way down the concrete steps, using the rail to spin himself round the mid-flight landings. He ran through the briefing notes he had memorised, identifying various arms and equipment stashes within the city, selected a suitable vehicle and calculated the quickest route to its location. A distance through the city streets of about two and a half klicks was a risk, but it was one he would have to take. He paused in the exit to the street and pulled up the hood of his top, concealing his face in shadow.

On the street, traffic was light and pedestrians lighter still. Walker forced himself to slow down and walk at a casual pace. He recalculated his route and veered into a side street, heading to the old part of the city, which remained a warren of twisting, narrow streets, the upper storeys of the buildings leaning into one another. The distance was longer but with sparser securi-cam coverage, the cams locked in a constant war of attrition with the local underclass, who had good reason to avoid surveillance.

Walker hung a left, then a right, navigating the maze via the GPS on his com-unit. Five minutes in, he heard footsteps behind him. One … no, two sets. He stopped suddenly and a second later the following footsteps also stopped. Not coincidence, then. Street punks or junkies looking for an easy mark. Too bad for them. He slid the knife from the sheath strapped to his left forearm and started to walk again. His pursuers increased their pace, closing the distance. Walker waited until the first man was in striking distance before pivoting round. His arm swung an arc, the edge of the blade slicing open his would-be assailant's throat. The man coughed and spluttered as he clasped his hands to his throat in a vain attempt to stem the gushing blood. His companion stopped short, looked from his dying partner in crime to Walker and then turned and ran. Walker stepped past the fallen man, drew back his arm and threw the knife. It struck with a meaty thud and buried itself up to the hilt in the robber's shoulders. He uttered a ragged gasp and fell face first on the ground. The aspirated gurgling told Walker he had punctured one of his victim's lungs. He planted his foot firmly on the man's back and pulled the knife free, then took a hold of his hair, hauled back his head and slit his throat. His forehead bounced off the ground as Walker released his hold; he was already wiping the blade clean on the man's jacket. He replaced the knife in its sheath, took a quick glance round, and walked away.

The killings lifted his mood. They might have been nobodies, but Walker was in no doubt that he had meted out justice to sinners. The city was full of such scum. They riddled the entire continent like a contagion. When the RSA finished with the Caliphate in the Middle East, they should come here and finish what the missionaries began all those centuries ago. And why stop there? India, Pakistan, Iran: godless heathens, the lot of them. Those they could not convert should be purged.

Walker took a deep breath and mastered his hatred. He was alone in a foreign city without allies, and the police, however corrupt and inefficient, were sure to be closing in on him. Vengeance, however righteous, would have to wait. Ahead, a bulky figure stepped out of the shadows. Walker palmed the knife.

'You want some of this?'

The man melted back into the darkness.

'No. Didn't fucking think so.'

He pressed on, moving into the heart of the old Medina. Where once the narrow lanes and market stalls had thronged with tourists, now only boarded-up windows and litter-strewn doorways remained, the domain of brutal-looking rats. A particularly vile specimen hissed at him and Walker resisted the urge to lash out with his boot, knowing better than to put his leg within biting range. He paused to check the GPS and adjusted his course to the right. Word of the pair of corpses he had left behind had apparently spread among the underclass, for although he felt eyes watching him from the shadows, no one else challenged him.

The alley opened into a square, previously home to a shopping arcade. A series of arches decorated with geometric designs ran along the northern edge, their openings shuttered by steel roller doors. Walker made his way to the second arch from the left and opened the access pad. He typed in a lengthy alphanumeric code and heard the thrum of an electric motor, followed by the rattle of chains. He ducked beneath the still-rising door and slapped his hand against the light switch. Pale light illuminated the far reaches of the unit, delineating the tarpaulin-shrouded outline of a car. Walker waited for the roller door to close again before making his way forward.

He pulled back the tarp to reveal the sleek lines of a Chevrolet Corvette, its fire-truck red bodywork muted in the dim lighting. His fingers brushed along the wing, feeling almost zero resistance. A touch ostentatious, perhaps. But it had some very special features. He opened the door, slid into the bucket seat and pressed the starter. The motor purred instantly to life; battery systems at one hundred per cent. The Agency had quartermasters embedded in major cities across the globe, local sleepers tasked with maintaining equipment, munitions and dead drops. Old school tradecraft but still highly effective, which made the risk of their being compromised acceptable.

Walker strapped himself into the four-point harness and initiated the Corvette's auto-drive. The roller door rattled upwards at the car's approach. He tapped the dash and opened an encrypted comms channel. Time to get his ass handed to him again by the deputy director.

CHAPTER 29

The cell was a three-metre plascrete cube, its unpainted walls off-white in colour. Aside from the prisoner it contained two items, a foam mat and a galvanised bucket. The mat was too thin to cushion the hardness of the floor or to insulate against the cold, while the bucket, after an indeterminate period of time, was close to full. Light came from a bulkhead in the centre of the ceiling, or occasionally filtered through from the corridor when the guard slid back the inspection hatch in the steel door. Inspections were irregular, as were meals, which were issued through the same hatch. Food consisted of bottled water, stale bread and a thin, tasteless gruel. While the calorie count was low, Cooper's captors clearly did not intend for him to starve to death. But the psychological and physical effects of the restricted intake as an aid to breaking him was readily apparent; he had been trained in the same methods.

On arrival, still bound and hooded, Ismail's men had cut off his clothing, leaving only his shorts. They had then pinned his arms and legs while they removed the flex cuffs. He had been warned to lie flat and to look at the floor as the hood was removed. At the time the dim light had seemed dazzlingly bright after what felt like days of darkness. He had lain there squinting until he heard the door bang shut and the clicking of the deadbolts.

Examination of the cell was swift and fruitless, the walls smooth and without weaknesses, the door equally impenetrable. The only way out was through that same door, and it had remained closed since his arrival. Try as Cooper might, he could hear no sound beyond the arrival and departure of his guard. Was Goodman still alive? Was he being held in an adjacent cell? Cooper's shouts and banging on the walls went unanswered. He settled down to wait. Each time the hatch slid back he wondered if this was it, the time he was finally dragged away for interrogation, torture or execution. Instead, he'd received four servings of tepid water, coarse bread and grey gloop. As best as Cooper could reckon, he had been held there for three days, four at an absolute stretch.

The Templar selection process had drilled discipline and routine into Cooper's soul. He rolled up his bedding, placed it in the corner and used the side of his foot to push the bucket and its evil-smelling contents into the corner diagonally opposite. Crossing his arms over his bare chest, he attempted to rub some heat back into his chilled flesh before dropping to the floor. He did three sets of thirty push ups, squats and crunches, resting in between; keeping warm, killing time and preventing himself from brooding. Despite less than a week having passed since his capture, he had already seen a reduction in muscle mass. He needed to stay strong and fit, physically and mentally, to maximise his chances of escape. If his routine disturbed the guard, he gave no sign.

Cooper heard approaching footsteps and jumped to his feet. He backed up against the wall, giving himself as much room to manoeuvre as possible. The hatch slid back and a pair of dark eyes looked through. This time, instead of the expected tray of food, it slid shut again. Cooper's pulse quickened as adrenalin surged through him. He tensed as he heard the deadbolts pull back. The door swung open to reveal two heavily built men, dressed alike in olive combat trousers and black vest tops. Their knuckles were taped with cloth, like boxers waiting for their gloves. They stepped forward, moving to either side to reveal the presence of a third man. He was short and heavyset, with iron grey hair and a neatly trimmed moustache. The rank insignia on his epaulettes was unfamiliar to Cooper.

The officer introduced himself, his English clipped and precise.

'I am Lieutenant General Ahmad.'

'Templar-Private Billy Ray Cooper. Service number 26647155.'

Ahmad waved a dismissive hand. 'Yes, yes. We already know your name, rank and number. If you would just answer my questions it would save us all a considerable amount of time.'

'Templar-Private Billy Ray Cooper. Service number 26647155.'

'Very well. Turn around, face the wall and put your hands behind your back.'

When Cooper hesitated the two guards stepped forward, eyes bright with malevolence. He obeyed Ahmad's instruction and felt a fresh pair of flex cuffs tighten about his wrists. A hood blotted out the light and he was turned round and directed towards the door. They turned to the right and Cooper counted thirty steps before a brief halt. He heard a door click open and he was steered to the right again and ushered into the room beyond. The movement of air suggested a room considerably larger than his cell, a supposition verified as fact as he was marched a dozen paces forward before being spun about and told to sit. Cooper felt cold metal against his bare thighs. Hands grabbed his feet and pushed his legs back until his calves touched the legs of the chair. A click sounded as metal brackets were fastened about his ankles. The flex cuffs were cut and his forearms were similarly shackled to the arms of the chair. Cooper felt the cloth of the hood stick to his face as his breathing quickened.

'How many troops do you have stationed in Damascus?'

'Templar-Private—'

Cooper's breath whooshed out as a fist buried itself in his gut. His instinct was to double over but the restraints held him firm as he gasped for air. Ahmad waited for his breathing to return to normal.

'Again, what is the strength of your battalion?'

'More than you've got fingers and toes.'

This time the punch came from a different angle, suggesting the two guards were tag-teaming him. Presumably they didn't want to tire themselves out.

'Tiresome.' Ahmad sighed. 'That is the perfect adjective for you Americans. Perhaps a different question – what are your objectives after securing Damascus?'

'Just another day at the beach – beers and a barbecue. Maybe check out the local talent.'

The uppercut cracked Cooper's teeth together and snapped back his head. Lights danced behind his eyes even in the darkness of the hood. Were they really such amateurs as to let him goad them into knocking him unconscious? He doubted he could be that lucky.

'You think this is a joke, or a game? I can assure you it is not. I have tried to be civilised, one soldier talking to another, but I can see you require more robust methods of persuasion.'

Cooper grunted as a wooden pole or baton cracked against his right shin. It was followed a moment later by a blow to the left. The tempo of the blows increased as they alternated between each leg, the pain building steadily as the flesh was pulped and bruised. He loosed a scream of rage and frustration. The blows stopped.

'What is the strength of your forces in Damascus?'

'Fuck you!'

'Out of witticisms so soon? This will indeed be tiresome.'

The brackets were unfastened from Cooper's wrists and ankles, and he was thrown to the floor. He rolled onto his back and tried to breathe through the pain. As he reached up to pull off the hood a boot caught him on the side of the head. The kick was pulled, serving as a warning. Cooper reacted instinctively, protecting his face with his forearms and pulling his knees up to his stomach to cover his genitals. He moaned as the kicks thudded into his back and his tenderised shins. He heard a rib crack or break and tried to twist away from the kicks. Then, as suddenly as it had begun, the attack stopped, leaving him shuddering and gasping for breath.

As he had done so long ago, during the VR torture sim of his selection, he started to recite the catechism, focusing solely on the 107 questions and answers. Everyone broke sooner or later, but military information had a limited shelf life. The longer he held out, the less use anything he gave up to his interrogators would be. Always assuming they hadn't broken Goodman already and weren't doing this just for fun.

Cooper gasped as a jet of icy water battered his body. A second jet joined it and the hosing down continued for several minutes, turning his flesh painfully numb. He shivered and shook, teeth chattering away, the hood's wet fabric clinging to his face.

'I do not enjoy this unpleasantness,' Ahmad said. 'But if you insist on being recalcitrant, you leave me no choice. Are you ready to answer my questions in a civilised manner?'

Cooper stammered, 'T ... Templar-Private Billy Ray Cooper. Service number 26647155.'

Ahmad uttered the sigh of a long-suffering teacher, disappointed in his pupil.

'Take him back to his cell. Water only this evening.'

Strong hands grabbed Cooper by the upper arms and hauled him to his feet. Dispensing with restraints, the guards dragged him back to his cell, leaving a watery trail in his wake. They stopped at the door, removed the hood and thrust him forward. He landed painfully on his hands and knees and slid forward to lie prone. Cooper pictured the words of the catechism as if on the printed page, tuning out the cold and the pain as he shivered on the hard plascrete floor. When the hatch opened sometime later Cooper found himself too spent to move. He heard the plastic water bottle hit the floor and roll into the corner.

They came again at what Cooper reckoned to be some point in the night. It might have been as little as an hour or two later, as his discomfort stretched the minutes into hours. The hood and flex cuffs were again applied, but this time they turned to the left on exiting the cell. After the third turn Cooper lost track, the burning pain in his shins blotting out all other thoughts. At the point he could endure no more, he was sat down, allowing his escort to remove the hood and cuffs. Cooper blinked and took in his surroundings; he was on a bench pressed against the white wall of a short corridor. To his right, on the opposite side, was a single door with an Arabic nameplate.

One of the guards pointed to the neatly folded black shirt and trousers on the bench. Cooper pulled on the loose-cut clothing and found the size about right. The other guard handed him a pair of slip-on canvas shoes.

'Speak English?' Cooper asked.

Neither man had uttered a word in his presence and this trend continued as the guard who had given Cooper the shoes motioned for him to rise. He followed the instruction and the guards led him through the now open door.

Ahmad, sitting behind a simple wooden desk, looked up from an antiquated workstation. He nodded to the guards, dismissing them.

'Please, take a seat.'

Cooper looked round the office. The blind behind Ahmad was drawn, shutting out the night. A single filing cabinet stood against the wall on the right, and a battered office chair sat unoccupied in front of the desk. Soft white light shone into the room via panels set into the ceiling. No immediate danger or obvious threat.

'You may stand if you wish. But I assure you there is no trap waiting to be sprung.'

Cooper stepped forward and sat in the chair. The relief at taking the weight off his legs was instant. He tried not to let it show.

Ahmad lifted a small cup to his lips and took a sip of thick black coffee made in the Turkish style. He carefully placed the cup back on its saucer and selected a pistachio finger. Flakes of green pastry dropped to the desk as he bit into it. He chewed thoughtfully for a minute then used his forefinger to brush crumbs from his moustache. Cooper's stomach grumbled rebelliously as Ahmad worked his way through the remainder of the pastry. He washed it down with another sip of coffee and finally turned his attention back to the Templar.

'I expect you're wondering why you are here. Perhaps you expected another interrogation. Well, that is no longer necessary. Corporal Goodman has told us all we need to know. He is a reasonable man.'

'I doubt Pete's told you shit. You probably said the same to him – told him I'd spilled my guts.'

'You can believe that if you wish. But you have no value to me in terms of providing military information.'

'So, I'm now worthless to you?'

'As a Templar you are still a high value target – you represent the pinnacle of American fighting forces. Not only your military skills, but your devotion to Christ. Doubtless you have heard we are all heathen devils and yet you can see we are not so very different. The truth is that your commanders are lying to you. We are not the aggressors. Islam wishes to live in peace with the West. It is your government that seeks a state of perpetual war in order to maintain its control over its citizens, to distract them from the failings of their domestic policies. All I'm asking is for you to acknowledge this.'

'I don't understand.'

Ahmad smiled benignly. 'We have prepared a statement – one in which you will confess to the crimes you have committed against Islam and the Caliphate and apologise for the suffering you have caused. You will say the war is wrong and all American troops stationed in Caliphate territories should be withdrawn immediately. Read this on air and you and Corporal Goodman will be free to return to your people.'

Cooper examined Ahmad closely but nothing in his expression or body language suggested he was anything but deadly serious. He tried to stifle his laughter but it burst uncontrollably from him, loud and shrill.

Ahmad pursed his lips. 'I'm afraid I do not share your amusement. However, they say humour is a great comfort in times of adversity.'

The guards re-entered the room, seized Cooper's arms and pulled them behind his back. He heard the whine of the flex cuffs being fastened and then the hood was drawn over his head.

'If you won't cooperate, I'm sure Corporal Goodman will prove more reasonable. Take him away.'

CHAPTER 30

The SOC oversuit rustled as Albright checked the surveillance feed on his HUD. They had three drones in play, including a micro one no bigger than a fly, inside the Cathedral of the Sacred Heart itself. Evening mass was nearing its end and the subject of Albright's surveillance stood in front of the altar, surrounded by the pillars of the cathedral's great dome. Bishop Gibson wore a red mitre and matching chasuble over his clerical robes, the latter in some part concealing the fact that his once powerful frame was now running to fat. With his flowing silver hair and beard, Gibson had something of the Old Testament prophet about him. It was fear of his ability to inspire and potentially command the masses that had brought him to the attention of Albright's bosses at the Agency.

Mass ended and Albright switched the feed to one of the external drones as the bishop made his way to the portico, which was supported by six Corinthian columns. He stood framed between the two central columns as he shook the hand of each of his departing parishioners. Some were flashed a smile, others given a curt nod, but all were apparently known to the bishop. Albright counted close to two hundred in total, none of whom were on any watch list.

Having concluded his duties for the evening, Gibson pulled the cathedral doors closed with an echoing boom.

According to intel, Gibson normally spent a couple of hours in his office following mass, reviewing and dealing with the business of the diocese. Albright tracked him with the drone, following him first to the toilet and then down a flight of stairs to his office in the sub-basement. He gave it a further fifteen minutes to ensure Gibson was settled before making his move.

Albright pulled out of his parking space, drove past the portico and the pair of towers that surmounted it, and parked up on the sidewalk at the side of the cathedral. He shifted the focus of one of the external drones and confirmed there would be no witnesses to his entry. His final prep was to pull on a pair of plastic overshoes before snapping on nitrile gloves.

A biometric lock protected the rear door. It was a basic system for which the Agency had long since obtained override codes. Albright transmitted the code and let himself into the vestry. He paused at the door as the drone picked up a cleaner in the corridor outside. She was using a polisher to buff the parquet floor, shaking her hips in time to the music of whatever song was playing on her oversized headphones.

Albright was a patient man. He unwrapped the silver foil from a stick of gum, folded it in half, and then folded it again before popping it into his mouth. He chewed slowly, identifying the flavour as wintergreen. It was a little game he played with himself, keeping five or six sticks of gum in his pocket with the outer wrapper removed. A tiny bit of randomness in a life that otherwise depended upon and was dominated by precise planning, timing and discipline.

Albright always had a plan. If that plan went south, he had a backup plan and, situation permitting, a backup to the backup. In nine years of service, he had seen two directors and three deputy directors come and go. Not one of them had ever had reason to fault his work. He was the best, a fact acknowledged by his superiors and peers alike.

The cleaner switched off the polisher and wrapped the cord about the handle before opening a broom cupboard. Her back was to Albright for less than three seconds, but it was all the time he needed to step out of the vestry and make his way silently to the stairs leading to the sub-basement and his quarry.

He removed the pistol from the holster beneath his left armpit and cocked it. The door to Gibson's office was closed, a chink of light showing beneath the roller blind that had been drawn down over its window. Albright turned the handle, stepped through and pulled it closed behind him.

'I gave instructions I wasn't to be disturbed,' Gibson barked, without looking up. 'Cat got your...' His voice trailed off as he finally looked up and saw the gun in Albright's hand.

The pistol coughed once, burying a tranquiliser dart in Gibson's shoulder. The fast-acting drug quickly subsumed any relief he felt at still being alive. Albright reached him as his head thudded against the desk. He manhandled him out of the chair and hoisted him onto his shoulder, grunting beneath the burden.

Albright checked the drone feed; the cleaner had moved into the main body of the cathedral and was wiping down the pews. No other life signs detected. He settled the bishop's weight more evenly across his shoulders, grunting as he scaled the stairs, and made his way back to the vestry. Another check of the external feeds showed no one in the vicinity of the cathedral and he pushed open the door and popped the trunk of the car, which had been lined with plastic sheeting in preparation.

Albright laid Gibson on his left side in a foetal position. Having checked his airways and pulse, he secured Gibson's wrists with zip cuffs, inserted a ball gag into his mouth and buckled it tight. Wouldn't do for the bishop to die ahead of schedule.

With the evening rush over, traffic was light and Albright

took the direct route along North Laurel Street, turning left onto West Cary, arriving at the Jefferson Hotel inside of five minutes. He had already booked a suite in Gibson's name and paid for it from the bishop's account. The audit trail would show he had siphoned the money from one of the church's many charitable foundations. Other sums of money had already been transferred to a dummy corporate account, allowing forensic accounting to identify a long and slow history of embezzlement, with some of the proceeds converted into bonds and shares.

Albright parked at the rear of the Jefferson and used an electronic skeleton key to gain admittance to the laundry. He wheeled a laundry cart back out to his car, loaded the still unconscious bishop inside and covered him with towels. A cloned key card provided access to the service elevator, which he rode to the top floor. The doors pinged open, revealing an empty corridor. Albright pushed his charge into the corridor and made for the executive suite.

Albright took in the details as he made his way through the main living area; a sky-blue Balenciaga dress draped across the back of the sofa, matching Saint Laurent shoes and clutch bag at its base. An empty bottle of Krug Grande Cuvée and two flutes sat on the glass coffee table, the rim of one stained with vermillion lipstick. The holo-display on the back wall displayed pornography, frozen midframe. Albright caught himself turning his head ninety degrees. He smiled ruefully and hurried through to the bedroom where one of his colleagues, also dressed in SOC overalls, was in the process of dressing the scene.

Albright watched him as he chopped out lines of cocaine on a hand mirror on the bedside cabinet. His eyes flitted to the corpse of a strangled call girl laid at right angles across the foot of the bed; long blonde hair fanned across the rumpled sheets, right breast exposed through the torn PVC of an S&M nun's outfit. But it was the huge rubber strap-on that caught and held his attention. Given the bishop's sermons on sodomy, they might be gilding the lily. Then again, maybe not. The public liked a hero to fall, and fall hard.

Albright crooked a finger towards the other agent.

'Paxton, give me a hand with His Excellency here.'

Paxton threw the towels aside and grasped Gibson by the ankles. Albright nodded he was ready and together they heaved the bishop free of the cart and deposited him on the bed.

'Jesus, fat fuck needs to lay off the communion wafers!'

'Quit grousing and help me strip him.'

Even unconscious, Gibson's limbs seemed to fight them as they struggled to pull the cassock first over his hips and then up to his chest, exposing a fish-pale belly tufted with grey hair. Albright cut the plastic ties binding Gibson's wrists and wrestled his left arm free while Paxton struggled with the right. Losing patience, he tugged hard, splitting the seam as the garment came free. Albright examined the broken stitches and then tossed the cassock across the room.

'We'll put that down to the throes of passion. Get his shorts off.'

Paxton looked set to argue but Albright's expression swiftly disabused him of the notion. He removed Gibson's boxers, revealing his flaccid penis.

Albright retrieved a pair of leather chaps from the back of a chair and threw them at Paxton, whose lips puckered with distaste.

'You were the one who said he wanted more field work.'

'Yeah, but—'

Albright cut him off. 'But nothing. Remember, we're acting in the national interest here.'

Together, they got Gibson into the chaps and propped him up against the headboard. His eyes fluttered open as he started to surface from the tranquiliser, but his limbs remained immobile.

Albright removed the needle-gun from the inside pocket of his suit jacket and fitted the ampoule. He had loaded it previously with a speedball, a mix of heroin and cocaine. Paxton applied a tourniquet to Gibson's left arm and tapped up a vein. He stepped aside to allow Albright to administer the fatal shot.

Gibson's eyes went wide and froth spilled out around the ball gag, while a faint tremor shook his right hand. Albright's lips twitched in a faint smile as he triggered the needle-gun, delivering the drugs. He monitored Gibson's vitals on his com-unit. An initial rise in heart rate was followed by dropping oxygen levels due to the push-pull of the cocaine demanding oxygen while the heroin slowed his breathing, putting a strain on his lungs, heart and brain. The levels dropped further and the ECG reading spiked as his heart went into fibrillation, followed closely by lung failure. Thirty seconds later, all vital signs ceased.

Albright clapped his hands together. 'You know the drill – tissue samples under the girl's nails, his and her prints on the bottle and glasses, razor blade and snorting tube – no one else's. Are we clear?'

Paxton nodded and Albright pulled out his com-unit and hit the speed dial for one of the Agency's partisan journalists. He glanced at the time; looked like Bishop Gibson was about to lead the nine o'clock news.

CHAPTER 31

Vanderbilt looked away from the screen and pinched the bridge of his nose. The latest reports from the front made for grim reading; the Syrian insurgents were proving better equipped and, above all, better motivated than anticipated. But he really should have anticipated it; history was littered with examples of small bands of devout actors triumphing over larger forces. Whatever else could be said of the Caliphate, no one could deny that they were motivated by sacred values. The Templars' training was intended as a direct reflection of the Islamists' fanaticism. For the most part it worked, the problem being that their military presence in Israel and ongoing operations in Jordan assisting the rebels made it necessary to dilute their forces with regular troops. He needed to find a way of tipping the balance of power back in their favour. But how? Deploying a targeted nano-virus, even covertly, was out of the question following the backlash after its use by the Israelis in Jerusalem. As Orthodox Christians, the Greater Russian Collective had a vested interest in liberating Jerusalem, but it was clear little or no appetite existed for attacking the Caliphate in their own territory. And with the RSA's continuing low standing with their allies in Europe and Africa, blanket bombing would also appear to be out.

A knock sounded on the door and it swung open to admit Lachlan. His expression and the tense lines of his body indicated that he had arrived as the bearer of bad news. At his bidding, Vanderbilt switched on the holo-screen and brought up a news feed. The flawless features of a computer-generated avatar flashed to life in 3D. Her tone had a condemnatory edge as she recited the story.

'The Diocese of Richmond was shaken to its core earlier this evening by the shock discovery of Bishop Bartholomew Gibson's body in a suite at the Jefferson Hotel. The body of a twenty-five-year-old woman, a known sex worker, was also discovered at the scene, the apparent victim of a sex game gone tragically wrong. Police are not seeking further suspects in relation to either death at this time.'

Vanderbilt shut off the holo, leaned back in his chair and steepled his fingers, leaving his adjutant uncertain as to his mood. Long seconds passed before he finally broke the silence.

'It would appear Gerrard is not quite as stupid as he appears.'

'We still have Connors,' Lachlan offered.

Vanderbilt shook his head. 'Not after this. The coup will have to be purely military. Connors and his cronies will avoid taking sides, or even expressing an opinion, until it becomes clear who the victor will be. Still, I have one card left to play.'

'Sir?'

Vanderbilt waved Lachlan away, indicating he wanted to be alone with his thoughts. It seemed the Lord, in His infinite wisdom, had sent him another test to add to his growing list of tribulations.

Decision made, he hit dial on his com-unit. The encrypted call was picked up on the third ring, the responding voice gruff and impatient.

'Who is this? How did you get this number?'

'Thaddeus Vanderbilt. As to your other question, Lee, I have my sources. Sources that tell me all sorts of interesting things.' Vanderbilt let the silence stretch, ratcheting up the tension, before moving in for the kill. 'I gather you're … unhappy with the current administration's direction of travel. Could be we have a common cause. One that would merit having a discussion.'

'As I'm sure you're aware, Grand Master, we're in the middle of a war – my diary is full for the foreseeable future.'

'Oh, I'm sure you can free up a small window. After all, what could be more natural than a meeting between the Templar Grand Master and the Secretary of Defense to discuss strategy in the Middle East?'

'I don't know…'

Vanderbilt picked up on the uncertainty in Morrison's voice.

'Nonsense. This is the opportunity you've been waiting for. Tell me I'm wrong and we'll forget this call ever happened.'

'Say you're not wrong. How do we keep this under the radar? Gerrard will have my balls if he finds out I've been speaking with you. He's paranoid as to your intentions and with good reason, apparently.'

'We don't hide it. We have a formal meeting to discuss the Syrian campaign. I'll feed you some tidbits you can pass back to Gerrard. Let him believe he's coming out on top. In his arrogance, he won't know he's being played until it's too late.'

'Sounds like I'd be taking all the risk – to what end?'

Vanderbilt chuckled hollowly. 'Heavenly reward not enough for you? The end should be obvious – once we have dealt with Gerrard, Kordowski and that Jezebel, Hopkins, someone will have to occupy the Central Office.'

'And the public are just going to vote for me, are they?'

'Try not to be any more obtuse than you have to be, Lee. Short term, there won't be any elections. Much is rotten in this once-mighty republic of ours. There will have to be a winnowing of the corrupt and godless, as unpleasant as that may be. The people need a Good Shepherd to lead them out of their indolence and depravity. Only then can they be entrusted with the reins of democracy again.'

'Why do I get the feeling I'm the sheepdog here?'

'There are no insignificant roles in God's work.'

'Is that what you told Bishop Gibson? Didn't work out so well for him, did it? What's to stop me taking all that you've told me straight to Gerrard?'

'Nothing at all. But it will only confirm what he already suspects while you remain trapped in a corrupt administration you hate and fear. If the previous president was no obstacle to Gerrard's ambition, he certainly won't hesitate to have you removed. Particularly should rumours begin to circulate as to your loyalty.'

'Seems to me I'm swapping one boot on my neck for another.'

'Perhaps. But your current master has given you precious little by way of reward for your services. I'm willing to place the crown on your head. I'm equally wiling to drive home the nails instead. The choice is yours.'

'If I agree to this, I want assurances – the safety of my family, regardless of the outcome. I'm willing to take my chances, but Kathleen and the children—'

'If this goes against us, I won't be in any better position to help them than you will.'

'Bull. You have wealth, influential friends and a cadre of the most highly trained soldiers on the planet. You can have them safely in Europa City with new identities with a click of your fingers. That's my price. Allowing for inflation, it's not much greater than thirty pieces of silver.'

'Very well. But if it eases your conscience any, whatever else Gerrard is, he's not the Messiah.'

Morrison closed the connection and Vanderbilt raised his eyes heavenward and said a silent word of thanks. He had taken a gamble and it had paid off. Not that he had any intention of installing Morrison as president, puppet or otherwise. The new order he envisaged would be ruled over by the Templars. After all, he was the Grand Master.

Vanderbilt sighed and opened the desk drawer. He took out the leather scourge and ran his fingers along the tails. As ever, sinful pride must be kept in check. The mortification of his flesh served as a reminder that everything he did was for His glory and His glory alone.

CHAPTER 32

Tazi's uniformed escort pressed his finger against the button for the top floor of the Police Prefecture and the elevator door slid shut in front of her. His partner kept his sidearm discreetly pressed against his thigh, trigger finger parallel with the slide. She rocked back and forth on her heels as the carriage climbed its way to the offices of the National Brigade, fingers interlaced, the chain of her handcuffs dangling below. Commandant Idrissi had requested to see her in person, which indicated there might be a deal to be done. Whether that deal was to her liking remained to be seen, as did on whose behalf he would be offering it. Idrissi was a careerist and that made him susceptible to pressure from above, and the politicians would not want to unduly rock the boat with the RSA.

The elevator door pinged open, her escort waving her forward as they formed up either side of her. Tazi threaded her way through the open-plan office. She counted three officers bent over their terminals; if they were following regulations their sidearms would be stowed in their desks, magazines removed. A green sign identified a fire exit ten metres to her right. A clear run from her present position, but on reaching Idrissi's office there would be three desks and one of the detectives between her and the exit. Tazi shook her head and followed her guides.

The officer on her right knocked once on the door and waited. At Idrissi's terse 'enter' he turned the handle and swung the door inwards. Tazi stepped into the office without waiting for an invitation. She sensed the guards tensing behind her.

'Thank you, Boucher. That will be all.' Idrissi waited for the door to shut before continuing. 'Captain Tazi, please take a seat.'

Tazi folded herself into the chair and held up her manacled wrists. 'Perhaps we could dispense with the cuffs? I've no intention of trying to escape.'

Idrissi opened his desk drawer, took out a key and threw it towards her with a lazy underarm lob. Tazi noted approvingly that his eyes never left her face. She caught the key deftly and unlocked the cuffs. They fell to the desk with a clatter. She smiled ruefully as she massaged her wrists.

'Is this the part where you tell me how much trouble I'm in?'

Idrissi crooked a finger and used its edge to smooth down his moustache.

'Dangerous driving. Reckless endangerment. Illegal occupation. Aiding and abetting. Would you like me to go on? I'm sure there's a few more we can add to the list, but that's more than sufficient for us to revoke your licence.'

'Aiding and abetting? Is Jefferson Lynch a felon? Have you issued a warrant for his arrest? Last time I checked, he was the victim.'

Idrissi's eyes narrowed, creating a 'V' in his forehead. 'That's yet to be determined. But he remains a person of interest. Someone who can assist us with our enquiries. Or would have been able to, had you not helped him evade protective custody.'

Tazi leaned forward and Idrissi pushed his chair back instinctively, butting it against the wall. His eyes flicked to the top right drawer of his desk and Tazi placed her palms flat against the desk to show she had no intention of attacking.

'Person. Of. Interest.' Tazi parroted his words back to him. 'To the *Sûreté Nationale* or to the Religious States of America?'

Idrissi's body stiffened. She appeared to have struck a nerve.

'I don't appreciate that insinuation.'

'No? That's a shame. Because we both know it's largely true.' She held up her hand to forestall any further protest. 'I know you're a straight arrow and run the National Brigade as best you can. But the rank-and-file cops on the streets can be bought for less than half their monthly paycheque. Placing Lynch in protective custody would effectively be signing his death warrant.'

'Perhaps.' Idrissi wagged a blunt forefinger. 'But one thing I know for certain is that you've overstepped the mark. Whatever corruption does or does not exist within the force, I cannot simply waive the laws. If I allow Red Phoenix Security to run around the city as it pleases, who will be next? Anarchy will engulf the streets.'

'I'm not asking you to turn a blind eye, but let's be clear about the victims. Some wealthy diners got a story to impress their friends with. Some cops got embarrassed. How much actual harm are we really talking about here?'

'Are we forgetting the high-speed car chase through the city?'

'Self-defence. In case you've forgotten, we were fleeing from a psychopath who had just destroyed an entire apartment block! One most likely operating under instruction from a foreign government.'

'And I'm sure the judge will take that into account at your trial.'

Tazi folded her arms and remained silent.

'All right. I can probably have the charges reduced to the driving and resisting arrest, although the owners of Rick's may well decide to press civil charges. In the circumstances, you should consider yourself fortunate.'

'Bail?'

'That rather depends.' Idrissi narrowed his eyes. 'As a free citizen, not connected to or employed by the *Sûreté Nationale*, I trust you can be relied on not to do anything rash – such as taking justice into your own hands?'

Tazi met his gaze, but Idrissi refused to blink.

'I think we understand one another, Commander.'

'Good. In that case bail will be set at two hundred thousand.' Idrissi pressed the intercom. 'Boucher, please escort Captain Tazi back to holding, pending the posting of her bail. Our business here is *finished*.'

Tazi noted the stress on the last word. A deal had been struck; one that she would have happily pursued of her own accord. She would be on Walker's trail before the end of the day.

Images flickered across the dash display as the AI sifted through the live feeds from the city's surveillance cams, pulling up thousands of feeds and comparing them with the fragmentary images of Lynch's attacker previously caught on cam. A separate algorithm parsed the *Sûreté Nationale*'s radio traffic, searching for incidents that could be related to the would-be assassin's escape. The killing of two petty criminals in the Old Medina was flagged as a ninety-three per cent certainty when matched with footage of the man police had now identified as Jon van Dijk entering the warren of streets. Surveillance coverage was poor, as it was with any of the slums, which made the exit of the Corvette all the more noticeable. Confirmation had to wait a further five minutes until a stoplight halted the car, affording the first clear image of the driver.

'Got you!'

Tazi watched the Corvette as it turned on the screen. No doubt about it; her Tango was heading for the coast; most likely to rendezvous for an extraction. She started the

Maserati and pulled out into the flow of traffic. From his driving it was clear van Dijk, or rather Walker, thought he was home and dry. All she had to do was hang back and follow him to his destination. And then what? She wasn't sure. She hadn't killed anyone since she left the Paratroop Brigade; had tried to put that part of her life behind her. But maybe the time had come to make an exception?

Tazi swore as she spotted two patrol cars closing on the Tango. A third cop car appeared and the Corvette sped away. Looked as though factions other than Idrissi's were active in the *Sûreté Nationale*. She hit the accelerator herself in response.

CHAPTER 33

Walker checked the securi-cam feeds and police broadcasts as he navigated the car towards the coast. Deputy Director Hannah had made it clear that the only reason he had approved his access to a covert vehicle was that his arrest would make a bad situation worse. The implicit threat of disciplinary action on his return to the RSA was clear; he had fucked up for the last time. No point arguing that Lynch had to be the luckiest motherfucker in the whole of Creation.

He returned his attention to the dash display; two points of contact were closing rapidly from the south. Up until now, he had been driving just below the speed limit to avoid attracting attention. A third contact pinged up from the south-east; the cops had made him. He disengaged the safety protocols and ordered the auto-drive to take evasive action. The sudden acceleration pressed him back in his seat as the car started to weave in and out of the traffic, cutting sharply across all four lanes.

Leaving the AI to do its job, Walker took out his pistol and ejected the magazine. Fifteen rounds, plus one in the chamber. The police might be as incompetent as they were corrupt, but they had far more bullets. Fighting wasn't an option, which meant shaking his tail. The opportunity lay half a klick ahead: the Mohammed V tunnel. He instructed the AI to change course. The motor howled as the car accelerated to top speed, slowly lengthening the distance between itself and the pursuing vehicles. Walker counted down the distance to the mouth of the tunnel – one hundred metres, fifty, twenty, ten, contact! He hit the countermeasures and the cam displays went blank. Ten seconds later the tunnel lights went out. Walker initiated the car's chameleon mode, changing the colour from red to silver and altering the plates, as the emergency lights fluoresced to life. He reckoned he had ten, maybe fifteen seconds at most before the cams came back up. It would be tight, but if he could just clear the tunnel he would be home free. He leaned forward in his seat, trying to force extra acceleration by will alone. The tunnel exit loomed ahead, the cams still dark. He blinked in reaction to the sudden daylight. Luck, it seemed, was finally with him as he spotted one of the giant cargo trucks that ran above the road, straddling all four lanes, using high-level rails parallel to either side of the freeway. At his direction the car moved into the outer lane and slid below the truck, matching its speed.

Walker permitted himself a tight smile as the securi-cams came back online. The three dots of his pursuers converged on his position and then sped past, seeking a non-existent target. He initiated a coded burst to the Jericho instructing it to prepare for his extraction.

Unobserved behind him a Maserati dropped back, putting an additional two vehicles between them as it ticked along at 60 kph.

A couple of klicks later Walker left the shelter of the truck and followed Avenue TanTan to the coast, the white stone finger of the El Hank lighthouse visible ahead. A reply from the Jericho advised it was thirty minutes out but would prefer to wait until nightfall for extraction. Walker's response was terse and to the point; he needed extraction now. He had studied the capabilities of both the Royal Moroccan navy and air force and knew neither had the power to challenge a Seraph class submarine. They were already heading for a major diplomatic incident; violating their territorial waters would just be another drop in the ocean.

Walker parked up in the lot adjacent to the lighthouse. The day was bright, the water calm and visibility good for miles, almost as if to spite him. Didn't matter. Thirty minutes from now he would be skimming across those blue-green waves, leaving this godforsaken continent behind. Hopefully for good.

For all his bark, Hannah was a reasonable man. He would review the mission logs and conclude there was little, if anything, Walker could have done differently. A show would doubtless be made – desk duty for a month, maybe – but Walker would be operational again before long. And if he knew one thing about that redneck loser, it was that Lynch would find it impossible to remain silent. It might take six months. Maybe a year. But sooner or later Walker would get another crack at him. This time there would be no last-minute reprieves.

The powerful whine of an electric motor drew his attention and he looked up in time to see the Maserati reverse alongside him, leaving a gap of only a couple of inches. Tinted windows prevented him from seeing the driver and he leaned over irritably, popped open the passenger side door and scooted across the seats. His anger gave way to a cold resolve as the woman stepped out of the Maserati and walked over to meet him. About five foot six, with caramel skin and a lithe build, long black hair pinned on top of her head. At first glance her clothes were casual, but the black combat trousers, vest top and high-top boots were all combat grade. Walker recognised her instantly: Alia Tazi, owner and manager of Red Phoenix Security. She had interfered with his mission for the last time. He made to draw the pistol holstered below his left armpit.

Tazi's hand was a blur of motion as she reached for her belt buckle. The shuriken thudded into the back of Walker's hand as the SIG cleared the holster. Walker let out a grunt of pain as his pistol clattered on the tarmac. He met Tazi's cold eyes and his resolve faltered.

'You know we don't have to do this,' he said through gritted teeth, as he pulled the shuriken free. 'Twenty minutes from now I'll be gone and you'll never see me again. Your client is alive – so no harm, no foul.'

Tazi shook her head. 'No harm? You put a slug through my shoulder. Brought down a tower block full of innocent people. Can't let that stand. Bad for business. Worse for my reputation.'

Walker took a couple of steps back, giving himself room to manoeuvre. His eyes flicked down to the SIG and back up again. In that split second Tazi closed the gap between them. Her left leg swung up in a kick that connected with his right arm with numbing force. He swung wildly with his left; Tazi darted back out of range and allowed his momentum to carry him forward. Her leg lashed out again, connecting with the back of his knee to send him sprawling on the tarmac. Walker curled instinctively, protecting his head and face with his forearms, but the expected blows failed to materialise. He risked a glance through his fingers and saw Tazi had stepped back a pace or two. The bitch was playing with him.

Rage lent him the strength to spring to his feet. At heart, Walker was a Templar; he'd passed through the toughest selection process in the world. He would be damned before he let some female best him. He feinted to the left and Tazi turned to follow, opening her guard. Walker drove his foot into her crotch and was rewarded with an explosion of breath. Tazi staggered back, opening the gap between them again.

'That's just a taste of what's coming. Going to kick your cunt right in.'

Tazi spat as she straightened up, her pain apparently

mastered. Walker circled her warily, looking for a fresh opening. She turned as he turned, right arm held diagonally across her body, palm outward. Walker swung a right hook, which she deflected easily, spinning nimbly out of reach of the following left uppercut. He threw another punch and she danced away again, a faint smile playing across her lips. Despite appearing to have the advantage, she made no effort to land any further blows, apparently seeking to wear him down before moving in for the kill. Walker couldn't afford to let that happen. Time to make use of his bulk and greater strength.

Walker spun in a series of roundhouse kicks, driving Tazi back and keeping her off balance as she blocked the blows. His opening came five kicks in as her right knee buckled. With her guard down, he sprang forward, pushing her to the ground and pinning her upper arms with his knees. He locked his fingers round her throat and started to squeeze. Tazi tensed the muscles in her neck, fighting in vain to stave off the inexorable tightening of his fingers. Her hips bucked beneath him as she tried to throw him off and he pressed down harder; her fear excited him. He ground against her as the loop of his fingers closed, laughed as he saw her fingers frantically scrabbling on the tarmac. In another second or two she would slip into unconsciousness and death would swiftly follow, leaving one less godless heathen in the world.

Walker screamed as a hot stab of pain lanced through his thigh. He rose instinctively and Tazi's back arched beneath him, throwing him clear. As he rolled over onto his back, he saw the previously discarded shuriken buried deep in his right thigh, a crimson stain spreading outwards. The kick, swift and brutal, caught him under the jaw, snapping his teeth together. He spat out a mouthful of blood and the severed tip of his tongue as Tazi stamped down on his balls. Pain followed by nausea flashed through his body and his stomach heaved, spattering bile on the tarmac. He willed his limbs to move but they refused to obey. A third kick thudded into his ribs and he heard the snapping of bone.

Tazi stepped back and drew a ragged breath, the skin of her neck and throat already purpling. Another kick thudded into his torso, taking with it a couple more ribs.

Tazi's hands grabbed his lapels and hauled him off the ground. She knelt on her left knee and planted her right foot on the ground to form a square. Her body pivoted sharply as she bent his back over her knee, bearing down with all her weight. The crack of breaking bone sounded loud as a shot.

Momentary relief flooded through Walker as the pain of his crushed testicles and wounded thigh disappeared. Panic followed as he realised that he couldn't feel anything below the waist.

Tazi pushed his body off her knee and staggered to her feet. Walker fought to push his torso up with his arms, straining at the same time to move his legs.

'Not this,' he pleaded. 'Kill me.'

Tazi fixed him with the full artic force of her gaze. 'Death's too good for a prick like you. Enjoy the rest of your life.'

CHAPTER 34

Lynch slid back the door and stepped out onto the balcony. He turned his head from the wind as he bent it towards the flame of his lighter. Paper hissed, leaving ash in its wake as he sucked hard on the cigarette. For a brief instant there was only the hit of the nicotine, then all his problems washed over him anew, raising goosebumps on his skin. He exhaled, twin plumes of smoke issuing from his nostrils, and rested his forearms on top of the cold metal rail. Europa City stretched around him in all its night-time glory. A million twinkling lights, the bright neon corporate logos crowning tower blocks, and the ever-shifting shimmering enticements of the holo-ads. It looked beautiful, in its way, but then darkness hid a thousand sins. Daylight would soon reveal the leprous plascrete blocks, the functional and unlovely forms of the prefab housing, the squat manufactories, the acrid smell of which floated on the night air. Two generations had been born here, but every man, woman and child who had first occupied those dwellings had come to the city as a refugee, their homes drowned in the Great Flood of '49. Different nationalities, colours and creeds, all thrown in the deep end and left to sink or swim. And yet the city state and its forty million inhabitants had somehow prospered. While it was no rival to the African Tech Corps, its economy far outperformed that of the RSA, to which it was a major exporter of arms. A fact that made Lynch very uncomfortable, given the extradition treaties that existed between the two states.

Lynch lit a second cigarette from his first and ground the original under his heel, sending sparks out into the space beyond the balcony. Despite his misgivings, two days earlier they had passed through customs at Angela Merkel International without incident. The med-kit on the plane had limited pain relief and a sheen of sweat had covered Russell's face as Lynch helped him into a taxi. Russell had given an address in the Eindhoven district of the Dutch Quarter and collapsed back into his seat, leaving Lynch to stare out of the window at the unfamiliar surroundings. An hour later, they had drawn up outside one of the more aesthetically pleasing apartment blocks; ninety storeys of steel and glass. The safe house was on the seventy-first floor.

Lynch smoked his second cigarette down to the filter and dropped it to the floor. He took one last look at the pretty lights before heading inside. He found Russell where he had left him, sprawled on the sofa with a datapad in his hand. The privacy setting was on, so the screen remained dark to Lynch no matter how he angled his head. Russell's expression suggested the contents weren't entirely to his liking; or maybe it was the pain. The promised doctor had failed to show, since when Russell had stoically crunched his way through a series of over-the-counter pain meds. The sheen of sweat on his face spoke to their limited effectiveness, but it was the colour and smell of his wound that concerned Lynch most. You didn't need to be a doctor to tell infection had set in. For all that Russell tried to pretend otherwise, something was wrong. Lynch decided to press him again.

'Any word on when we're moving out?'

Russell's finger stopped mid-swipe. He lay the datapad

on his chest, screen down.

'Shouldn't be more than another two or three days. A week at most.'

'A week?'

'Worst case. These things take time. Not like you have anywhere to go. Is it?'

'Still don't see why I can't go out.' Lynch tried his best not to sound petulant. 'It's a big city. Nobody knows me, right?'

'Until you get picked up by facial recognition software and some RSA stooge finishes what they started in Casablanca. I didn't risk my ass to get you out just so you could go and blow it sightseeing.'

'I risked my ass for you too. In case you've forgotten. Even if we're not moving, surely this resistance of yours can rustle up a doctor?'

Russell fell silent and Lynch shook his head and crossed the open-plan living area to the kitchen. He picked up a bottle of bourbon, pulled out the stopper and poured a couple of fingers into a glass. He drank half of it down, enjoying the comforting warmth in his stomach, then topped it up again. Definitely an improvement over what he'd been drinking in Morocco. But a well-stocked cage was still a cage.

He picked up the remote and pointed it towards the holo-emitter, bringing up rolling coverage of the latest Templar attack in Syria. Thirty seconds of missiles detonating was all he could stand. He had witnessed enough in person to know the cost in human flesh. Russell looked up as the remote clattered on the worktop.

'Jesus, Lynch. Can't you sit at peace for five minutes? You're worse than a child.'

'If you'd let me in on the plan I might rest easier. Who knows, I might even be able to help.'

'Better you don't know. That way, if you get picked up you can't tell them anything when they waterboard you.'

'And what happens when they pick you up?'

'They don't. Not alive.'

'You got a cyanide capsule in your tooth or something?'

'Something.'

Lynch's laugh tailed off as he saw Russell's expression.

'Holy Mother of God, you're not joking, are you?'

Russell put the datapad aside and swung his feet off the sofa.

'You don't get it, do you? We're fighting for America's soul. It isn't a game. This is for keeps. We have to stop Gerrard and his cronies before it's too late.'

'Stop treating me like some dumb sap! I know what's at stake here. I've played my part – you've seen the stats; my broadcast of the leaked CIA document has gone viral. The more Gerrard tries to deny it, the more shade it throws on his legitimacy. Give me access to the leadership, let me tell their story. Words are going to be every bit as important as bombs and bullets in defeating the RSA.'

'Talking to an ex-Agency spook here, remember? I know all about the value of propaganda, black or otherwise. I just need you to sit tight a few more days and then everything will become clear. Can you do that?'

Lynch ran his hand across his scalp and felt the prickle of stubble. He'd been a journalist long enough to know when a source was bullshitting. Russell would hang himself soon enough. In the meantime, he might as well make use of his other contacts.

'Yeah,' he said, grudgingly. 'I can do that.'

'Good. I'll order us some food. Chinese okay?'

Lynch nodded. He hesitated, trying to appear casual. 'You got contacts in the RSA – sleepers, spies, whatever you want to call them?'

'We've got assets. What's on your mind?'

'My daughter, Christine. I want to know she's okay. I've made myself pretty unpopular back home – I don't want there to be any blowback on her, or her mother. Tabitha and me might not see eye to eye, but she's still the girl's mother. Whatever I'm getting into here, I need your guarantee it won't hurt them.'

'If you and the wife were still together, or you had any kind of relationship with your daughter, it might be a problem. As it stands, they have no reason to believe you give a damn. Harsh as it sounds, the best thing you can do for them right now is to keep letting them think that.'

'I know I'm not exactly father of the year, but seriously?'

'Trying to see her, contacting her, it's only going to put the girl in danger. For better or worse, you're going to have to see out what you've started. It's your only hope of a fresh start. Your only chance at avoiding being a fugitive for the rest of your life.'

Lynch downed his drink. He hated that Russell was right, but not as much as he hated the knowledge the problem was largely of his own making. He'd spent his life putting himself and the story above everything and everyone. And if Tabitha and Christine had still been in his life, would he have chosen to broadcast the footage of Tyler calling in the airstrike? Much as he wanted it to be otherwise, he knew the answer was 'yes'. Because everything else was secondary to the pursuit of his version of the truth.

'Can you at least confirm she's okay, without tipping anyone off?'

Russell sucked his teeth as he appeared to consider; possibly weighing up the resource he had in the area against any potential risk. Or maybe he was wondering if it was worth the price to keep Lynch sweet.

'I'll see who we've got in Lexington – but no guarantees. Now, how about that food?'

Lynch nodded. If he wasn't going anywhere, he might as well fix himself another drink. Maybe see if there were any beers left in the fridge. He needed to think things through.

Lynch paused the video and ran his finger along the outline of his daughter's face on the screen. Christine was twelve, going on thirteen, already turning into a young woman. He had missed so much of her life, and looked set to miss much more if he kept to Russell's advice. But as he looked back, he couldn't see himself taking any other path. He had been at the height of his fame or, more accurately, notoriety when Christine was born. His articles often put him at the centre of the story, a larger-than-life figure trailing drug-and-booze-fuelled chaos in his wake. But as addiction set in the persona he had created swiftly turned to parody. Chat show hosts, acquaintances and hangers-on expected the full 'Jefferson Lynch Experience' and were disappointed if they received anything less, until it eclipsed the work itself. His frustration turned to violence and his marriage collapsed, Tabitha rightfully choosing to protect their daughter from his unpredictable mood swings. From there it had been a steady downward spiral, finally culminating in his arrest for drug smuggling. In many ways he ought to thank Hannah for having press-ganged him into covering the Templar liberation of Israel. The horrors he had witnessed had finally purged him of his demons and given him fresh purpose.

Realising he was stalling, he focused again on the clip. The timestamp was six days ago, filmed at a school recital. Lynch didn't recognise the song; probably whatever sim was currently hot on the vidcasts. He remembered when people wrote and performed music; now it was all AI generated and fronted by CGI avatars. No one died young. No one got old and fat. But then again, even the most successful sims rarely held the public attention for more than a few months before the algorithm shuffled them into something new. Pop stars, actors and writers had all become redundant, reduced to a series of data mappings that could be endlessly combined to create new content. They hadn't managed to do the same for journalists yet. Least, not the credible ones.

Lynch resumed play; his daughter's performance was approaching the big finish. In those few minutes she looked happy, confident and untroubled by her renegade father. The applause that followed seemed to bear this out, although he doubted the assembled parents would be less than polite. How much stigma had she suffered because of him? More than he could ever make up for. But he knew if he ever got back to her he would have to try, even if it took the rest of his life. He just hoped he hadn't left it too late to try and be a father to her. The thought knotted his gut and made him feel sick as he continued to watch. The focus was tight on Christine, which meant he couldn't see the audience, sparing him from looking at his ex-wife. He realised, to his surprise, that when he thought of her the anger was gone, replaced by a dull emptiness. Was that what forgiveness felt like? Had he really changed that much?

Russell had refused to explain how he came to be in possession of the video. Had someone hacked his daughter's or his wife's social media accounts, or did Russell's mysterious backers have someone in place, shadowing them? Lynch found he was equally uncomfortable with either option, but he was the one who had asked for evidence of his daughter's well-being. Now, conflicted by doubt and longing, he understood why the ex-spook had counselled against it.

Lynch reluctantly put his com-unit down on the worktop and made his way over to the sofa to speak to Russell. He appeared to have drifted off, but the sweat on his face and shallowness of his breathing told a different story. Lynch shook his shoulder, gently at first and then with more force. Russell's eyes remained closed. He pulled up Russell's shirt and examined the wound. Puss had seeped through the dressing, exuding a sweet smell of decay.

'Shit.'

Lynch's gaze flitted around the room, but neither antibiotics or a doctor magically appeared. If he wanted those things, he would have to go out and find them. It was a risk, but without them Russell was dead.

CHAPTER 35

Cooper blinked in response to the sudden influx of
light as his captors removed the hood from his
head. Instead of the interrogation, he found himself
in a well-lit and well-appointed dining room. Geometric
patterned rugs covered the varnished boards of the floor,
the table and chairs were made from richly carved wood,
and the walls decorated with antique scimitars and shields.
He recognised the man sitting at the head of the table as
Marshal Ismail, his beard and hair unnaturally dark, the
chest of his olive drab uniform decorated with medals. A
pair of armed guards stood one either side of the door, eyes
seemingly fixed on some faraway point. By now Cooper
recognised it as sufferance of being in the presence of an
American infidel.

He attempted to rub some life back into his hands, the
angry red welts from the recently removed flex cuffs still
visible. Ismail motioned him to take a seat. Cooper looked
around suspiciously, the marshal nodded his
encouragement, and so he sat midway along the table,
adjacent to his host.

'Please, help yourself to food and drink,' Ismail said, his
voice surprisingly soft and melodious. 'It's quite safe, I

assure you.'

Cooper, ignoring the food, asked, 'Is this some new form of torture?'

Ismail smiled wistfully. 'You torture men for one of two reasons – information or pleasure. I have established that you and your comrade have nothing worthwhile to tell me, and I am not a sadist. So, there will be no more torture.'

'Not by you,' Cooper sneered.

'I make no apologies for Lieutenant General Ahmad's methods. It is all in the game. One that you yourself are familiar with the rules of.'

'The same rules that mark me and Goodman as being of value, but not Sanchez. Remember him? The guy whose brains you splattered across the floor.'

'His misfortune was to be an engineer in a service battalion. The world is not so interested in such men,' Ismail explained, as if to a slow child. 'But Templars – the elite of America's Special Forces – the world knows you and your fearsome reputation. Warrior monks – the scourge of the Islamic Caliphate.'

Cooper pulled a face. 'Don't believe all the propaganda.'

'Rest assured, I do not. But regardless, you have an undeniable cachet. If your government won't negotiate a hostage exchange, then there's surely mileage in showing the world the Templars are not invincible. That you can be captured and tamed like other men.'

'And where is Corporal Goodman?'

'You shall see him soon, but for now I thought it best to talk with you separately. You have my word of honour, one soldier to another, that he is being treated well.'

'Divide and conquer, eh?'

'This distrust is what separates our cultures unnecessarily. There's no reason why we can't co-exist peacefully. Like America, we simply want to govern that which is rightfully ours.'

'Somehow I doubt either the Israelis or the Saudis share that point of view.'

Ismail raised his shoulders in a shrug. 'It is possible that my predecessor, may he dwell eternally in Paradise, overreached himself. While I do not accept the right of the Jews to occupy the land we call Palestine I acknowledge, given the blood spilt on both sides, it would be best to reach some form of compromise. That, however, is a topic for another discussion. Come, you should enjoy your food while it is hot.'

Cooper, appearing to accede to Ismail's wishes, spooned some food onto his plate, using it as an excuse to pick up the knife and fork. Unlike the ornate silverware set before his host, these were functional stainless steel, the knife lacking an edge or a point, although he might manage to remedy that in his cell. He forked a piece of meat into his mouth and started to chew. The goat was tender, lightly spiced, with a smoky edge suggesting a barbecue or flame pit. Realising he could not recall when he had last eaten, he attacked the rest of the plate and made short work of it, washing it down with cold water. His stomach rumbled appreciatively.

Cooper looked up, met Ismail's amused gaze and felt a sting of shame.

'If you're expecting me to break my vows I'm afraid you're in for a disappointment. Neither torture nor goat, however excellent, will persuade me.'

'I have other means of persuasion — those of rhetoric and logic. You are a long way from home, Templar. The proverbial stranger in a strange land. It is past time you understood the history and culture of those whose lands you have invaded.'

'I'm not an invader.'

'Your lips say one thing, but the sound of your voice says another. I look forward to our conversations together. I have much to teach you.'

'You can try. But don't expect me to be a willing student.'

'I did not say it would be easy. After all, you've been

taught that those who serve the Caliphate are monsters and barbarians. That sort of programming cannot be overcome with a single conversation.' Ismail smiled ironically. 'No matter how excellent the goat.'

Cooper looked at the serving platter and then looked away. But out of sight was not out of mind as the smell of roast goat filled his nostrils and his stomach grumbled in complaint. Surely it was better to eat his fill now and gather his strength? His next meal might be a long time coming. Deciding this was wisdom, not weakness, Cooper helped himself to another serving. He would need all his strength to escape.

Ismail lifted a wine bottle and poured about a quarter of a glass. 'You must try the wine – Bargylus, Grand Vin de Syrie. The eighty-four is a most excellent vintage.'

Cooper hesitated, but only for a second, before taking the proffered glass. Used to beer, he took a large gulp and coughed.

Ismail uttered a soft sigh.

'A wine like this needs to be appreciated.' He raised his own glass and nosed it to demonstrate. 'First, inhale the bouquet. Enjoy the delicate hints of fruit. Next, a small sip. Hold it on your tongue and see how the flavour changes. After you swallow, note the long finish with the surprising hint of wood. Now, you try.'

Cooper sniffed; the wine was sharp and pungent. He took a sip and was surprised to get the taste of blackberries and pepper. Wasn't wine made from grapes? Ismail was right, the taste did linger, although he thought it more of the same. He took a slightly larger mouthful and returned to his meat. For a while there was only the clatter of cutlery on porcelain.

Marshal Ismail looked on and smiled paternally. Cooper vowed silently to wipe that smile off his face as he palmed the knife and tucked it into the small of his back.

After the meal the guards escorted Cooper to a fresh cell. He pondered the absence of hood and restraints as they walked him along an eggshell-coloured corridor in what appeared to be a sizeable mansion. The doors and facings had the scarred and worn appearance of salvaged materials, but Cooper didn't need to touch them to know they were genuine wood. They entered the living area, in the far corner of which a spiral staircase provided access to the upper storey. The patio doors were open and Cooper looked at his guards and received a curt nod of affirmation.

The sun was already bright in the sky and Cooper shaded his eyes with his hands as he stepped into the courtyard. A two-metre-high wall encircled the compound, obscuring the landscape beyond. Sprinklers played across the well-tended lawn, shrubbery and palm trees, doubtless the only green for many miles. Double gates were set into the south wall in front of a gravel turning circle, indicating the existence of a road and, by extension, vehicles. All this Cooper observed in the instant before he was directed across the courtyard to the middle door of a group of three chalets. He noted the padlocks on the shutters and one of the guards used a swipe card to unlock the door.

The room beyond was certainly an improvement on his bare plascrete cell. It contained a bed with crisp white sheets and a pillow, a small bedside table and an easy chair. A sliding Perspex door gave access to a compact bathroom with a shower, sink and toilet. Cooper's nostrils twitched, reacting to the smell of strong bleach. He opened the mirrored door of the cabinet above the sink and found soap, deodorant, a toothbrush and toothpaste, but no razor. The clicking of maglocks alerted him that he was imprisoned once more. He closed the cabinet and returned to the main room.

Cooper tried the door as a matter of course; locked, as expected. The windows were also sealed, preventing access to the shutters beyond. He circled the room slowly, searching for hidden cameras or listening devices, even though he knew it to be a futile exercise. Microscopic cameras and microphones could be concealed anywhere, in the power outlets, light fittings or the air vent above the bed. His captors would be watching him, which meant he had to be careful. Regardless of what Ahmed said, there was zero chance of Goodman and himself being repatriated to the RSA. The only hope he had of seeing his family again was to escape, and two fugitives had a better chance of making it through enemy held territory. That made discovering Goodman's whereabouts imperative.

He completed an inventory of the room, sliding open the door of a built-in wardrobe to reveal a couple of towels and a further three sets of shirts and trousers identical to the ones he was wearing. Not quite prison stripes, but distinctive enough to mark him out. The bedside cabinet contained boxer shorts and an English translation of the Quran. Cooper flicked idly through it before replacing it in the top drawer. He was bored, but he wasn't that bored. Dropping to the floor, he looked under the bed and discovered only dust. He quickly slipped the pilfered dinner knife between a couple of the slats and stood up.

Dust shone whitely on the chest of his shirt and knees of his trousers. As he brushed it away Copper became aware of the smell of his body. Apart from his hosing down, he couldn't remember the last time he had washed. As with the food, he decided to take advantage of the facilities. Both could be withdrawn at any time; throwing the prisoner off guard with unpredictable punishment and reward was 101 of the softening-up process.

Once he was clean he would get some sleep, then see about formulating a plan. Thus far he had only seen ten people: Ismail, Ahmad, the pair of guards who escorted him back and forth, and a changing roster of six other guards who protected the marshal. But someone had prepared the food, just as someone serviced his room. He had no reason to believe they would be sympathetic to him, but for a Templar, these were not insurmountable odds.

CHAPTER 36

Lynch's finger hovered over the dial icon. He hated to involve Hirsch again, but he was desperate. As someone who had worked the Europa City streets as police, he had vital knowledge of its black market, information Lynch needed if Russell were to survive. He hit dial.

Hirsch picked up on the third ring, his voice guarded.

'Steve, what can I do for you?'

'Er … Johnny's not keeping so well,' Lynch replied, playing along. 'It's the old trouble. But I'm having a problem filling his prescription. Can you recommend a suitable drug store?'

'Hmm. Should be a couple can fill that for you. Give me five and I'll message you.'

'Thanks. That's appreciated.'

Lynch killed the connection. He had wanted to ask a lot more, particularly if Tazi was okay. But it was obvious Hirsch suspected someone was listening in. Good people had put themselves on the line to get him out of Casablanca. It was on him to make sure their sacrifice was worth it.

Ten minutes went by, during which he imagined Hirsch making calls of his own, then Lynch's com-unit pinged. He swiped it open and read Hirsch's message: Docks, German Quarter, Hamburg district. Ask barman for Lothar. Say Dimitri sent you.

Lynch's mouth quirked in a smile; how very clandestine. He looked across to where Russell lay on the couch and the smile faded. His fingers danced across the screen of his com-unit as he called up directions to Docks. Fastest route was three stops on the subway to a transfer station where he could pick up the cross-city monorail, followed by another two hops on the subway to the Reeperbahn, with the station practically on the club's doorstep.

He crossed to the kitchen isle, opened the top drawer and helped himself to the pile of disposable credit-chits Russell had stashed there. Picking up the diplomatic pouch, he unzipped it and took out the gun Tazi had given him. Probably best not to get caught with an unlicensed firearm in a foreign state. He was about to turn away when he caught sight of a package on the counter. The box was about eighteen inches square and marked with the Bamako Tech Corp logo. Ignoring the fragile labels, Lynch shook it and was rewarded with silence. He split the seals with his thumbnail and lifted off the lid. His brow wrinkled and then smoothed out as he recognised the contents.

He lifted out the wraparound HUD glasses, peeled off the protective coating and raised them towards his eyes. They hummed with power as his implant activated and he attached the glasses to the fasteners on his temples. He unpacked the camera drones next and placed them side by side on the worktop. The model was newer, but they were the same design as those he had sacrificed to save himself from the missile attack in Casablanca. He initiated the uplink and they rose into the air, flitting around like a pair of bats, their feeds projected directly onto his retinas. Up until now he hadn't realised how much he had missed his eye in the sky. But that was a pleasure that would have to wait. He recalled the drones to their docking station and fastened it to his belt.

Lynch stopped at the couch. Russell's chest was barely moving as he drew in a series of shallow breaths. His pulse was slow and weak, skin burning hot to touch.

'Thought you spooks were meant to be tough bastards? Hold in there, buddy.'

Lynch locked the apartment door behind him and rode the elevator down to street level. At the underground station he pre-loaded a multi-zone ticket onto his com-unit and made his way through the night-time press of bodies as a train drew up at the eastbound platform. Subways, he observed, had the same smell the world over: body odour and flatulence. They also had the same basic rule, avoid eye contact, which suited Lynch to a tee.

On leaving the train, Lynch crossed the concourse and made his way to the monorail, the city's famed wire. Here, at the terminus, the monorail started at ground level, rising vertiginously as it exited the station. Lynch stared out of the window, noting the steady stream of traffic; mostly freight and delivery trucks, feeding the city's twenty-four-hour economy. The vehicles dwindled away as the train accelerated into its climb, rising to weave between the towering blocks. Holographic advertisements flickered across the glass and steel. The familiar logos were all present: Tessler, Walther, Heckler & Koch, corporations grown fat from feeding on the military-industrial complex, the bulk of their wares, like those of the African Tech Corps, destined for America. He couldn't guarantee anything he wrote would ever change that, but he had to try. That meant getting out of Europa City and contacting the Free America movement.

The 'O' in the 'Docks' neon sign was out, suggesting the club had seen better days. A bored-looking doorman gave Lynch a cursory glance before waving him inside. The carpet sucked at Lynch's feet as he made his way over to where a girl with bright green hair stood framed in the top half of a split door, tattooed forearms resting on the base. She raised a languid arm and pointed a scanner in Lynch's direction. He tapped his com-unit against it and accepted the charge with his thumb.

'Wanna check that bag?'

Lynch shook his head.

'Whatever.'

She pointed him towards a steep flight of stairs edged with metal chequer plate. Low-wattage bulbs protected by wire mesh illuminated the way.

The industrial motif continued inside the club, with exposed pipework, cables and vents. A curved bar, heavily decorated with mirrors, stood above the recessed dance floor on which a solitary dancer threw shapes while darting between the lasers. A series of booths with banquettes of green leather lined the left wall. Lynch spotted two drug deals and a hooker plying her trade as he made his way to the bar. He heard the jabber of his personal monkey and gritted his teeth. Now was not the time to succumb.

The barman had the kind of good looks and easy manner that was sure to make him a hit with the female customers. He looked up from where he was polishing a glass and smiled.

'What can I get you?'

'Not so much what as who. I'm looking for Lothar. Dimitri sent me.'

The barman's smile vanished. 'Are you quite sure about that?'

'Absolutely.'

'All right.' He pointed to the booths. 'Take a seat. But first, you need to order a drink.'

'Got any bourbon?'

The barman scanned the shelves and then took down a bottle of Maker's Mark cask strength. 'How about this?'

'Large one. Straight up.'

Lynch took his drink to the nearest free booth. Even in the dim light he spotted a patch on the banquette darkened by some fluid or other and scooted past it to sit facing out towards the dance floor. The lone dancer was working himself into a frenzy, one that seemed unrelated to the beat of the music as his feet pounded against the boards. Suddenly, he froze, put a finger to his ear and then turned to stare directly at Lynch's booth.

Lynch examined him as he approached; a tall, wiry man with close-cropped brown hair, dressed in a sweat soaked T-shirt, jeans and boxing boots that came up to his calves. He grinned, showing a surprisingly white set of teeth that contrasted with the almost black of his irises.

'How is Dimitri?'

'Enjoying sunnier climes.'

'I doubt that. But you are here for product?'

'Cefazolin – to be administered intravenously. Gauze, tape, sterile dressings and fentanyl.'

'I am not a pharmacy.'

'Our mutual friend says different.'

'True. But this is boring. You want, I can get frenzy, rapture.' He looked Lynch up and down. 'Maybe some old school meth?'

'Just the medical supplies.'

'Fine. But my time and contacts cost the same.'

Lynch extracted the disposable credit-chits from the diplomatic pouch. 'Think you'll find my money's good.'

Lothar counted out the chits, stacking them carefully on his side of the table. Lynch got the impression that however much money was there was precisely what the medication for Russell would cost. He cursed himself silently for not holding some back.

'Delivery address?'

Lynch hesitated, not wishing to give up the location of the safe house. But he knew Russell didn't have the time to spare. Lothar, noting his reticence, placed his com-unit on the table.

'Send encrypted coordinates. A drone will deliver the merchandise within the next two hours.'

Lynch sent the address and Lothar returned the com-unit to his pocket. He stood and scooped up the credit-chits. Lynch picked up his glass and drained it. Time to ride the wire.

The drone arrived twenty minutes after Lynch, deposited its package on the balcony. Lynch worked quickly, setting up the IV meds and then cleaning the wound and applying a fresh dressing. Russell murmured incoherently throughout, which Lynch reckoned preferable to lapsing into a coma. The next few hours would be make or break for Russell. Lynch dragged an armchair across and settled down to wait.

Lynch must have dozed off, for the dawn light woke him as it filtered through the balcony doors. His neck was stiff and, when he shifted his weight on the chair, pins and needles ran up and down his right leg. He swore loudly.

'Jesus, Lynch! Ain't you done grousing yet?'

Lynch sprang up and Russell tried ineffectually to bat him away as he placed his palm on his forehead.

'Fever's broke.'

'You don't say. How's about you get me some water? Parched, here.'

Lynch fetched an isotonic drink from the fridge and handed it over. Russell drank slowly and carefully, looking round the room to orientate himself. His gaze alighted on the now-empty IV pouch.

'Thought we agreed you weren't to leave the safe house?'

'That's what you said. I never agreed to anything. If I had, you'd be dead. But don't worry, I was careful.'

'That remains to be seen. But the damage is done. What day is it?'

'Wednesday. You've been out of it since Monday night.'

'Shit.'

Russell threw off the blanket covering him and tried to stand. He got halfway to his feet before collapsing back on the sofa. Lynch, seeing his grimace of pain, handed him a bottle of fentanyl tablets. Russell looked away as he levered off the cap and shook a couple of pills into his hand. He dry-swallowed them before sinking back into the couch.

'Just need a minute or two.'

Lynch took out another IV pouch and attached it to the butterfly needle in the back of Russell's right hand. He hung it on the makeshift stand he had fashioned by stacking a pair of stools on top of one another.

'I get this isn't easy for you,' Lynch said, 'but you need to rest up. If you feel like eating, there's some leftover noodles I can reheat?'

'What? No chicken soup?'

'I could always add boiling water to the chow mein.'

Russell's laugh turned into a wince. Lynch turned away and went to busy himself with the food. He was midway through plating up when he heard a ping. He checked his com-unit and then turned to see Russell staring at his own, his forehead puckered in a frown.

'Bad news?'

'Bad timing. Finally got the go-ahead – flight leaves Angela Merkel at twenty hundred hours tonight. No way I'm making it.'

'When's the next one?'

'Who knows? Maybe next week, or next month. Maybe longer. Logging a flight plan to Richmond and not arriving isn't a trick you can pull too often, no matter how much money you spread about. Sooner or later, someone talks.'

Lynch mulled that over. Time was a luxury he could not afford, which left one option.

'I'll go on my own.'

'Absolutely not. You need someone to vouch for you, to make the necessary introductions.'

'So you let them know I'm coming. I'm one man. How much of a threat can I be? If they're scared of me this little revolution of yours is never going to get off the ground.'

'Anyone ever tell you that you're a stubborn, crazy bastard?'

'Only almost everyone who got to know me.'

'Fine. I'll make the calls. But know this; if you get on that plane by yourself I can't be responsible for what happens to you at the other end. They get spooked, they might ditch you in the ocean, or shoot you on arrival.'

Lynch raised himself to his full height.

'Your former colleagues at the Agency couldn't take me out with the full backing and resources of the RS government. Reckon I'll take my chances with Free America.'

CHAPTER 37

The knock on the door was followed by an instruction to stand clear. As Cooper was already sitting on the bed, he remained as he was. The door swung open and the younger of the two guards, whose name Cooper had learned was Faezal, placed a tray on the floor. He stepped back and closed the door, leaving behind the smell of strong coffee and sweet pastry.

Cooper swung his legs off the bed. How long was it since he'd last had coffee? He sniffed it cautiously, despite knowing there were many tasteless and odourless drugs his captors could use, if so inclined. Reasoning they had no need for such subtleties, he took a sip and sighed. The pastry was some kind of baklava, drenched in syrup with lemon cutting through. He would have liked to save some for later but, lacking any means of concealment, he ate both slices, washing them down with what turned out to be very good coffee.

A knock sounded again and when the door opened Faezal was accompanied by the older and more serious Nabab, who now did all the talking. Cooper obeyed his instruction to put on his shoes and exit the chalet. He stopped short as he saw Goodman next to the door of the adjacent building. The corporal was dressed in the same loose-fitting shirt and trousers as Cooper, a prison uniform sure enough. As he stepped closer Cooper noticed the yellow and blue of fading bruises on his face and the scab on his top lip. Beyond these superficial injuries the corporal looked fit and well, evidenced by the intelligence that shone in his eyes.

'Don't suppose you got a room with a view?'

Goodman smiled, revealing a missing eye tooth.

'Have to say the resort facilities are a little Spartan.'

'No talking,' Nabab warned. 'You are to exercise. Move.'

Cooper fell in step with Goodman as he cut across the lawn to the narrow flagstone path that surrounded it. He examined the walls for handholds, cracks or gates and found only white, unblemished plascrete. Objects that could be used as climbing aids were likewise unavailable, the palm trees set well within the perimeter of the wall. His ears heard only the soughing of the desert winds; no traffic, planes or voices. The scent of cloves and violets from the shrubs was strong enough to taste. At a little after eight o'clock in the morning the temperature was already forty degrees, only rendered bearable by the fine mist of the sprinklers. To leave the compound without water and transport would mean certain death.

Goodman's stony expression indicated his own survey had been equally fruitless. With no clue as to their location or the make-up of the surrounding terrain they would be operating blindly. If Faezal could be separated from Nabab he might be tricked into providing information, but such an opportunity looked unlikely at present.

As they completed their first circuit Nabab paused to light a cigarette, prompting Faezal to do likewise. When they moved on, the distance between them had stretched to six or so metres.

'Take it your initial accommodation was less hospitable?' Cooper whispered. 'When did they move you?'

'Yesterday. You?'

'Three days ago. You met the big guy yet?'

'Ismail? Yeah. Tried to convince me that we're the bad guys.'

'Uh-huh. Seems to be their game plan for now.'

Cooper's voice trailed off into silence as the guards, having finished their cigarettes, closed the gap. He turned the problem over in his head. Ismail had been keen to assure him Goodman was still alive and now here he was, doubtless presented as part of a strategy to win Cooper's trust. Maybe he should play along and see where it led, try to subvert the marshal's plan. In the meantime, he needed to find the opportunity to talk with Goodman so they could pool their knowledge.

The air vent slid aside to admit the drone. Its motor whirred softly, masked by the air-con, as it crossed the room and descended towards the foot of the bed. The operator held it steady as Cooper shifted in his sleep. He let out a grunt and rolled onto his belly, his right arm throwing back the sheet to expose his naked back. The drone hovered patiently until his body grew still, then skimmed above his sleeping form to take up station by his left shoulder. Cooper twitched in response to the needle-gun as it delivered a 0.3 milligram dose of scopolamine.

The guards gave it five minutes before entering Cooper's cell. He squinted in response to sudden flare of light and shielded his eyes with the back of his hand.

'Where am I? Who are you?'

Nabab handed him a set of grey coveralls. 'Get dressed and follow us.'

Cooper obeyed the guard's order. The material was coarse and irritated his skin, and the plastic sandals were cold on his feet. Was he dreaming? If so, he'd had this dream many times before. The thought slid away before it could trouble him. He fell in step with the guards; Faezal in front, Nabab behind. They led him down a long corridor, past various doors that opened off to the right and left. This, too, felt familiar, as did the opaque glass-panelled door at the end of the corridor. Faezal held the door open for Cooper.

The room was tiled in sterile white, a single medical couch positioned below a ceiling-mounted tech console. A man of middle height and years, with a shaved head and greying beard, stood at the couch's head, his eyes concealed behind the mirrored lenses of a wraparound HUD. He motioned Cooper to come forward.

'I am Doctor Mahmoud. You won't remember me, although we have met many times. This is perfectly normal. You will now lie on the couch.'

Cooper swung his legs up onto the couch and lay back. The gel base moulded itself to his body, engendering a sense of weightlessness. Mahmoud skimmed his fingers across a datapad and servo motors kicked in, raising Cooper into a sitting position. A holo-screen fizzed to life in front of the console. Cooper recognised a flight of RSAF F-27 Hellcats, the unmanned strike jets operated remotely by pilots thousands of klicks distant. He heard the familiar roar as they launched their full complement of Hellfire missiles, could almost smell the fuel as he remembered a dozen similar airstrikes in Israel. The focus shifted to the adobe and whitewashed blocks of a small village. A pair of old men sat playing chequers and drinking coffee outside a single storey, flat-roofed house. Further along the street a teenage boy was using a stick to drive a bony cow ahead of him. The camera panned to reveal a small market, a single row of stalls occupying the middle of a dirt track. A robed woman picked through the dates, pomegranates and olives while talking to the elderly proprietor. A second woman cradled an infant in her arms. All three looked up in response to the howl of the incoming missiles. The village dissolved in flames, plumes of oily black smoke rising into the sky. At the edge of the destruction lay a single child's shoe, its white fabric splattered with red.

The image dissolved to be replaced by a baking desert plain, the air shimmering with heat. A line of Caliphate POWs knelt on the edge of a trench, their hands secured behind their backs with zip ties. The camera panned along, focusing on the bruised and bloody faces of the prisoners. Sweat mingled with blood as the midday sun beat down on their uncovered heads. Those whose eyes weren't swollen shut stared resolutely ahead, ready to accept their martyrdom. A man dressed in the uniform of a Templar captain stepped forward and drew his pistol. He placed the muzzle against the base of the first prisoner's skull and pulled the trigger. Blood and brain matter splattered across the trench as the corpse fell forward. The captain stepped up to the next POW and repeated the procedure, working his way along the line. At the end of the line, he ejected the magazine from the pistol and slotted in a replacement before working his way back up the trench, kicking into it those bodies that had not fallen automatically into its depths. The camera zoomed out, revealing a parked-up flatbed truck with a tarp cover. A pair of Templars armed with assault rifles motioned for the next sixteen prisoners to step down.

Cooper felt the bile rise in his throat as he recognised the school bus with its flat front tyre; he was to have a starring role in the next atrocity. Mackinlay's voice was harsh as he warned the two refugees not to ignore him. When one of the men, surprised, whirled round with a tyre iron in his hand, Mackinlay opened fire, spraying both men with bullets. Cooper joined in a second later, emptying an entire magazine into the bus. He tried to look away as the rear emergency door opened, but the gel held his head and neck immobile as the bloodied arm of a child flopped forward.

The holo-screen shut down and the couch reclined. Doctor Mahmoud checked the readings on his datapad and then ordered the guards to return Cooper to his cell.

CHAPTER 38

I t had taken all of Lynch's powers of persuasion, but practicality finally won out and Russell accepted his decision to travel on alone. He had made Lynch commit the GPS coordinates of the Free America command base to memory and provided him with the location of a jeep and its access codes. As he sat on the tarmac at Angela Merkel waiting for the night flight to take off, Russell's parting words returned to him: 'I can't guarantee your safety. They smell anything off about you, they will put a bullet in you.'

Spooked, Lynch declined the offer of a reheated meal in favour of a couple of sleeping pills washed down with whiskey. Skimming through the in-flight music collection, he found some blues but couldn't concentrate on the words. He cued up some freeform jazz instead. His mind began to drift as the zolpidem kicked in and he racked back his seat and sank into the warm darkness.

The pilot shook him awake seven hours later. Lynch smacked his lips and wiped a line of drool off his collar. It took a few seconds for him to place where he was; the memory jolted him back to full consciousness. He rubbed his eyes, found a bottle of water in the seat pocket, cracked it open and took a long drink. The water was warm, but it didn't matter.

'How long was I out?'

'Long enough.' The pilot pointed at the window. 'Take a look.'

Lynch raised the blind and looked out of the window as the plane turned towards the coast. The verdigris-stained spiked crown of the Statue of Liberty appeared ahead, its right arm still raised defiantly, bearing its flaming torch. The swollen waters of New York Harbour submerged Liberty Island, covering the statue's pedestal and base and rising to its knees. A bitter taste formed in Lynch's mouth as he recalled the statue's official title; Liberty Enlightening the World. How had their once-great republic gone so wrong? Liberty: it died by degrees without anyone noticing until one day it was suddenly gone.

Beyond the seemingly wading Libertas the remains of derelict skyscrapers crowded the horizon. Sunlight burnished the jagged shards of glass and highlighted the leprous concrete. The Great Flood had heralded the end of Manhattan's Financial District and sent the global economy into meltdown, Mammon proving far more mortal than the markets had credited. The economies of America, Russia and China might have recovered to some degree, but forty years later they remained much diminished.

The plane turned north-west, flying inland over the city as it commenced its descent. Makeshift barriers and abandoned vehicles blocked the streets; weeds and small saplings sprouted from the cracked concrete and broken tarmac as nature reclaimed the city.

Lynch jerked back from the window as he spotted the crosses that lined the road, still bearing the skeletal remains of the crucified.

'Holy Mother of God! That shit's medieval.'

The pilot shrugged, inured to the grisly spectacle.

'Some of the fiercest fighting took place here when the original states of the USA seceded. It was an easy victory for the separatists as the remnants of the police and National Guard were overwhelmed dealing with looters and rioters. As you can see, they felt it necessary to make an example of them.'

'And nobody's thought to bury the poor bastards?'

'Guess not. I better get ready for landing.' The pilot winked. 'Hope you've enjoyed flying with Free America Airways.'

Lynch buckled his seatbelt. As a rule, he wasn't a nervous flyer but the apocalyptic landscape made him question exactly what they were going to land on. In the end he needn't have worried. The plane completed its descent and landed on what looked to be a recently constructed runway in an open area of grassland. He retrieved the diplomatic pouch from the overhead locker, took out the SIG Compact and tucked it into the waistband of his trousers. *Thank you, Tazi.* As soon as he got things squared away with the rebels he would try to contact her.

He paused on the stairs of the plane, patted down the pockets of his gilet, found his smokes and lit up. Felt good to be back on American soil after two long years. Even better to finally visit a state that wasn't under the tyranny of a bunch of religious zealots. Times were a-changing. He could feel it.

Lynch was barely clear of the runway when a fuel tanker sped past. The unfriendly gaze of the groundcrew bored into him as he walked towards the hangar. It seemed to be his fate to report from hostile territory. He wondered how to best sell himself. He was renowned for being what they called a colourful character, someone who polarised opinion. But editors and news anchors didn't normally carry guns.

He typed the first of the codes entrusted to him by Russell into the keypad on the hangar door. The LED turned from red to green and the door slid open. At least they hadn't changed the code, suggesting an element of trust. PIR sensors detected him and the lights hummed to life, illuminating the cavernous space and the jeep that sat in its centre. The vehicle looked new, which meant money was filtering into the resistance from somewhere. Lynch made a note to ask the FA leaders about it. The fob was tucked inside the front offside wheel arch. He plipped the locks and the dash luminesced to life. The controls remained locked out and he typed in the second code. Anxious seconds passed before its acknowledgement.

Lynch patted the dash. 'Never doubted you for a second.'

He entered the memorised GPS coordinates in the nav-comp and waited for it to plot a course. The destination looked to be 120 klicks to the north-east of his present location, wherever that was. He dug out the SIG, placed it on the passenger seat and hit auto-drive. The engine hummed to life and the jeep rolled forward.

After clearing the airfield, the jeep turned onto the scarred and potholed surface of a long-abandoned freeway. It jolted and bumped its way forward for twenty klicks before turning off and cutting cross-country, travelling along dirt roads that passed several small settlements composed of prefab buildings surrounded by the fields and managed woodlands that sustained them. Russell had referred to it as 'the public face of a population reduced to a pastoral existence, too weak to be a threat and too poor to be worth incorporating into the RSA'. Personally, Lynch doubted it offered much protection. He had seen how those fuckers operated, knew exactly what they were capable of. The legislature was equally corrupt, the Church filled with hypocrites. America deserved better.

The jeep continued its bouncing journey, eating up the terrain at a steady 55 kph. It navigated an area of managed forest and forded a stream, passing the decaying ruins of a long-forgotten settlement. Lynch, for all his nostalgia and belief in the ideals of the old republic, had never given much consideration to the reality of what lay beyond the borders of the Religious States. In his mind he had equated them with the prosperity of old, imagined a world of well-kept lawns with white picket fences, the stars and stripes flying proudly on the veranda. He felt foolish and humble in equal measure. And yet surely the whole point in having a dream was the belief you could make it reality.

A truck loaded with animal feed cut across the jeep's path, its driver slowing long enough to subject Lynch's transport to suspicious scrutiny. He wondered how openly Free America was known. Did the common people view the movement as a threat or a possible means of salvation? Were any of them sympathetic to the Religious States, or envious of its structure and order? More than a generation on from the second civil war, what reason did any of these sons and daughters have for laying down their lives for the dream of a reunited America? These and more questions would have to be asked, and he might not like the answers.

Thirty klicks out from his destination Lynch thought he caught the whine of a drone. A scan of the slate grey sky revealed not so much as a bird. But then a tactical drone had an operational ceiling of 18,000 feet. Lynch scrubbed his face with his hands. The unknown was always more unnerving than a clear and present danger. He lit a cigarette and in deference to the no smoking sign lowered the window. Free America was welcome to charge him for valeting.

The jeep rolled to a halt thirty-five nerve-wracking minutes later and Lynch stepped onto a grassy plain, seemingly little different from the half dozen or so they had passed through. A low ridge of rock bounded the plain to the east, while a copse of scrubby trees shielded the south-west. He waited. Nothing happened. It continued to happen for several minutes. Russell, in his traumatised condition, might have misremembered the coordinates. Lynch initiated the uplink and launched his camera drones, which whirled into the sky to provide a bird's-eye view of the plain. The grass stretched all around, the wind producing swirling motifs in the purple seed heads.

A flash lit up the sky directly above and his HUD went dark, as did the jeep. He watched the drones spiral to the ground. Had to be some form of localised EMP, which meant he wasn't alone.

What started as a gentle vibration in the soles of Lynch's feet travelled up his shins and into his thighs as the ground dropped away to reveal a ramp descending into the earth. Lynch stepped forward and stared into the gloom, noting the distant glow of electric lights. The sudden glare of headlights dazzled him, and he staggered back towards the jeep as a trio of JLTVs cleared the ramp and blocked his forward exit. He hauled open the passenger door and snatched up the SIG as the JLTV disgorged a dozen combat troops wearing camouflage body armour.

Lynch looked at the series of red laser dots on his chest as he aimed the pistol at a soldier with captain's pips on the shoulders of his body armour.

'Lose the weapon,' the captain barked.

'Not sure I can do that.'

'Then I suggest you get sure before you get dead.'

'You'll be dead too.'

Lynch tightened his finger on the trigger as the stand-off continued. He felt sweat trickle down his neck as he locked eyes with the officer. The kid looked determined, as did his men. The dots on his chest were now rock steady. This wasn't some gung-ho militia. He was dealing with professional and disciplined soldiers. If they had wanted to, they could have taken the kill shot by now. He eased his finger off the trigger.

'Okay, I'm going to raise my hands. We cool with that?'

'Drop your gun. Turn around, kneel, and place your hands on the back of your head. Make any kind of move I don't like and I'll aerate your skull for you.'

Lynch complied with the order. Two soldiers came forward and removed his HUD and docking station. They patted him down, emptying his pockets of cigarettes, lighter and hip flask.

'He's clear, Captain Jones.'

'Get the jeep and those damn drones of his. Hopefully nobody noticed this stupid fuck advertising our position.'

Lynch was hauled to his feet and frog-marched down the ramp. As they descended, he wondered what he had let himself in for. Was he merely exchanging one set of militarised fanatics for another? He was pulled to one side as the jeep and JTV's drove down the ramp into a vast floodlit underground cavern. Lynch stared at the tanks and drones that were lined up ready for deployment, at least three dozen of each. Beyond the lot, laid out in a neat grid, were a series of command buildings and barracks. Soldiers, male and female, shuttled back and forth, either on foot or utilising electric buggies, the headlights of which disappeared into the far distance. It was an impressive display of wealth and logistics, not least of which was its concealment from the RSA. No wonder Russell had been twitchy about its location.

Lynch's expression must have given his thoughts away, for Captain Jones turned to him and said, 'We have friends in Canada, Europa City and Africa who, like us, believe in the values of the old republic. We've been organising and building for years, determined not to be the next Oregon or Idaho. We've been building our military capability and embedding sleeper agents in the RSA. It's been more than a decade in the planning and execution. We've had our share of setbacks, but finally, we're ready.'

'But,' Lynch said, waving his hand around to encompass the underground silo, 'this must have cost billions.'

'It came together for less than you might imagine. Jerusalem definitely loosened a few purse strings. Gerrard's administration might have tried to hide behind the Israelis, but no one is in any real doubt as to who sanctioned and supplied the nano-virus that literally liquified those Caliphate schmucks. What they won't say in public, they ask themselves in private: could we be next? The RSA is a rabid dog. It needs to be put down before it infects anyone else.'

Lynch chewed that over as he was escorted to the command centre, a single-storey prefab building, the narrow windows of which were bright with electric light. Jones knocked once on the door before pushing it open and ushering Lynch inside. The woman who rose from behind the desk in response to their entry was in her mid-seventies, whipcord thin with washed-out blue eyes and a deeply lined face, her grey hair pulled back in a severe ponytail. She wore a charcoal trouser suit with a white blouse, kitten heels taking her height to five foot six. In the history-vids her hair was blonde and her face relatively unlined, but Lynch still recognised her as Gina Pulaski. She had served as a senator for New York in the final Democrat government of the USA, first under Garcia and then, following his death, Williams. Refusing to acknowledge the secession of the original twenty-nine founding Religious States, she had advocated military action against them. But the reality of the flood-ravaged country quickly made such action impossible, with the police and military struggling to maintain control of states descending into lawless anarchy after the collapse of Congress and the Federal governments.

'Welcome to the Eagle's Nest, command centre for the Free America movement.'

Lynch held out his hand, which Pulaski ignored.

'Senator Pulaski, I heard you were dead.'

'And I heard you were a mean, drunken sonofabitch with more dirty habits than a convent laundry room.'

Lynch couldn't tell from Pulaski's expression if she was joking or not and decided it best to move on.

'You put all this together?'

'It's fair to say I had a lot of help. Keeping it under the radar is the hardest part – up until now we've managed to avoid idiots flying drones overhead. I've half a mind to order Captain Jones to take you back outside and shoot you.'

'And the other half?'

'Hank Russell speaks highly of you. Damned if I know

why, because what I've seen of you is far from impressive.'

'Is that so? Because I'm the sonofabitch who exposed Colonel Tyler's war crimes. The same bastard who first made it out of Israel and then Morocco with the RSA hot on my heels. Had a lot of help, but it was grit and determination saw me through every step of the way to stand before you now. You can curl your lip all you like, Pulaski, but I happen to know that means something!'

'Even if it does, what good are you to me? We find ourselves on the brink of war and while your patriotism can't be disputed, you're no soldier.'

'Never claimed to be one. Never wanted to be one. Looking round, seems to me you have more than enough of those. But you didn't help me escape Casablanca and fly me across the Atlantic just to bust my balls. So why don't you stop blowing smoke up my ass and get to the point?'

'Why you—'

Pulaski raised her hand, cutting Jones off. 'I don't need you to defend me, Captain Jones. Besides, I like a plain speaker. So let me do some of my own. You're a loose cannon, Lynch. You've stumbled through life more by luck than good judgement, particularly of late. But you've a nose for a story, a thirst for the truth, and a unique way of presenting it. After decades in the shadows, the time has come to reveal ourselves. Our agents have informed us of a growing conflict within the RSA, with Grand Master Vanderbilt poised to mount a military coup and seize control of the RSA in the name of the Church. Such an occurrence would plunge the country even further into darkness. But that doesn't mean we can't exploit the chaos caused by a coup to launch an attack of our own. That said, military strength alone will not carry the day. Unless we win the hearts and minds of those who swear fealty to the Religious States, we will never be more than an occupying force. And if history has taught us nothing else, it is that such occupations always end in failure.'

'Once again, it's all about controlling the narrative.'

'Same as it always was. Question is, are you the man for the job? Personally, I still have my doubts. Are you here because you truly believe in the cause or because you have nowhere else to go? A roach scuttling for cover.'

'And what's Russell's assessment of me?'

'That the only thing you really care about is the story, and by extension your own personal standing. It was the story that brought you here, right?'

'The story and a little thing we journalists like to call the truth. You say you want to overthrow the Religious States and reunite America. But what will you put in its place? What does Free America actually stand for?'

'It stands for the most simple and basic of truths. "All persons are born free and equal, in dignity and in rights, and, being endowed by nature with reason and conscience, they should conduct themselves as brothers and sisters one to another." Is that good enough for you, Lynch?'

The fire in Pulaski's eyes and the unflinching certainty in her voice reminded him rather too much of Colonel Tyler; two sides of the same coin. But he was in. The story was his to uncover, including any hidden agenda.

'Reckon so.'

CHAPTER 39

Cooper sat up in bed and scrubbed his face with his hands. He felt tired, as though something had disrupted his sleep, but whatever nightmares haunted him slipped away with the words of the call to prayer. As had become the habit, Marshal Ismail would send for him and Goodman after the *Salat Ul Fajr*, the morning prayer, and invite them to break their fast with him. Breakfast would come with another lecture of the history and achievements of Islam which, if Ismail were telling the truth, were many and varied.

The table was laden with the usual assortment of small dishes, a stack of pitta breads serving as both plates and utensils. Ismail smiled warmly and indicated they should sit. Cooper's stomach grumbled as he looked over the table. In addition to balls of sheep's cheese, hard-boiled eggs and olives, there was *ful medames*, a stew of cooked fava beans, and *makdous*, tiny oil-cured aubergines stuffed with a mixture of walnuts, red pepper and garlic. The latter had become something of a favourite, and he scooped one up with a still-warm pitta and bit down into it.

Ismail, playing the role of mother, poured coffee into tiny cups. Although served black, it was brewed with cardamom and sugar. Cooper took a sip, conscious of the layer of grounds lurking at the bottom. The marshal, meantime, had steepled his fingers.

'Despite what your instructors have told you, ours is a predominantly peaceful religion. Like the Templars, we are simply defending our faith from aggressors. As I have said before, there is no reason why our two faiths cannot coexist peacefully – apart from American intransigence.'

Goodman threw down a half-eaten boiled egg.

'Just once, I'd like to enjoy a meal without the lecture.' He looked questioningly at Cooper. 'Don't tell me you're going to sit and listen to this BS? We've heard it half a dozen times already. Repeating something doesn't make it fact. Your scientists might well have advanced the fields of algebra, calculus and geometry but that was hundreds of years ago. Your recent history is one of tyranny, violence and bloodshed.'

Cooper shot a glance at Goodman, warning him not to deviate from the script. He was no fan of Ismail's lectures, even if he had to admit they were starting to latch onto his earlier doubts, expanding the cracks in his already shaky beliefs. The Five Pillars of Islam were certainly not incompatible with living a good life or fundamentally incompatible to the tenets of Christian belief. Cooper shook himself; lack of sleep was starting to blur his thoughts. He didn't belief that shit, did he? They were playing along with Ismail to win his trust and aid their escape. Time to get back on mission.

'Why don't you take a breath, Pete? We've talked about *this*. Two sides to every argument. Sometimes you have to listen, gather information and analyse it.'

'Maybe I'm all analysed out, because some things you can't let slide.' Goodman placed his napkin on the table and scraped back his chair. 'I think it's time I went back to my cell.'

Ismail gathered up his own napkin and threw it on the table.

'I had hoped we might be civilised about this but I see, despite my many attempts, there's no reasoning with you, Corporal Goodman. You treat my kindness and forbearance with suspicion. Worse. You throw it back in my face. Very well, then, we will do this the hard way. But mark my words, one way or another, you will serve my purpose.' He waved for one of the ever-present guards to come forward. 'Take him back to what he deems a cell.'

'The most luxurious apartment is still a cage if you can't leave it as and when you choose,' said Goodman.

He shot Cooper a venomous glance as Nabab led him away. Ismail smiled benignly, keen to put the corporal's outburst behind him. Cooper, acquiescing, helped himself to another stuffed aubergine. Food, while not excessive, had been plentiful over the last ten days and he had instigated a strict exercise regime in his chalet, building up and maintaining the muscle mass lost during his initial period of confinement and interrogation. It helped to pass the time and prevented him from brooding about his family although he spent many an evening composing lengthy letters to his mother and father, his sister, Shania, and the twins, Dale and Wade. Some of the content mirrored the letter he had written to them prior to going into combat for the first time. How naive that young man now seemed, proud to be serving his country and willing to lay down his life for the cause. The reality of war had proved very different to what he had imagined. But his family had to be shielded from the horror to prevent the benefits of his service to them being soured, although by now, a month after his capture and with no word, they must be fearing the worst. Officially, he and Goodman would be listed as missing in action, but with each passing day the hope would slowly fade.

'Tell me.' Ismail's urbane tone broke into Cooper's thoughts. 'Have you thought any more about Lieutenant General Ahmad's request?'

'The one for troop numbers or the one about future objectives? I think both would be rather out of date.'

'Come, now, I thought we were past such insincerities. Do not let your comrade's churlish mood colour your attitude. You know very well of what I speak.'

'That I should confess to war crimes on behalf of the American people? I'm sorry, but I can't do that.'

'Are you sure? Because you don't sound so certain. During our discussions you have freely conceded that war crimes have been committed, yes?'

'I believe I said there had been atrocities on both sides. That's just the nature of war.'

'In which case I fail to see your objection to telling the truth. Especially when it will set you free. One short broadcast and then you and Corporal Goodman can return home. It seems a small thing to ask of you.'

'From your perspective, I'm sure it is. But I would be returning home as an apostate, a traitor, a man who has shamed his family. I'd rather let them continue to think I was dead.'

Ismail smiled. 'Excellent. Spoken like a man of honour. This is why I like you, Billy Ray Cooper. In many respects you are a simple man, but you understand the principles of duty and love. These are worthy qualities in an opponent.'

Ismail's sudden change of tack threw Cooper into confusion. The more you talked with him, the more reasonable he appeared. Cooper groped for a comeback.

'Is this some sort of game?'

'Precisely – a game where the ultimate stakes are life and liberty. Right now, you are weighing the odds prior to rolling the dice. Will you come up snake eyes?'

A shiver ran down Cooper's spine. Was Ismail generalising or had he intuited his plan to escape? Was he unknowingly dancing to Ismail's tune, a tiny cog in the great machine of the marshal's ambition? Cooper tried to get a grip on his thoughts. Subscribing near-supernatural powers to an enemy was a sure road to a self-fulfilling prophecy. He picked up his coffee and blew on the surface, leaving Ismail's question unanswered.

'I see we are playing poker, not craps. Very well, hold your cards close to your chest. In the end it will not mean so very much.' Ismail pointed to the table. 'Have you eaten your fill?'

Cooper, finding his tongue curiously thick in his mouth, nodded.

'Very well. Faezal will escort you to your "gilded cage" and you can get cleaned up. At ten o'clock I wish to tell you about the great Doctor al-Zahrawi – around the year one thousand he produced an encyclopaedia of surgery that was used in Europa as a reference book for the next five hundred years. I am certain you will find his story quite fascinating.'

Cooper kept silent as a sudden surge of rebellion rose inside him. He fought his impatience, remembering the maxim of his instructors during selection: slow is smooth, smooth is fast. He folded his napkin, dipped his head to his host and carefully pushed back his chair.

Faezal fell in one step behind him on his left, a solid presence with a hint of menace. Both men relaxed once they were in the courtyard and away from the scrutiny of the marshal.

'I really like the *makdous*,' Cooper said conversationally. 'Are they made here or brought in? Must be the former, right? We're pretty far from civilisation.'

'No, we have deliveries.'

'Really? I've not seen any. Do they come in the dead of night?'

'That's because we haven't had one for several weeks. But I'm sure there'll be one soon. You Templars have hearty appetites.'

Cooper caught the ghost of a smile on the young soldier's lips. Humour, a sign that he was relaxing around his charges. Nabab displayed no such tendencies and Cooper felt a twinge of conscience at exploiting Faezal's naivety. He quashed it as Faezal pushed open the chalet's door and ushered him inside. The door closed and he heard the maglocks click into place. He felt confused, uncertain as to his objectives. Ismail had treated them with nothing but kindness. Cooper slammed the heel of his hand into his temple, focusing on the pain. He was letting Ismail get inside his head. He needed to remember his training. The primary duty of every prisoner of war was to escape.

CHAPTER 40

Cooper turned the shower on, twisting the temperature dial to maximum. The mirror fogged over quickly, with any camera lenses presumably being similarly affected by the steam. Hunkering naked beneath the sink, he tapped out a series of dots and dashes on the pipe with the flat of the stolen dinner knife. He listened carefully for the reply, translating the stuttering Morse code. The supply truck had arrived just after the morning prayer. They would take breakfast with Ismail as normal and make their move afterwards. Time to roll those dice.

After secreting the knife in a hand towel, Cooper stepped under the shower. He let the steaming water play over him for a few seconds before turning the dial to the opposite extreme. The sudden cold was like a physical blow, jolting him to full consciousness. He knew the odds of success were low but the longer he delayed the less able he would be to make a move. Whatever the cause, Stockholm syndrome or a more deliberate manipulation, each day saw Ismail's influence over him increase. Goodman had noticed it too and began pushing back until Cooper cautioned him against it. Their conversation had been heated at first but he had managed to talk the corporal around. Now their patience was about to finally bear fruit.

The sun beat down on the courtyard, an uncompromising and merciless heat. Cooper had begun to hate that sun, viewing it as another obstacle to be overcome on the road to freedom. Despite their efforts, neither he nor Goodman had been able to ascertain their precise location, but reckoned they were far enough north to make crossing the Turkish border the best means of escape. If relations between the RSA and Turkey were not exactly cordial, the Turks' distrust of their immediate neighbour would most likely see them seek to secure a political advantage through the repatriation of the Templars. Unless they decided to simply make the problem disappear.

Cooper looked over to where the supply truck sat parked on the turning circle. Goodman gave him the briefest of nods. Nabab glowered and pushed him roughly forward, causing Goodman's shoulder to bounce off the edge of the patio door. Cooper saw him tense, but he mastered his anger, doubtless adding it to the account that would shortly be settled.

Ismail stood and smiled in welcome, waiting until both men were seated before resuming his own seat. He indicated they should eat. Cooper resisted the temptation to fill his plate, reminding himself that today should appear to be a day like any other. He sipped his coffee and made a show of pondering his selection before spooning fava beans onto his plate.

'Today,' Ismail said, 'we shall discuss *Ayat al-Kursi*, the 255th verse of the second chapter of the Quran. Many believe this to be one of the most powerful, as when it's recited it confirms the greatness of God.'

'Are you one of those many?' asked Cooper.

Ismail smiled indulgently. 'Ah, always looking a chink in the armour. But a student who challenges is better than one who blindly accepts.'

Cooper stuffed his mouth with pitta to avoid answering.

If Ismail found it rude, he gave no sign, eating sparingly of the mixed olives. The remainder of the meal passed in silence and concluded with Ismail checking his watch.

'I have other matters to attend to today, so we shall meet at oh nine thirty.'

Cooper and Goodman pushed back their chairs, stood and bowed to the marshal as Nabab and Faezal stepped forward to shepherd them back to the chalets. The Templars waited until they were clear of the dining area before making their move. Goodman's right elbow powered back and up, smashing into Nabab's nose. As he turned instinctively away from the blow Goodman slipped his arms beneath Nabab's armpits and brought his arms up to clasp his hands on the back of his neck. The sound of breaking bone reverberated as Goodman pushed forward. He dropped Nabab's twitching corpse to the ground. Cooper simultaneously stamped down on Faezal's shin, running the edge of his foot downwards as he pulled the sharpened dinner knife from where he'd secreted it in the small of his back. He twisted Faezal's left arm behind his back and wrapped his own right arm across the young man's throat, pressing the point of the knife below his left ear.

Ismail, apparently unperturbed by Nabab's death, gave them a slow handclap.

'Very good, you have a hostage. Now, what are your demands?'

Cooper kept his eyes fixed on Ismail as he walked Faezal backwards to the patio doors.

'We're going to get in the truck parked out there and you're going to let us drive away.'

'That is not going to happen. Release Faezal and I will be merciful. Otherwise…'

Ismail's unspoken threat hung in the air as Goodman slid back the patio doors. Faezal started to struggle and Cooper twisted his left arm further, eliciting a gasp of pain.

'Please. We are friends,' Faezal pleaded. 'You don't have to do this.'

Cooper gritted his teeth. Faezal was the enemy. Faezal was a barrier to his escape and reunion with his family. He had a duty to use any and all means to escape. The life of a single enemy combatant was nothing in comparison.

Ismail clapped his hands. 'Jaamal!'

Footsteps sounded and Cooper recognised the muscular olive-garbed figure as one of the guards who had beaten him during his initial interrogation. He pressed his forearm tighter, restricting Faezal's oxygen supply. The young guard's eyes widened with terror as Cooper continued to drag him towards the truck. Ismail looked on impassively as the hastily summoned guard waited for instruction. Cooper checked out of the corner of his eye that Goodman was keeping pace with him.

Cooper pressed the knife deeper, producing a bead of blood. 'I will kill him.'

'That I do not doubt,' Ismail replied. He held out his right hand. 'Sidearm.'

The guard unbuttoned the flap of his holster and handed Ismail his pistol. The marshal thumbed off the safety and pulled back the slide. He raised the pistol and sighted carefully. The left back quarter of Faezal's head exploded. Cooper staggered back, releasing the corpse and the knife. The gates opened behind the truck and marching boots crunched across the gravel as Caliphate soldiers swarmed inside and formed a circle around Cooper and Goodman.

'You think I did not anticipate an attempt to escape?' said Ismail. 'That the kitchen did not notice a missing knife? That your furtive glances and hurried conversations went unnoticed? I saw all this and more and I allowed it in the hope that you would see the light. But both of you have gravely disappointed me.'

Cooper pointed at Faezal's body. 'Guess he must have disappointed you too.'

'Faezal's martyrdom will be remembered,' Ismail replied, ignoring the sarcasm. He pointed to the two Templars. 'Take them back to the cell block.'

Cooper's arms were wrenched back as he was forced to his knees. He felt the plastic cut into his skin as the flex cuffs were tightened about his wrists. It had always been a long shot, but at least this way they would perhaps die with some measure of honour. Better that than being used as pawns in some propaganda game.

Ismail handed the pistol back to the guard.

'Inform Doctor Mahmoud that he is to intensify treatment. And let Ahmad know he has a video to make. It's time we let the Americans know about our guests.'

CHAPTER 41

Besides herself, Morrison and Kordowski were also present in the Central Office, clustered around the president's desk. Hopkins watched Gerrard as he watched the video playback of a live broadcast that had gone out earlier that morning; the set of his jaw indicating the rage that simmered just below the surface. Grey had started to overtake the brown in his hair, and he had visibly lost weight over the last six months as the war ground inexorably on. What they said was true; be careful what you wish for, you might just get it. Not that she felt a great deal of sympathy for him. Gerrard, like the rest of them, had gone into this with his eyes wide open. But even the hawks got squeamish when they saw the bodies coming home.

Victory in Jerusalem had proved to be a false dawn, since when the Caliphate had entrenched their forces and begun fighting with fresh ferocity. The speed at which Paradise was filling with martyrs didn't seem to deter them at all, something that could not be said about the American public's reaction to Arlington's rapid expansion. The anti-war movement was gaining strength with each passing day, while Gerrard's approval rating shrank accordingly. The video would only add to Gerrard's reputational decline.

The courtyard, enclosed behind high walls, was an oasis of green, sprinklers playing over the well-tended lawn, shrubbery and palm trees. The camera swept briskly down to the south, where a pair of steel cages sat at either side of a gravel turning circle. Turning to the left, the camera zoomed in on the first captive, who sat with his knees drawn up to his chest, head angled back into the patch of shade that had so far escaped the heat of the sun. Sweat beaded his stubbled features and begrimed his uniform. The camera paused on the name tape on the right breast of his tunic, identifying him as Cooper, before panning across to the other cage. A similar process revealed the name Goodman.

Gerrard paused the video.

'Uniforms can be appropriated. Are we certain these are our men?'

Hopkins ignored Morrison's look of mute appeal, forcing him to deliver the news.

'Biometric analysis confirms their identities as Corporal Peter Goodman and Templar-Private Billy Ray Cooper. They disappeared while on patrol in Tadmur six weeks ago.'

Gerrard's arm tensed. For a moment, Hopkins thought he was going to launch the remote across the room. He pointed it back towards the holo-screen instead and the video resumed. The focus shifted to a tall, straight-backed man dressed in an olive uniform, its epaulets decorated with gold braid, chest festooned with medals. His dark hair fell to his shoulders, his beard to his chest. Marshal Abu Salman Ismail, de facto leader of the Caliphate following the assassination of Abu Ahmad al-Nasr al-Qurayshi via a drone strike on the Al-Aqsa Mosque in Jerusalem. He spoke in concise English, calling for the immediate release of seven high-ranking Caliphate officers held by the RSA in return for freeing his own captives. Failure to comply within three days would result in the Templars' public execution. The screen went blank.

'Ideas?' Gerrard asked, a hint of desperation shading his voice.

'Compliance is a non-starter,' Kordowski replied. 'The RSA doesn't negotiate with terrorists. Anyway, it's a moot point; el-Abboubi and al-Furkan are dead. Complications resulting from the use of enhanced interrogation techniques.'

'So we either confess to torturing prisoners to death, or accept the backlash from allowing American soldiers to be beheaded live on air. That's some shitty optics either way, prior to the midterms.' He threw his hands up in exasperation. 'You're killing me here. Give me some other options.'

Hopkins shook her head in response to Morrison's questioning look, and Kordowski did likewise. The Secretary of Defense had the floor.

'Just the one – high-risk, high-reward. Intelligence has managed to trace the signal back through its various relay points and confirmed its origin as a villa located to the south of Aleppo. As you'd expect, it's heavily defended on all land approaches, but we could use a stealth plane to drop a retrieval team via HAHO, while staging a diversionary ground assault. A VTOL suborbital hopper would provide extraction.'

Gerrard rubbed his chin thoughtfully.

'Least-worst option so far. But let's get one thing straight – if we can't rescue the prisoners their propaganda value is to be neutralised by terminating them.'

Hopkins said what they were all thinking. 'Vanderbilt isn't going to like that. Not one bit.'

'I don't give a rat's ass what that scheming sonofabitch does or doesn't like. It's time he saw where the true power lies. Am I clear on this?'

'Perfectly,' Hopkins replied, biting back her anger. She'd warned him about antagonising Vanderbilt further until Hannah evaluated how much of a threat he posed, based on Morrison's recent intel. Depriving him of Bishop Gibson, and by extension the formal backing of the Church, had only made him more dangerous; a rabid dog backed into a corner. Current polling put control of both Houses on a knife edge. A daring rescue mission would go a long way towards tipping the balance. Failure, on the other hand, wasn't an option. She'd worked too long and too hard to get her shot at the Senate. Fuck it up and there wouldn't be a second chance.

'I want that bird in the air inside of twelve hours, Lee. Not a minute later,' Gerrard warned.

'Understood, sir. If I may?'

Gerrard waved him away, but when Kordowski made to follow he raised a hand. 'Not you, Gene. I want to go over the speech for tomorrow.'

Hopkins caught the edge of the door and slipped round it. A couple of quick paces drew her level with Morrison.

'Take it you got someone in mind for the job?'

Morrison stopped and regarded her carefully. 'Not like you to take an interest in military matters, Susanna.'

'Cut the bullshit. We both know if this goes south Gerrard's administration is toast. He's denying us our best shot by cutting the Templars out.'

'Says you. I won't deny they're good – God knows, the money we spend on them, they ought to be. But they still comprise less than two per cent of our military. The boys of the Eighty-second Airborne Division are more than capable. Major Robert Stanley of the First Brigade will lead a team of his choosing.'

'He's good?'

'A solid and expert soldier. Career military, third generation. Won't hesitate to do the needful if required.'

'Just so long as your boy understands that's the last resort. Dead heroes won't win us any votes.'

'I'll be sure to pass that along, along with any other strategic advice you wish to offer.'

Hopkins glowered but said nothing. Morrison would get what was coming to him in due course, but for now she needed him.

CHAPTER 42

S tanley linked his HUD into the live satellite feed of the villa's courtyard. Night-vison imagery confirmed the two captives were still being held in cages near the south wall. No other signs of movement were detectable.

He toggled on his mic. 'Raider King to Goliath Command. You are clear to commence assault.'

'Copy, Raider King. Goliath out.'

The satellite feed shifted to show the commencement of the ground assault to the north-east of the villa. A dozen JLTVs, modified with jacked-up rear axles and swivel-mounted M60 machine guns, roared into action, closing on a line of Caliphate entrenchments that secured the main land approach to the villa. Tracer rounds lit up the night sky, arcing towards the enemy defences in a display of sound and fury. Retaliatory fire commenced within thirty seconds, indicating a high state of readiness. Stanley terminated the feed; the drop zone was fast approaching and what was happening on the ground was out of his control.

The modified Northrop Grumman B–21C was cruising at an altitude of 35,000 feet; outside air temperature –45°C, air pressure a quarter of that at sea level. Stanley and the other members of the six-man extraction team had been breathing one hundred per cent oxygen for the past thirty-five minutes to flush the nitrogen from their bloodstream to prevent the bends. Stanley checked his oxygen supply as a red warning light illuminated above the rear ramp, indicating the depressurisation of the hold. He looked to his second in command, Sergeant Chisholm, and received a thumbs up. Patterson, Rodriguez, Simpson and Conrad completed their own check-in. They formed a line with Stanley at its head as the rear ramp descended, exposing them to the freezing air outside.

Stanley checked his GPS and jumped as the readout registered fifty-seven klicks from target. The air whistled past as he fell towards terminal velocity; the remainder of the team jumped at two second intervals. The readings on his altimeter display ratcheted downwards, reaching 27,000 feet after twelve seconds of freefall, at which point he deployed his chute. He counted off the intervals between the opening of the other chutes, registering all five. As the lowest member of the stack, it was Stanley's task to set the travel course. Distance to landing zone, wind speed and direction scrolled across his HUD and Stanley adjusted the angle of his canopy to compensate, zeroing in on a point two klicks south of the villa; a natural hollow concealed by sand dunes. The air temperature had risen to $-12.7°C$, but even with his polypropylene knit undergarments he felt the chill in his bones. Not that he would trade that feeling for anything in the world; the extended under-canopy time of a HAHO jump was the closest a man could come to flying.

With the drop zone less than ten seconds away, Stanley ran through a final comms check; his team were on course and ready. Not that he had any doubts. He'd fought alongside each man numerous times and knew he could trust each one with his life. Would do so again before the mission was over.

Stanley brought his legs together and braced for impact. He bent his knees automatically as his boots hit the ground. He watched the other members of the extraction team drop in perfect formation as he gathered in his chute. An explosion lit up the horizon as the diversionary force continued to engage with the Caliphate defences. The clock was ticking. He snapped open a folding entrenching tool and worked quickly, digging through the soft desert sand and burying his chute, jumpsuit, and oxygen mask and bottle. He wiped the sweat from his brow, the numbing cold of the jump a distant memory.

Time for a weapons check. The squad were all armed with UCIW rifles which, with the stock fully collapsed, measured just twenty-two inches. Chambered for a 5.56 x 45mm round, they were fitted with a SureFire suppressor and an Aimpoint Micro red dot sight. Stanley ejected the thirty-round STANAG magazine, checked it and clicked it back into place. He repeated the procedure with Walther Q4 Tac he'd chosen for his sidearm. A Marine Recon knife, based upon the second pattern of the classic Fairbairn–Sykes fighting knife, hung hilt down from the PALS webbing on the left side of his vest. Two M68 fragmentation grenades, fitted with electrical impact fuses, were affixed on the right. He'd included a couple of flash-bangs for good measure. While the success of the mission would rely on stealth and speed, it was prudent to be well-armed.

Locked and loaded, Stanley signalled the squad to move out and they fanned across the top of the dune. He scanned the horizon, his night-vision goggles transforming the desert into an eerie green. Motion sensors and infrared detected nothing between the landing zone and the villa, and Stanley broke into an easy run that quickly ate up the distance to the target.

Chisholm and Rodriguez reached the compound first, the heavyset sergeant boosting the lighter man to the top of the wall. Rodriguez signalled it was safe and dropped into the courtyard. Stanley waited for Simpson and Conrad to scale the wall before making his own ascent, leaving Chisholm and Patterson to secure their exit.

Conrad and Simpson were in position, weapons trained

on the villa's patio doors. Heat signatures showed four figures clustered around the kitchen table, with another three prone bodies distributed in rooms towards the rear of the building, presumably sleeping. The body count was too low for Stanley's comfort; intel suggested closer to twenty Caliphate soldiers operating from the building, which begged the question, where were the other dozen or so?

Rodriguez signalled Stanley towards the cages. Both captives were slumped against the bars, limbs splayed out as far as the confines would allow. Stanley identified the occupant of the cage in front of him as Cooper. He reached in and gently shook his shoulder, silencing him when he started awake.

'Major Stanley, Eighty-second Airborne.' He identified himself in a whisper. 'We're here to take you boys home. Orders from the president himself.'

The young Templar went from drowsiness to high alert in an instant and Stanley felt himself being scrutinised.

'Easy there. We'll have you out in a couple of minutes.'

Stanley applied a nano-corrosive to the lock and moved across to the next cage. Rodriguez had already briefed Goodman, who was on his haunches, attempting to loosen his cramped muscles. Stanley gave him the thumbs up as he destroyed the cage's lock. Still zero movement in the villa. He signalled the hopper to commence its descent. A textbook operation.

Powerful spotlights lit up the courtyard as Stanley pulled open the door of Goodman's cage. He grunted and tore off his night-vision goggles. The patio doors shattered as Conrad and Simpson sprayed the villa. Motion sensors detected fourteen enemy contacts emerging from a shielded basement. Stanley switched his UCIW from auto and targeted the spotlights, pivoting round as he took out each one with a single round, while Conrad and Simpson continued to lay down suppressing fire.

'Rodriguez, we need an exit!'

'On it!'

Stanley pulled his goggles back down as he shot out the last of the lights. He directed a burst of fire into the villa and his target spun back into the room. Conrad and Simpson clicked empty at the same time; the moment the Caliphate troops were waiting for. They emerged through the shattered patio doors in two waves, spraying bullets randomly. Stanley's hand wrapped round a grenade as he hit the ground. He pulled the pin and the spoon spun away. The throw was intentionally weak, relying on the rushing Caliphate troops to close the distance after the impact had armed the fuse. It detonated two seconds later, peppering the first wave with deadly steel fragments. A second explosion sounded behind Stanley as Rodriguez blew through the doors in front of the turning circle, shaped charges expelling the debris safely into the desert.

Stanley rose to one knee, weapon back on auto and firing bursts at the remaining Caliphate troops. Conrad and Simpson fell back, loosing off tightly controlled shots. Chisholm appeared at the breach and helped Rodriguez shepherd Goodman into the desert beyond. A round thudded into Stanley's chest, the impact spinning him about and forcing the air from his lungs.

CHAPTER 43

Cooper saw Stanley go down; even with the vest the bullet would have hit him with the force of a sledgehammer. He darted forward as the major struggled to rise, Caliphate bullets buzzing like a swarm of angry wasps. Cooper ignored the burning pain as a bullet creased his thigh, his right hand scooping up Stanley's UCIW. He fired off a couple of bursts, using the muzzle flashes of their weapons to target the Caliphate soldiers. The shots found their target and he used the brief hiatus in the attack to hoist Stanley in a fireman's lift.

'Reckon it's time we left this party,' Cooper said.

He fired off another burst, his rifle stuttering to silence as Conrad and Simpson ducked through the shattered wall. Seizing the opportunity, the remaining Caliphate troops rushed forward. Cooper drew the Walther from Stanley's holster and snapped off a couple of shots as he felt his way to the breach. Bullets bit chunks from the plascrete wall to his left. His groping hand hit space and he paused to fire one last volley before ducking through.

Cooper lowered Stanley to his feet. 'Can you walk?'

'Yeah, vest caught it. Winded me pretty bad, but that's all.'

Chisholm patted Stanley on the shoulder and pointed to the sky where the navigation lights of the hopper were visible as it commenced its descent. Stanley nodded and opened a comms channel.

'Looks like we've woken the neighbours, Rivera. See if you can't put them down again.'

'Will do, Major.' The pilot's voice was clear, despite the fact she was operating the hopper from thousands of miles away.

Stanley signalled the squad to make for the dunes. The darkness lit up as a pair of missiles streaked towards the courtyard. The ensuing fireball mushroomed towards the heavens, casting a ruddy glow over the sand.

Cooper fell in beside Goodman as they sprinted towards the descending aircraft. The corporal's breathing was quick and shallow, as though he was on the verge of hyperventilating. Cooper slapped him on the back reassuringly.

'We did it, Pete. We got clear. Fuck Ismail and the rest of those fucks!'

The hopper dusted down, scattering blinding sand far and wide. Chisholm and Rodriguez all but bodily lifted Goodman inside the aircraft as the side door slid open. Cooper waved them away and kept his borrowed pistol trained on the now smoking ruins of the courtyard. He pulled Stanley past and held position as the remaining squad members climbed aboard, turning at the last moment to take Chisholm's hand as the hopper started to lift. The ground fell away with dizzying speed as the VTOL aircraft accelerated towards orbit. The real mission accomplished, the JLTVs broke contact and sped towards the border with Turkey, their size diminishing from that of small dogs to ants in the space of a breath as the hopper climbed rapidly. Cooper tracked back towards the Caliphate position in time to catch the flash, unmistakeable even at a distance.

Stanley toggled on his comms. 'Rivera, we got incoming.'

'I see them. You boys better hold tight.'

The angle of the hopper's ascent increased and Cooper heard the dull thudding of chaff deployment charges, followed a couple of seconds later by the far louder detonation of a surface-to-air missile.

'Damn it!' Rivera cursed over the intercom. 'The other's still locked.'

Cooper twisted one of his arms through a cargo netting strap as he heard the sonic boom of a pulse detonator. The hopper shook, taking shrapnel as the remaining missile exploded at close range. He heard the tortured whine of a failing engine, the squeal rising in pitch as Rivera coaxed the stricken craft towards the edge of the atmosphere. Cooper's knuckles whitened as the nails of his free hand dug into his palm. It couldn't end like this. Not when he was so close to finally seeing his family again. The random cruelty of such a death was almost too much to bear. If there was a god or any kind of justice in the universe he had to live. He offered up a rare moment of silent prayer. The whining ceased as the hopper levelled out, skimming the atmosphere before commencing its descent towards Akrotiri Air Base in Cyprus. Cooper flicked his eyes towards the heavens and let out a whoop of joy, which was taken up by the rest of the crew.

'Talk to me, Rivera,' Stanley barked

'We're down to one engine and the tail assembly has taken some damage, but nothing I can't compensate for. Suggest you sit down, strap in and enjoy the rest of this RSAF flight to freedom.'

Chisholm clapped Stanley on the shoulder. 'Fortune favours the brave, Bob.'

'It does that.'

Cooper watched Stanley move down the cabin, his brief nod to each man a silent acknowledgement of the part they had played in the success of the mission. It was the kind of easy camaraderie Cooper had imagined when he enlisted. But neither Tyler nor his replacement, Willard, had ever shown that kind of warmth to the men under their command. Were Templars meant to be above such things? If so, why impress on them that they were sworn brothers with a sacred duty to one another? He looked over at Goodman; the corporal was white as a sheet, teeth clenched, sweat beading his brow.

'Relax, Pete. It's over.'

'Over? Yes, over for some!'

The tone in Goodman's voice alerted Cooper to the danger but he was too far away to intervene as the corporal grabbed the hilt of Stanley's Recon knife and pulled it free. Goodman's arm swung back and then forward, digging the point of the knife into the flesh below Stanley's vest. Chisolm leapt forward as Stanley spun away, his blood dripping on the decking. The sergeant swung a powerful haymaker that connected with Goodman's jaw and sent him sprawling. He gave Goodman no time to recover, rolling him onto his belly and securing his wrists behind his back with a pair of flex cuffs.

'Major?'

'I'm all right. Don't think he hit anything vital. Guess that's twice I've been lucky today.' Stanley rose shakily to his feet, blood seeping through the fingers of the hand he had pressed to the wound in his belly.

Cooper stared in shock at Goodman, unable to reconcile his sudden and unprovoked attack with the steadfast solider he had served with. It had to be PTSD or some other kind of mental break.

Stanley pointed at Cooper. 'Best secure our other friend.'

'Whoa there!' Cooper protested. 'I probably saved your life.'

'Yeah, which makes me all the keener to hold on to it. So don't make this any harder than it needs to be.'

Cooper looked round the cabin but found no allies in the shuttered expressions of the rescue team: guilty until proven innocent. His face darkened, but he held his hands out, wrists pressed together. Rodriguez looped the cuffs over his hands and pulled them tight, avoiding his eyes.

CHAPTER 44

Hirsch plipped the locks on the car and turned up the collar of his suit in response to the drizzle. He walked along the sidewalk, empty but for a trio of late-night revellers staggering their way towards a taxi rank. His hand crept instinctively towards the butt of the pistol holstered beneath his left arm. The men passed, laughing drunkenly, and Hirsch breathed out. Ahead, the garish neon signage of Rick's Café Americain lit up the boulevard. Hirsch hurried on.

The heat hit him like a blow as he pushed through the ornately sculpted doors. He saw the house hologram start towards him and waved it away. 'Not tonight, Bogie.'

The hologram shrugged, produced a cigarette case from an inside suit pocket and extracted a cigarette. It tapped the end of the cigarette three times on the case and put it to its lips. The hologram made a show of searching for a lighter and a couple of seconds later a woman with platinum blonde hair detached herself from the bar and walked across. The Bogart hologram inclined its head to accept the proffered light. Smoked curled up towards the lazily rotating ceiling fan.

'I thought I told you to stay away, Ilsa?'

'You did, but we both know I couldn't. Oh, Rick, you've got to help us. If not for me, get those papers for Victor.'

Hirsch tore himself away from the floor show. Looked like the café was expanding its repertoire. He scanned the room and caught sight of the lithe figure seated at one of the rear tables. The coloured beads of the table lamp painted Tazi's face a multitude of colours as she bent her head to take a sip of her drink. She nodded the briefest of acknowledgements as he pulled out one of the ornate wooden chairs and sat down.

He tapped the bar console on the table and ordered himself a beer. 'Can I get you anything, Alia?'

Tazi ran a finger along the rim of her half-full glass, apparently undecided. 'What the hell – Vesper martini.'

'Glad to see you made bail. How are you?'

'Looking over my shoulder. Some of your colleagues didn't take too kindly to me making fools of them. Some of the more hard of thinking might be tempted to try and even the score down the line. Otherwise, it's on to the next contract. Don't mind telling you that business is brisk.'

'Looks like your investment in Lynch paid off, huh?'

'Is that reproach I hear in your voice? It doesn't suit you. Not given your past.'

'I like to think I'm paying for my sins. Y'know, Lynch made me just before he left.'

'Did he, now? Well, I wouldn't worry. I suspect he'll have bigger stories to break than your resurrection from the dead. Speaking of which, have you heard from him?'

'Yeah, he needed a contact for some medicine. Russell took a turn for the worse. Hardly surprising. But he seems a tough old bird.'

'They do say atonement is a wonderful thing. But I guess you'd know all about that.'

'Funny. You know what the last thing my old partner said to me before I left was? "You've been sentenced to life. Whether you're behind bars or not, there won't be a day goes by you don't think about what you've done." Man, was he right. But you know what? I don't think it could have played out any other way. The city's a better place now. I have to believe that.'

Tazi shrugged. 'Whatever gets you through the day. Me, I'm all about the money.'

'The lady protests too much. Looks to me as if you might have caught a dose of that nasty bout of idealism that's going about. Turns out there isn't a vaccine for that shit.'

'At least I wasn't born with it. Unlike some I could mention.'

'You reckon? Did you know we got an anonymous tip off about the CIA spook responsible for destroying Lynch's apartment block? The same one that put a bullet in you. Found him lying in the parking lot of the El Hank lighthouse – no danger of him running away on account of the fact somebody had rendered him paraplegic by snapping his spine between the T7 and T8 vertebrae. Turns out his name is Joseph Walker – ex Templar special forces. Actually served in the same unit Lynch was embedded with in Israel.'

'And this is a problem?'

'Normally it would be. But the Agency is claiming Walker went off the reservation, was on some sort of personal vendetta. Point is that luck and good judgement aren't the same thing. I'd hate you to have to leave Morocco.'

'Much as I'm touched by your concern, Africa is a big continent. Plenty of places a woman like me can apply her skill set.'

'Maybe so. But I got to figure there's a reason you quit the armed forces. Figure you maybe decided it was time for a little stability in your life.'

Tazi shook her head and laughed. She picked up her drink and put it down again as the laughter continued. When it finally subsided she said, 'And you reckon you could be part of that stability?'

'What? No. That's not what I meant. I don't know if it'll make a damn bit of difference in the long term, but you did a good thing for Lynch. You didn't have to, and I appreciate the favour. I'd hate to see you get in trouble over it. So this is me telling you to be careful. Nothing more than that.'

For a second he thought Tazi was going to come back with another sarcastic comment, but then her face grew serious.

'Ok. Thanks for the advice and the drink. I need to head off. Look after yourself.'

Hirsch permitted himself a rueful smile as he watched her leave. He never did have any luck with women. He drained his beer and ordered another. He knew the advice he had given Tazi was as much for himself as her. Commandant Idrissi was no fool. From now on he would have to tread extra carefully.

Tazi's com-unit buzzed in her pocket. She pulled it out and saw the swirling fractals of an encrypted call. Her lips twitched in a smile as she hit answer and heard the distinctive drawl on the other end.

'This a courtesy call, Lynch, or is there something I can do for you?'

'What? No.' Lynch sounded taken aback. His voice was hesitant as he continued, edging into unfamiliar territory. 'I, well I guess I just wanted to check you were okay. Hope the cops weren't too hard on you?'

'Let's say they were no bigger assholes than usual. Commandant Idrissi is pragmatic enough to realise dragging me through the courts would be an embarrassment to the *Sûreté Nationale*.'

'So long as you're not in trouble. I'd hate to think I'd gotten you jammed up.'

'That's twice I've heard that today. But I'm a big girl. I can take care of myself.'

'I know that. And I know I can be a total pain in the ass. I just wanted to let you know I appreciate everything you've done for me. It's no exaggeration to say I owe you my life.

I won't forget that.'

'Hey, the clue's in the job title – close protection officer.'

'If you ever need a testimonial…'

'No need. You're already trending off the scale. Got more offers of work than I know what to do with. Should more than cover whatever fine they slap me with.'

Tazi heard the clank of tracks and the sound of running feet in the background. Someone called out Lynch's name and an engine revved.

'Look, I gotta go. But check my socials – my next broadcast will be viral!'

The call cut out before Tazi could reply. She smiled ruefully. Lynch was certainly one of life's originals. She doubted her next client would be half as interesting, but while he was right, he was a pain in the ass.

CHAPTER 45

I smail put his shoulder to the hatch and pushed. The resistance was heavy but he felt some give and pressed with all his might. The hatch moved upwards and he heard rubble slide clear as the angle increased, then the weight was gone and the hatch clattered to the side, sending up plumes of dust.

Ismail coughed as he emerged into the ruins of the villa. He stood within the narrow pool of light cast from the basement and surveyed the damage. The missiles had detonated outside the villa, blowing in the patio doors and ripping through the main living area. Part of the ceiling had collapsed and beyond it the stars were visible through a hole in the roof. The American infidels were nothing if not predictable. He knew they would come for his captives and had recognised the attack to the north-east as a feint. Many had embraced martyrdom to convince the infidels that their ruse had fooled Ismail. But the marshal knew their sacrifice would not be in vain.

He picked his way through the ruins of the villa, emerging into the courtyard and skirting round the crater left by the missiles. He was careful not to look away from the bloody remains of his fallen troops; severed limbs, coils of spilled intestines, the eyes that now stared sightlessly. These deaths were upon his orders and to shrink from them would be to dishonour the fallen. He would see to it that their earthly remains were recovered, bathed, shrouded and buried within twenty-four hours.

Ismail traversed the length of the courtyard, arriving at its southern wall. He surveyed the two empty cages and the jagged hole blown through the wall to provide an exit. It would have been simple to boobytrap the cages to prevent the two Templars being extracted alive, but that did not suit Ismail's purpose. He had forged his arrows carefully and let them fly. If it was the will of Allah, they would reach their target. If not, he would form another plan, and another, not resting until either death claimed him or the Caliphate drove the infidels from their lands.

Cooper looked round the foxhole, uncertain how he had got there. Sergeant Jackson was to his left, rifle held at the ready, lips moving soundlessly. Goodman's dead eyes stared up at him from the base of the foxhole, a neat hole in the centre of his forehead, the left rear quarter of his skull missing, blood and brains oozing onto the dull earth. No. That wasn't right. Was it?

'Cooper, pull your shit together. Did you see where the shot came from?'

Cooper shook his head, as much to cover his own confusion, as to provide a reply. He had no memory of the shot. No recollection of how they came to be in the foxhole or even where they were or who the enemy was.

'Shit. Get ready to fire.'

'Sarge?'

His question went unanswered as Jackson heaved himself from the foxhole and sprinted towards the carcass of a burned-out car, weaving from side to side as angry hornets took chunks out of the tarmac around his feet. Cooper caught the muzzle flash, one fifty metres to his right, elevation ten metres, third-storey window of a long-abandoned department store. He checked his rifle was on auto, raised it to his shoulder and loosed a long, rattling burst. Glass and cladding panels fell to ground in a rain of razor-sharp shards.

Jackson peered tentatively round the front of the car. Silence. The sergeant raised his arm and swept it forward; move out. Cooper squatted, removed Goodman's dog tags and placed them in an empty magazine pouch on his vest. He hesitated, then closed Goodman's eyes.

The room spun and Cooper swayed on his stool. A series of empty beer and shot glasses littered the bar. His blurred vision swam into focus and he took in the wood panelling and corroded tin-plate signs that lined the walls of Tipsy McStagger's. Wasn't all leave cancelled? Yet here he was. Home. And that was all that mattered. He picked up his shot glass and drained it. Dropped it back on the bar with a clunk.

A mop of unruly blonde hair blotted out the surroundings as Donny bent in close to whisper in his ear.

'You get what I'm saying, right? There's plenty of folks in these parts, across the whole damn country, who are sick of the way things is being run. The government, the Church – they don't care about the little people, the workers, the ones who keep this country of ours running. They took away our right to protest. Hell, they even took away our right to comment. You post some shit on the socials they don't like, the man comes in the middle of the night and puts you in some off-book hole you never get out of. It ain't right. You know it ain't right, Billy Ray. You been out in the sandpit, seen first-hand the shit we're doing in the name of the people. Well, there's a group of us ain't gonna stand for that no more. Time was, we was a proud nation of fifty states – the time has come to restore the union, make our country whole again. If they won't let us do it at the ballot box, we just gonna have to take it by force. Storm the Capitol. Show those pigs we mean business and our business is mean. You get me?'

Cooper pulled away.

'Jesus, Donny! You can't be saying that shit in public. They'll lock your ass up and throw away the key.'

'That's my point, bro. We don't live in no democracy no more. We gotta fight like those first Founding Fathers. Make this a country we can all be proud of again. More than half the country is out of work, living on state handouts. Where's the dignity in that? Yet every year we spend billions fighting a war that never ends. What for? Not like we can use the oil no more. And who cares if the Jews have a country to call their own? Not me. Not my dog. That terrorist threat they keep going on about? Reckon those A-rabs would be happy to leave us be if'n we let them be too. The militia could use a man like you, Billy Ray. A soldier. What you say? You in?'

Cooper pushed himself to his feet. 'No way. That's… Shit, I don't know what that is. But I'm having no part of it. You hear me?'

The room was cramped, packed full of hastily assembled equipment to convert it into a lab. Steiner's complaints as to its inadequacies had fallen on deaf ears; examination of the subject was of critical importance, a point underlined by the fact he had been all but thrown on a suborbital flight to Akrotiri Air Base. His equipment requisition had followed on a Galaxy Ultra transporter a day later, during which time he had examined Goodman. A lassitude had overcome the corporal following his attack on Stanley, and when questioned he could provide no reason or motive. But in every simulation he had shown a desire to kill, destroy or betray friends, family and comrades. Steiner would have liked to dig deeper, identify the means of programming, but the decision had been taken to prioritise Cooper to determine if it was safe to ship him back stateside. The president wanted a success story to parade before the voters.

Steiner looked up from the screen. Cooper lay prone on the VR couch, head and eyes covered by the helmet and its visor. Lightly sedated, his chest rose and fell in a slow and steady pattern.

'Well, doctor? Are we dealing with another Manchurian Candidate? The last thing we need is to send a sleeper agent back home, particularly one with a Templar's training and experience.'

Steiner looked over at the holo-screen through which Deputy Director Hannah was viewing the proceedings.

'His behaviour, in terms of social and moral values, appears unaltered. Or as unaltered as you can reasonably expect for someone with his combat experience.'

'I'm sensing a "but" here.'

Steiner swiped up an image on his datapad.

'These are images of Cooper's memory engrams taken just before he completed the Templar selection process. And these I took this morning. We see substantial changes. Some could be attributed to trauma, as evidenced by extensive PTSD studies.'

'But not all,' Hannah interrupted.

'No. Here, in the hippocampus, we can see both degradation and strengthening of episodic and semantic memories – a rewriting of personal experience and factual understanding. To what end, I have yet to determine.'

'Perhaps you'd care to indulge me with some speculation?'

'Based on Goodman's behaviour, I'd say he's been programmed to react to a specific person or persons – your Manchurian Candidate theory.'

'Can you determine who or what?'

'Not from the scans. I'd need to implant a neuro-link, a brain–computer interface. The procedure is not completely without risk, the brain being a delicate instrument.'

'Cooper signed the standard release forms when he enlisted. Get him prepped for surgery.'

Steiner looked from the now blank screen to his patient. Sleep had relaxed his features, making him look almost child-like. Then again, twenty wasn't so far into adulthood. He sighed and put through a call for Cooper to be transferred to the medical wing.

Neuro-link technology had originally been pioneered as a means of treating paralysis and diseases such as Parkinson's, allowing stimulation and control of neurons within the neocortex. But the ability to augment the brain and link it directly to technology that could be controlled by thought had been recognised from the outset and the technology developed accordingly.

Steiner watched as the robotic neurosurgeon installed the links to the neurons that controlled movement, memory, thought and emotion, using a laser drill to penetrate the skull to allow insertion of thousands of flexible micron-scale threads. The interface chip would be constructed by injectable nanotech and communicate wirelessly, the programmable units enabling upgrades while in situ. On completion, he would be able to decode and visualise Cooper's memory engrams.

A cue flashed up on the neurosurgeon's screen and Steiner tapped it to confirm delivery of the nanotech. He keyed the screen to full magnification and watched the formation of the chip's key elements, starting with the processor and its linking to the threads, followed by the inductive charger that would wirelessly charge the battery. As each link was made data flowed to the diagnostic screen, where it was analysed and decoded. Steiner sifted and filtered the code, quickly revealing a recognisable pattern. Crude, but no less effective for all that. Sometimes it paid to keep it simple. He closed the link and ordered Cooper to be removed to recovery.

Deputy Director Hannah picked up on the first ring.

'I trust you have an answer for me?'

'I do. He has been subjected to a form of aversion therapy. First, to erode his faith and loyalty, then to engender fear and hatred of a specific target to such a degree as to induce a homicidal rage. Had we run a tox scan on Cooper's arrival, I suspect we would have found traces of emetine in his blood.'

'You can save the explanations and details for your formal report. Just tell me who the target is.'

'President Gerrard.' If Steiner had been hoping for a reaction to this revelation, he was disappointed. Nonplussed, he continued: 'It will be a simple process to remove it – severing the synapses between the affected neurons to prevent action potentials being sent from axon to dendrite. There may be some memory loss, but not to the extent where there will be a noticeable degradation of his cognitive abilities.'

Hannah tapped his lips with the edge of his forefinger. 'And would it be just as simple to alter the target? Say, for example, to Grand Master Vanderbilt?'

The colour drained from Steiner's face. 'I could program neurons of my own, certainly. But what you're asking is highly unethical, a violation of the Hippocratic oath.'

'Without quibbling over semantics, it would seem to me the harm has already been done. I'm merely asking you to redirect its outcome.' Hannah's lips compressed in a bloodless smile. 'You run a research fellowship, one that benefits from significant government grants which are up for review at the end of the year. It would be a pity if your funding was withdrawn.'

Indignity crept into Steiner's voice. 'You're blackmailing me?'

'I prefer to think of it as pointing out the realities of academia. There will always be someone coming up behind you, full of fresh energy and ideas, eager to cooperate. I take it we understand one another?'

'Absolutely,' Steiner said, sounding as though he would choke on the word.

'Good. Make the necessary changes and assign him six weeks R and R. Our boy is a war hero – make sure he looks like one when he returns home.'

'What about Goodman? Shall I remove his programming?'

'Do as you see fit. But lose him in the system for now. The official story is he's suffering from complex PTSD due to his treatment at the hands of the Caliphate. There's to be no talk of aversion therapy or brainwashing – I don't want anything to cast suspicion on Cooper. And Doctor, I trust I need not remind you that this is a matter of national security. If I hear even the faintest whisper of this, cancelled funding will be the least of your worries.'

CHAPTER 46

Cooper tilted the chair back until it was resting against the wall. At a little after four o'clock in the afternoon most of the day's heat had already dissipated, the faint breeze carrying the heady scent of honeysuckle. He looked out from the porch across the garden to where his father was skimming a mower across the already trim grass. Wayne Cooper, as if sensing his son's scrutiny, stopped and waved. Cooper saluted him with his glass of lemonade and rattled the ice before taking a sip. It tasted sharp and sweet, of lazy evenings spent on the porch after school, listening to the rattle of the cicadas. Life was full of simple things and idle pleasures that you never thought about or appreciated until you were thousands of miles away fighting for your life in a foreign country. He had imagined moments like this for so long he had started to believe the reality wouldn't live up to his fantasies. How wrong he had been.

They had flown him to Memphis where he was met by a handpicked selection of the press eager to know how it felt to finally be back on American soil. Cooper had reeled off the answers he'd been told to study on the flight back from Cyprus. *I feel blessed and grateful for my deliverance. I want to thank*

Major Stanley and the brave men of the Eighty-second Airborne Division for my rescue, and all those ordinary citizens for their thoughts and prayers during the long weeks of my captivity. Most of all I want to thank my family, who are waiting for me, so you must excuse me. And so he had departed in a storm of camera flashes.

Whatever else was propaganda, the words about his family were true. His escort had dropped him at a diner on the outskirts of Jonesboro where his mother, father, sister and brothers were waiting. That moment when he saw the joy and relief etched on their faces made everything he had been through worthwhile. Dale and Wade chatted excitedly while his mother tried to hush them; Shania sat kind of bashful, while his father, worried his emotions might bubble uncontrollably if he spoke, simply smiled. There had been good coffee and slices of an excellent blueberry pie, after which they had all piled into his father's beat-up Dodge Caravan MPV and covered the last few klicks to home.

Cooper rubbed his eyes with his knuckles in response to the treacherous pricking of tears. He set his glass aside and made his way round the side of the house. His mother was kneeling by the rockery, pulling weeds by hand, her face shaded by the ragged brim of a straw hat. White rockfoil, purple bellflowers and butter-yellow crocuses surrounded her in a riot of colour.

'Sure looks pretty, Ma.'

Patty Cooper pushed herself to her feet and wiped at the mud clinging to the knees of her floral print dress. She eyed the flowers critically.

'They're not so bad, but it was Granma Mae who had the real green thumb. I used to help her when I was a little girl. Guess some of it must have stuck.' She looked at his stubbled skull. 'You ought to put on a hat before you get burned. What did they say happened again?'

'I don't remember nothing, but I'm told I had some kind of bleed. They had to operate to relieve the pressure. Guess I'm real lucky they got me out when they did.'

His mother reached out patted his cheek. 'My brave

boy.'

Cooper reached up and took her hand. The nails were plain and unpainted, the skin callused from a lifetime of cooking, washing and cleaning, the hand of a hard-working wife and mother. She was good people.

'Billy Ray, you out in the garden?'

'Yeah,' Cooper answered his sister. 'I'm just talking to Ma.'

'You wanna come inside? I got something for you.'

Cooper shrugged his apology and made his way over to the screen door. It creaked as it opened onto the shade of the utility room. He found Shania in the kitchen, elbows resting on the table, a bright green apple held up for his approval. But his sister was no modern-day Eve; he already had too much knowledge of good and evil. What he needed instead were the waters of forgetfulness.

Cooper accepted the proffered apple and bit into it. He found it dry and slightly bitter, as was the case with most force-grown fruit. But it was the first fresh fruit he had tasted in months and he felt the weight of expectation as his sister looked on. He chewed the apple slowly, as if savouring it, before swallowing and licking his lips, a careful act to reassure his sister.

Memories of war were never far away. They haunted him in his moments of peace, turned dreams to nightmares that made him wake in a cold sweat, the enemy at his heels. Cooper forced the dark thoughts away, placed the apple core on the table and studied Shania.

She had matured still further since he had last seen her, but he saw care in her eyes that hadn't been there before. Had he put those worries there? Could he say or do anything to take them away?

Shania dipped her head and tucked a blonde curl of hair behind her ear, as she often did when nervous.

'You're staring.'

'Sorry, sis. Didn't mean to. There were times I never thought I'd see any of you again. This,' he waved a hand, 'still feels kind of unreal.'

Shania reached out, took his hand and gave it a squeeze. 'You know I'm here if you ever want to talk. Right?'

'I … appreciate that. I really do. But I don't want any of that darkness or horror touching you. I've got five more weeks of leave before I go back, and I'm going to need every good memory I can make.' He looked out of the kitchen window, saw his father still mowing the lawn. 'Let's just sit here and enjoy the morning.'

'Sure. If that's what you need.'

That was just it; Cooper wasn't sure what he needed. His family had welcomed him home like a conquering hero, the liberator of Jerusalem, scourge of the Caliphate. How could he tell them that their hero was a murderer of civilians and killer of child soldiers? Burden them with the knowledge he had committed those crimes for them? There were times he felt the words rush up inside him, ready to burst out. Then he saw his mother, carefree for the first time in years, like some heavy weight had been lifted from her. Or looked at his father's hands, the joints free from arthritic swelling after his nano-therapy. The truth would destroy their happiness; render all he had suffered through meaningless. So he would enjoy these few weeks of peace for their sake and then he would go back. Fight all the way to Baghdad if necessary. Whatever it took for them to release him from his vows.

Cooper looked round the bar room and felt a frisson of déjà vu. Hadn't he visited Tipsy McStagger's recently? But that was impossible.

Doctor Steiner had warned him he might experience flashbacks, memory loss, anxiety or anger as a result of his captivity and subsequent surgery. Was that what this was? Complex PTSD? If so, why wasn't the doctor treating him for it?

He took a deep breath and studied his surroundings, taking in the familiar: dark wood panelling, rusting tin-plate signs, the shelves that ran a couple of feet below the ceiling, stacked with foreign beer bottles and cans that had never been for sale in the bar. And there was Joe, the barman, polishing a glass as he waited for the next customer. As if on cue, the bell above the door rang as someone opened it and Cooper turned to see the squat figure of his childhood friend.

Mike's hair was thinner on top and his features were doughy from too much alcohol and junk food. Cooper waited a beat, but his initial assessment was correct; Mike had come alone. He suspected this would be the case, but it still hurt.

Cooper slid off his stool and held out his hand. Mike looked at him, laughed, and hauled him into a hug. Cooper noticed his clothes smelled of damp and his body of stale sweat. He pushed Mike away with a tap to the shoulder.

'No Donny?'

'Er…'

'Come on, Mike. Out with it.'

'Says he ain't drinking with anyone who murders Muslims for the government.'

Cooper staggered back against his stool as images of the school bus flashed before him.

'Don't take it personal, man. You know Donny's full of that conspiracy shit.'

'Yeah.' Cooper forced a laugh. 'Guess that first beer must have gone to my head. Speaking of which.' He held up two fingers. 'Joe.'

The barman nodded in response and moved over to the taps. Cooper waved Mike to the stool next to him. A beer slid across the bar to meet him as he sat. Cooper's own beer arrived a few seconds later. He gulped down half of it and stared moodily into the mirror behind the bar.

'You remember the last time we sat here? I'd just completed my selection for the Templars and was due to ship out for active service. Donny was so pissed at me. Guess he still is.'

'Like I said. Wouldn't take it personal. Man has got a lot of anger. He got to put it somewhere. Nobody likes to feel helpless. Least if it's a conspiracy he can do something to fight back against it. Otherwise, this is just random shit happening to us we ain't got no control over.'

'And what do you think?'

'Me?' Mike raised his glass and drained it. 'I try not to think at all. Get my welfare cheque and push as much of it as I can across this here bar. Like you said, it ain't much of a life, but it's the only one I got. Not everyone's as strong as you.'

Cooper signalled for another round. 'Don't know if it was strength or weakness made me sign up.'

'You say that. But you got to be one tough mother to make it through selection for the Templars. Don't want or need to know what you done over there. I can see enough of it in your face. But you got out like you wanted. Maybe that's come at a price you didn't expect, but shit.' Mike prodded himself. 'You really want to be a boozehound like me?'

'Being a bit hard on yourself there.'

'Don't feel sorry for myself and I don't need you to either. Made my choice. Same as yourself.'

Cooper fell silent. Mike was right. They had made their choices and there was no going back. But he should have known meeting in McStagger's was a bad idea. Next time he'd try to get him in the park, or maybe at the diner, somewhere with memories from when they were kids, somewhere they could both try to forget the present. In the meantime, food was a good idea. The burgers, if nothing special, were edible.

He waved to attract the barman's attention and then caught the tickertape across the bottom of the holo-screen.

'Joe, turn the sound up, will you?'

President Gerrard's voice crackled from the speakers.

'Today our forces have achieved a historic victory in Syria, with all cities and regions now under American control. The Caliphate is in full retreat, with much of Jordan also liberated from the Islamist yoke of terror. While we are not complacent in any way, we recognise the need for a period of consolidation in the wake of what has been a long and costly campaign. As I address you, two hundred thousand additional support troops are being mobilised to the Middle East, where they will be involved in the constitution of democratically elected governments in Syria, Jordan and Lebanon. For it is not this administration's way, nor the American way, to occupy foreign countries. Instead, we will remain in an advisory capacity to ensure the smooth transition to these newly founded democracies.

'Earlier, I alluded to the long and arduous campaign endured by the soldiers of our great republic. No force has fought harder or with more distinction than our Templar special forces. Throughout the campaign they have been in the vanguard of the action; first liberating Israel and then spearheading the ongoing attacks against Islamist insurgents in Syria. As devout and dedicated as these true Soldiers of Christ are, they are still but men. In recognition of this and of their glorious achievements on the field of battle I have agreed with Grand Master Vanderbilt that all Templars are to be withdrawn from the theatre of war and granted four weeks leave before being re-equipped and redeployed for the final assault against the Islamic Caliphate. May God speed them home and preserve the Republic.'

'What does that mean for you, man?'

The image of Gerrard filled Cooper's mind. He felt the sting of pain and looked down to discover he had clenched his fists tight enough to drive his fingernails into his palms. A wave of rage crept over him as Gerrard's face was replaced by another, and then the mood was gone, leaving behind an icy calm.

Mike waved his hand in front of Cooper's face. 'I said, what's that mean for you?'

'I guess it means a temporary stay of execution.'

'Say what?'

'We're effectively being furloughed until they're ready to throw us back into the meatgrinder.'

CHAPTER 47

F ree *America Interview Transcript #1: Jefferson Lynch in conversation with Gina Pulaski, leader of the Free America Movement, Capitol Hill, Washington, DC.*

Jefferson Lynch: I am joined this evening by former US Senator Gina Pulaski. For the benefit of younger subscribers, you served under President Garcia, the fiftieth president of the US Republic?

Gina Pulaski: That's correct, Jefferson. Santiago Garcia was the last duly elected president of the United States prior to the Great Flood, during which he, along with so many others in America and across the globe, lost his life. I continued to serve in the Democratic administration when Vice President Kecia Williams assumed the presidency in his stead.

JL: Some would say you did more than serve — yours was one of the most strident voices in Congress pressing for military action against the seceded states, which would ultimately become the Religious States of America under the presidency of Woody Lyndhurst. Would I be correct in saying that to this day you still do not recognise Lyndhurst's legitimacy, or that of any of his successors, including the incumbent, Charles Gerrard?

GP: Absolutely. They seized control of those states under a false manifesto and maintain power through falsehood.

JL: That's a strong claim. Care to elaborate?

GP: The Great Flood was a tragedy, but it was one of our own making – not the act of some vengeful Old Testament God. Years of ecological abuse, compounded by the detonation, either by accident or design, of a nuclear warhead over the Arctic Circle is the responsibility of humanity and humanity alone.

JL: But you do consider yourself a Christian?

GP: The operative word here is 'Christ'. I follow the teachings of the Gospels. God sacrificed His only Son so that our sins might be expiated.

JL: And yet you're not averse to an eye for an eye. Yours, as I've said, was one of the loudest voices calling for war against the secessionists. A second civil war, as we stand beside the ruins of the Capitol Building, that had fateful consequences.

GP [forced laughter]: I thought this was supposed to be a friendly interview?

JL: Then you haven't followed my work as closely as you claim. The truth has no friends. You're here, today, addressing the citizens of the Religious States, challenging their government and legitimacy; it's only right they should know who you are and what you stand for.

GP [angry]: I stand for the restoration of the United States and all that it stood for. An end to the costly ideological war in the Middle East, that only exists to make the arms manufacturers rich. I stand for truth and justice. Liberty and freedom.

JL: But do you? Or have you spent the last forty years harbouring a grudge and dreaming of former glories? You talk of ending ideological wars, but is the war you're calling for any less driven by belief?

GP: Of course it's driven by belief — faith in the Founding Principles that made our nation the greatest in the world. The Republic endured for two hundred and seventy-four years, before being torn apart by fundamentalists and zealots. It wasn't perfect but it was progressive, progress that has been steadily wound back for the citizens of the RSA, particularly women.

JL: Telling someone they're oppressed doesn't actually make them oppressed. Women in the RSA enjoy far more freedoms and rights than their counterparts in the Caliphate.

GP: It's easy to say they have the right to an education, to work, to drive, to go out in public without being accompanied by a man, to bare their faces and legs, and are accordingly 'free'. But what about the assault on women's reproductive rights? The dismantling of Roe versus Wade? The fact that women have all but disappeared from the boardroom and Congress? Where once it was the norm, now it has very much become an exception, even an aberration! Yes, women are free in the RSA — free to get married, stay at home and raise children. The clock has been turned back by more than a century! How is that progress?

JL: That's obviously something you feel passionate about, and I'll concede the point — freedom is indeed relative. But what about race relations? America is more unified than at any time in its history.

GP: That's another sleight of hand. America has swapped the Black bogeyman for a Muslim one. It's not equality, respect or mutual goals that binds the RSA together, it's fear of the 'other'. I am here today to serve notice that it's time for the fear to end. America deserves better. America can have better.

JL: Even if it means plunging the country into a third civil war?

GP: No one wants war. And it can be easily avoided. All President Gerrard has to do is step down, and for his administration to work constructively with us to restore the United States of America. I see no reason why this can't be a peaceful transition.

JL: But if Gerrard refuses to go, you will fight? That's what you've spent all these years preparing for, why you have built and equipped an army?

GP [pause]: As a patriot, dedicated to liberty, I will fight. However unwillingly.

JL: Thank you for clarifying that, and thank you for your time, Ms Pulaski. This has been Jefferson Lynch, broadcasting for Free America.

GP [low audio, caught on JL's mic]: Just what the fuck was that?

JL: That was me giving you some credibility. Your stage-managed puff piece wasn't going to win any hearts and minds. Frankly, I doubt much is going to make any impression on that bunch of sheep. I'd say it's your funeral, but it's going to be a lot of other people's, besides.

GP: Don't forget you're here at my sufferance, you arrogant sonofabitch. You ever ambush me like that again and you're done. Are we clear?

JL: Yeah. I understand you exactly.

Transcript Ends

Lynch unscrewed the cap from his hip flask and raised it in salute to the Capitol Building. He zoomed in via his camera drones, first taking in the cracked and shattered neoclassical pillars of the East Front Plaza, then rising up to view the streaks of rust that stained the once white Capitol Dome, finishing with the decapitated Statue of Freedom that surmounted it. Once, it had been home to the Senate and the House of Representatives. Now, it was just a shell, looted first by the conquering RSA troops and subsequently stripped of anything of value by those clinging to existence in the wasteland left behind. Symbolically, it still had to count for something. Why else make the trip out here for the broadcast? But if Lynch had learned nothing else, it was that stone, metal and wood could not define freedom and democracy. He uttered a sigh and recalled the drones to the docking station on his belt. He had named them Truth and Justice, marking each one with its respective name in Day-Glo paint. At least their mission was clear.

Lynch looked round, saw Jones and Pulaski huddled together in conversation, no doubt planning their better America. Pulaski still looked agitated. Maybe he should have stuck to the script, but he'd meant what he said; blandishments weren't going to win the people over. Even supposing Free America won, which was by no means certain, American reunification was a project that would take decades to accomplish. The remaining states of the Union were impoverished, their largely agrarian economy devoted to feeding their own people. The RSA's economy was firmly on a war footing, with high unemployment rates; the merging of the two would cause a drop in living standards and make prosecuting the war against the Caliphate impossible. Rebuilding the country would require a series of bold and imaginative public works programmes and reforms not seen since Roosevelt's New Deal. It would take a charismatic and ambitious leader, with the public's full backing, to push through such legislation. Pulaski clearly wanted the crown, but from what he had seen of her she was too bitter and hawkish to ignite widespread support. She had the chops for a war leader, but winning the peace was an altogether different matter. It would require a less partisan figure to reunite the American people.

Lynch turned his head in response to Jones' shout. The

jeep was ready to move out, Pulaski already inside, Jones standing expectantly beside the rear passenger door. Lynch stole another glance at the Capitol Building before nodding his acknowledgement and starting towards the jeep. He stepped round Freedom's giant bronze head, the eagle and feathers atop her helmet warped and bent by the impact of her long-ago fall. Maybe one day, when all of this was over, they would put Freedom's head back on her shoulders. Maybe not. It was only a statue belonging to a ruined building, symbolising something long lost.

APPENDIX A: TIMELINE

2030

Israel annexes the West Bank. International outcry follows and Jordan, Lebanon and the UAE sever diplomatic ties, leaving Israel increasingly isolated. Egypt admits thousands of Palestinians through the Rafah Border Crossing. US President Harris attempts to broker a withdrawal but fails to follow through on her threat to cut military aid in the wake of an increased threat to Israel from Iran.

American airstrikes target Iranian airbases. Iranian forces target American troops in Iraq, resulting in 53 fatalities. America seeks to legitimise war with Iran via the UN Security Council, but China and Russia use their vetoes. America responds by vetoing a resolution condemning Israel's annexation of the West Bank.

2031

China applies pressure to broker a peace deal after the escalating conflict closes the Strait of Hormuz, affecting trade. America reluctantly ceases military action against Iran in a bid to avoid a growing trade war with China.

2034

Hamas rocket attacks on Beersheba, Jerusalem and Tel Aviv kill 63 civilians and 11 IDF soldiers. Israel responds with airstrikes and a ground invasion of the Gaza Strip. Operation Bronze Spear lasts for three days, with 23 Israeli and 2,732 Palestinian fatalities. The operation destroys critical infrastructure, along with housing and hospitals. The US government again defends Israel's right to self-defence.

Defeated and destitute, much of the surviving civilian populace begins the exodus to Egypt.

2041

A resurgent ISIS in Iraq and Syria gains control of Lebanon and Jordan and cements itself as a new Islamic Caliphate. The USA deploys an additional 100,000 troops in an attempt to relieve Jordan and assist rebels in Syria. High casualties generate negative headlines in the US.

2043

Escalating tensions between India and Pakistan result in a minor nuclear exchange. Although targets are primarily military, civilian casualties are estimated at 250,000. Fallout affects areas of China and Afghanistan. China responds by sending relief aid and 'peacekeeping' troops to Afghanistan and Pakistan, strengthening the ties of the early twenty-first century Shanghai Cooperation Organisation.

The UN General Assembly attempts to broker an agreement on multilateral nuclear disarmament. China, Russia, the USA, Israel and North Korea refuse to sign. The UK, France, Pakistan and India disarm.

2044

The killing of 84 Turkish troops by Russian-backed forces in Syria results in escalating conflict between Russia and Turkey.

2045

Russian forces withdraw from Syria as part of an agreed peace deal with Turkey. The Islamic Caliphate takes advantage of the power vacuum to seize total control of Syria.

2047

American forces, brought to a standstill by the Islamic Caliphate, withdraw unconditionally from the Middle East. The withdrawal proves highly divisive with the American public, many of whom at a time of growing ecological disasters and global pandemics have embraced Creationist forms of Christianity.

2049

No one admits responsibility for the aerial detonation of a nuclear device over the Arctic Circle. Opinion remains divided between terrorist attack and the mal-operation of a military defence satellite. Either way, it makes little difference to the victims of the tidal wave that follows the vaporisation of the Arctic sea ice. North America and Western Europe bear the brunt of the disaster, with large tracts of Alaska, California, Hawaii, Maine, Massachusetts, Rhode Island, New York, Connecticut, New Jersey, Delaware and Maryland remaining under water. England, Norway, Denmark, the Netherlands and the west coasts of Belgium, France and Spain are similarly devastated.

US President Santiago Garcia is killed by the tsunami. Vice President Kecia Williams assumes the presidency, but with much of the infrastructure of the northern states destroyed she is powerless to prevent the country descending into anarchy. A short and bloody second American civil war ensues when 26 American states (South Carolina, Mississippi, Florida, Alabama, Georgia, Louisiana, Texas, Virginia, Arkansas, North Carolina, Tennessee, Kentucky, Missouri, Delaware, West Virginia, Maryland, Oklahoma, Nevada, New Mexico, Arizona, Utah,

Wyoming, Nebraska, Illinois, Indiana, Ohio), secede from the Union and form the Christian fundamentalist territory of the Religious States of America, with Richmond, Virginia as the capital. The secessionists' intention is to continue the decades-long war with the Islamic Caliphate in the Middle East.

Construction of Europa City begins, to provide emergency accommodation for millions displaced by the Great Flood.

2050

Woody Lyndhurst is sworn in as the First President of the Religious States of America. The remaining US states request financial aid from the International Monetary Fund, while refugees flee across the border into Canada. With no functioning federal or state governments, the former US states became lawless no-go zones ruled only by the gun.

The RSA withdraws from the United Nations. Russia follows suit, together with a number of the former Soviet Republics, which proves to be a precursor to what follows.

2051–2053

Following the financial collapse of many of the Eastern European Union countries, Russia steps in with financial and military aid, effectively annexing Estonia, Latvia, Lithuania, Belarus, Ukraine, Georgia and Kazakhstan into the Greater Russian Collective.

2052

Having requested direct military aid to restore law and order, South Dakota, Idaho and Oregon are formally admitted to the RSA.

2054–2055

Following the collapse of oil prices in the wake of green technologies, the majority of Saudi Arabia falls to the Islamic Caliphate. Oman and the UAE help preserve its southernmost regions. Diplomatic channels are opened with the RSA in the hope of securing military assistance.

2055–2070

A series of typhoons and rising sea levels devastate Japan, Taiwan, Singapore, Indonesia and the Philippines. An influx of refugees fleeing the damage allows North Africa to establish itself as a cyber technology capital, and the foremost supplier of the emerging nanotech market.

2056

In response to the expansion of the Islamic Caliphate, RSA President Lyndhurst signs off on the creation of a new military order of Templars. Drawn from existing special forces units across the military, they are an elite force dedicated to defeating the Islamic Caliphate. Like their predecessors, they take a vow of celibacy, believing that the lack of dependents will make them more willing to make the ultimate sacrifice.

2057

Templar forces establish operational bases in Jerusalem, Haifa, Tel Aviv and Eilat at the behest of the Israeli government.

2061

The Islamic Caliphate attacks Israel. Backed by the RSA and supported by an unprecedented airlift of vital supplies, Israeli forces hold out for two years.

2063

Caliphate forces finally overrun Jerusalem. A detachment of Templars covers the final air evacuation of Israeli forces. The Templars, led by Commander Maxwell Lewis, fight to the death. The Caliphate broadcasts images of their mutilated corpses worldwide.

2065

An accidental deployment of a targeted nano-virus kills in excess of two million people in the Khyber Pakhtunkhwa region of Pakistan before it is contained. In the wake of the disaster, governments around the world sign the North–West Frontier Accord, which outlaws all weaponised nanotechnology.

2066

First Crusade. Utilising Cyprus as a spearhead, the RSA launches a series of air strikes targeting military installations in occupied Israel and the surrounding countries of Lebanon and Jordan. A ground assault on Haifa led by Templar forces ends in a bloody defeat with sixty per cent casualties. The campaign is abandoned amid public outcry.

2069

Seeking fuel for its war machine and a staging point for future military action in the Middle East, the RSA annexes Kuwait, initiating a series of conflicts that will be known collectively as the Oil Wars.

2070–2075

RSA special forces engage in a series of covert actions in Iran, Iraq and Jordon, primarily with the aim of intelligence-gathering for a fresh crusade. Operations, including the assassination of high-ranking Caliphate officers, continue in these territories until the middle of the decade.

2071–2073

Second Crusade. Air strikes and a prolonged ground assault allow the RSA to take control of Israel and parts of Lebanon. Jerusalem remains out of reach and Islamic Caliphate counter-attacks soon wrest back control of the territory.

2074

Kuwaiti insurgents rebel against the American occupation. The RSA's response is led by Templar Captain Isaac Vaughan. Vaughan takes less than three months to put down the uprising, executing its leaders live on air. Vaughan is promoted to the rank of colonel.

2075–2076

Dubbed 'Vicious Vaughan' and 'Colonel Killcrazy' by the tabloid press for authorising the use of heavy ordnance and fuel-air strikes against the civilian populations of Iran and Iraq, Vaughan is recalled to Richmond in August following an official complaint by the United Nations and asked to account for his actions before a Senate inquiry. Believing himself betrayed by a government that will not commit to a war of total attrition to defeat the Islamic nations, Vaughan resigns his commission and embarks on a public-speaking tour of the RSA to promote his book, The Enemy Within.

2079

Vaughan assumes the position of Chairman of the Board of the Tessler Corporation in Europa City. Over the next three years he triples its profits by using his military contacts in the RSA to secure contracts for the supply of experimental cyber-ware.

2079–2083

Third Crusade (Saudi Campaign). Having twice failed to take Jerusalem, the next Crusade focuses on liberating Saudi Arabia from the Caliphate and depriving it of the oil reserves used to fuel its war machine. Islamic Caliphate forces are successfully driven back to Syria and Jordan.

2089

Fourth Crusade. Bolstered by Christian recruits from Eastern Europe and the Greater Russian Collective, the RSA amasses an army of one million frontline troops.

Saturation bombing lays waste to Lebanon and the western borders of Syria and Jordan. RSA forces then launch a three-pronged attack through Lebanon and Jordan in the east, via Egypt in the west, violating Egyptian airspace to land ground troops on Israel's western border, and by sea with direct beach landings. A protracted and bloody ground war of attrition follows as they fight to retake Israel foot by foot, culminating in the bloody siege of Jerusalem.

With the city devastated by long-range bombardment, the Templars, now joined by the Israel Defense Forces, launch a final assault on Jerusalem. No quarter is given or asked for as the surviving Caliphate forces are driven back to the Wailing Wall Plaza. Unwilling to sustain further casualties, the IDF deploys a targeted nano-virus to destroy the remaining Caliphate troops. Use of this banned weapon, together with the assassination of Caliph Abu Ahmad al-Nasr al-Qurayshi while he is at prayer in the famed Al Aqusa Mosque, draws international condemnation.

2090–Present

Buoyed by their success in Israel, Templar forces launch a fresh assault, seeking to drive Caliphate forces from Syria and Jordan. However, with stories of atrocities continuing to mount, opinion is starting to turn against the Religious States of America, with both Europa City and the African Tech Corps threatening to embargo the supply of arms.

APPENDIX B: MILITARY ACRONYMS

APS: Active Protection System
AMPV: Armoured Multi-Purpose Vehicle
ARV: Armed Response Vehicle
AWOL: Absent Without Official Leave
COSCOM: Corp Support Command
CSS: Combat Service Support
CROWS: Common Remotely Operated Weapon Station
CUSR: Covert Urban Sniper Rifle
ECH: Enhanced Combat Helmet
E-SAPI: Enhanced Small-Arms Protective Insert
E-SBI: Enhanced Side Ballistic Insert
FASCAM: Field Artillery Scatterable Mines
GEMSS: Ground-Emplaced Mine Scattering System
GSR: Ground Surveillance Radar
HAHO: High Altitude High Opening
HEAT: High-Explosive Anti-Tank
HUD: Head-Up Display
IFFN: Identify Friend, Foe or Neutral
IHADSS: Integrated Helmet and Display Sight System
IOTV: Improved Outer Tactical Vest
IRST: Infrared Search and Track
JLTV: Joint Light Tactical Vehicle

METT-TC: Mission, Enemy, Terrain, Troops available,
           Time and Civilian Considerations
MIA: Missing In Action
MILES: Multiple Integrated Laser Engagement System
MOUT: Military Operations in Urban Terrain
MRE: Meal, Ready-to-Eat
MSR: Main Supply Routes
NLAW: Next generation Light Anti-tank Weapon
NSTV: Non-Standard Tactical Vehicle
OCT: Observer, Controller, Trainer
OPFOR: Opposing Forces
POL: Petroleum, Oil, Lubricants
POW: Prisoner Of War
UAS: Unmanned Aircraft Systems
UCIW: Ultra Compact Individual Weapon
VTOL: Vertical Take-off and Landing

ABOUT THE AUTHOR

Leon Steelgrave is the author of the *Europa City* series – hardboiled science fiction that traces its genealogy back to the pulp stories of the 1930s. This dark and satirical world serves as a warning of the dangers of ecological disaster and totalitarian regimes.

Leon's early work includes articles and reviews for music fanzines *Take To The Sky* and *Glasperlenspiel*. But it was his attempt to secure a commission for writing one of a series of *Judge Dredd* novels published by Virgin Books that kickstarted his fiction writing career. Although ultimately unsuccessful, the editorial feedback was sufficiently positive and encouraging for him to complete his debut novel *White Vampyre*. He has published a further three books in the series and is currently working on the first of a new series set in the wider *Europa City* universe.

Leon is a member of the Alliance of Independent Authors and self-publishes his work through Ice Pick Books – fiction to make your ears burn!

Writing being a solitary profession, Leon loves to engage with his readers, so feel free to join his mailing list for releases, updates and exclusive material.

www.leon-steelgrave.com